SCORCHED EARTH

Also by John Gilstrap

FRIENDLY FIRE

"If you only read one book this summer, make sure it's *Friendly Fire*, and be ready to be strapped in for the ride of your life."
—*Suspense* **magazine**

"A blistering thriller that grabs your attention and doesn't let go for a second!" —*The Real Book Spy*

NICK OF TIME

"A page-turning thriller with strong characters, exciting action, and a big heart." —**Heather Graham**

DAMAGE CONTROL

"Powerful and explosive, an unforgettable journey into the dark side of the human soul. Gilstrap is a master of action and drama. If you like Vince Flynn and Brad Thor, you'll love John Gilstrap." —**Gayle Lynds**

"It's easy to see why John Gilstrap is the go-to guy among thriller writers, when it comes to weapons, ammunition, and explosives. His expertise is uncontested." —**John Ramsey Miller**

"A page-turning, near-perfect thriller, with engaging and believable characters . . . unputdownable!" —*Top Mystery Novels*

"Takes you full force right away and doesn't let go. The action is nonstop. Gilstrap knows his technology and weaponry. *Damage Control* will blow you away." —*Suspense* **magazine**

THREAT WARNING

"*Threat Warning* reconfirms Gilstrap as a master of jaw-dropping action and heart-squeezing suspense."
—**Austin Camacho**

HOSTAGE ZERO

"Jonathan Grave, my favorite freelance peacemaker, problem-solver, and tough guy hero, is back—and in particularly fine form. *Hostage Zero* is classic Gilstrap: the people are utterly real, the action's foot to the floor, and the writing's fluid as a well-oiled machine gun. A tour de force!" —**Jeffery Deaver**

NO MERCY

"*No Mercy* grabs hold of you on page one and doesn't let go. Gilstrap's new series is terrific. It will leave you breathless. I can't wait to see what Jonathan Grave is up to next." —**Harlan Coben**

"John Gilstrap is one of the finest thriller writers on the planet. *No Mercy* showcases his work at its finest—taut, action-packed, and impossible to put down!" —**Tess Gerritsen**

"A great hero, a pulse-pounding story—and the launch of a really exciting series." —**Joseph Finder**

"No other writer is better able to combine in a single novel both rocket-paced suspense and heartfelt looks at family and the human spirit. And what a pleasure to meet Jonathan Grave, a hero for our time . . . and for all time." —**Jeffery Deaver**

AT ALL COSTS

"Riveting . . . combines a great plot and realistic, likable characters with look-over-your-shoulder tension. A page-turner." —***Kansas City Star***

"Gilstrap builds tension . . . until the last page, a hallmark of great thriller writers. I almost called the paramedics before I finished *At All Costs*." —***Tulsa World***

"Not-to-be-missed." —***Rocky Mountain News***

NATHAN'S RUN

"Gilstrap pushes every thriller button . . . a nail-biting denoue-
ment and strong characters." —*San Francisco Chronicle*

"Gilstrap has a shot at being the next John Grisham . . . one of
the best books of the year." —*Rocky Mountain News*

"Emotionally charged . . . one of the year's best."
—*Chicago Tribune*

SCORCHED EARTH

JOHN GILSTRAP

KENSINGTON
PUBLISHING CORP.
kensingtonbooks.com

KENSINGTON BOOKS are published by

Kensington Publishing Corp.
900 Third Avenue
New York, NY 10022

All Kensington titles, imprints, and distributed lines are available at special quantity discounts for bulk purchases for sales promotion, premiums, fund-raising, educational, or institutional use.

This book is a work of fiction. Names, characters, businesses, organizations, places, events, and incidents either are the product of the author's imagination or are used fictitiously. Any resemblance to actual persons, living or dead, events, or locales is entirely coincidental.

To the extent that the image or images on the cover of this book depict a person or persons, such person or persons are merely models, and are not intended to portray any character or characters featured in the book.

Special book excerpts or customized printings can also be created to fit specific needs. For details, write or phone the office of the Kensington Sales Manager: Kensington Publishing Corp., 900 Third Avenue, New York, NY 10022. Attn. Sales Department. Phone: 1-800-221-2647.

KENSINGTON and the K with book logo Reg. US Pat. & TM Off.

ISBN: 978-0-7860-5183-0
ISBN: 978-0-7860-5184-7 (ebook)

First Kensington Trade Paperback Printing: March 2026

10 9 8 7 6 5 4 3 2 1

Printed in the United States of America

The authorized representative in the EU for product safety and compliance is eucomply OU, Parnu mnt 139b-14, Apt 123
Tallinn, Berlin 11317, hello@eucompliancepartner.com

To Michaela Hamilton
For guiding me to the real heart of the story

SCORCHED EARTH

CHAPTER ONE

As supervisor of the Wellington County, North Carolina, Emergency Operations Center, Esther Jeffries got to wear a white shirt while others wore blue, and she got to put an extra Benjamin and a half in her pocket every week, but she still had to take calls and dispatch deputies and ambulances and fire apparatus during ten hours of her twelve-hour shift. The other two hours—plus at least one more that was uncompensated now that she was management—she dedicated to scheduling, administrivia and human resources bullshit.

The extra money and loftier title were good, but they didn't come close to compensating for the extra aggravation.

Like everybody who signed on for a life in emergency services, she supposed, she was in it for the adrenaline rush. God help her, but she lived for hurricanes and forest fires. At thirty-five, she'd been doing this for fourteen years, and those multi-day marathon emergency fests were the reason why she couldn't imagine herself ever retiring.

The white shirt? Well, the jury was still out on that.

Esther sat in her chair and rolled into her workstation with its eight computer monitors—two rows of four, double-stacked, and four keyboards. Other dispatching stations only used six monitors. Her extra two helped her keep track of what those others were doing. She loved the ambience of the EOC, the NASA vibe of it. Bathed in perpetual low light to better see the screens, the workstations formed a semicircle around an array of large flat-screen televisions that could be set to display broadcast media—news reports, in the event of large events—but on normal days like today merely duplicated the information on all the call takers' screens.

The computers took care of distributing calls as they came in, first come, first served, delivered to the next available staffer. Esther had found over the years that people self-selected to prefer either taking calls or dispatching crews, but to keep everyone sharp, she switched people off, rotating three consecutive shifts on each. The two tasks, while closely related, required unique skill sets that could go stale if they were not regularly exercised.

Today's rotation had Esther in her happy spot, answering the incoming 9-1-1 calls. Of the six on duty that shift, she was one of four in that role, with Margorie Griffin dispatching deputies and Craig Tierny dispatching fire and rescue. The first three hours of the shift had been busy, but now they were in a slump.

Esther took advantage of the boredom to review their statistics from the last seven days. Impressive and improving. On average, incoming calls were answered within thirty-five seconds, a perfectly acceptable number that no doubt felt like hours to the terrified citizen on the other end of the line. After that the times were even better—total call-received-to-dispatch-made averaged one minute and twenty-seven seconds. She'd put that up against any jurisdiction anywhere.

But after that, the statistics fell apart, and that's where the skills of the call taker became so important. Wellington was a rural county that didn't have a lot of money. Its 73,000 residents lay across nearly four hundred square miles of mostly farmland, protected by five volunteer fire departments, each of which also ran an advanced life support ambulance, and twenty-four sheriff's deputies divided among three shifts. Dispatch to on-scene times *averaged* close to twenty minutes. For a true medical emergency, that was literally a lifetime. Three lifetimes, actually.

Esther's screen lit up with an incoming call. Three years ago, they'd been so proud of the enhanced 9-1-1 system they'd installed that instantly identified the location of every incoming call from a landline—just exactly at the time that everyone in the world stopped using landlines and switched exclusively to their cell phones. Now, this incoming call showed the identities of three cell phone towers, the triangulation of which—calculated by the computer—showed her the approximate location of the caller on a map.

Esther tried to sound as much like a robot as she could as she spoke into the boom mic of her headset. "Nine-one-one, what is your emergency?" As soon as the call connected, the voice-to-text transcription started.

"Uh, yes, ma'am, this is Griffin Smith, I'm on Hadden's Hill Road about a half mile south of Route Fourteen-Thirty." He sounded winded, like he'd been running. Or maybe he was just scared. "There's a pickup truck with two teenagers in it just ate a hickory tree. It's pretty awful."

Esther used her mouse to highlight the call on her screen and drag it over to the Fire and Rescue screen, where they would read the text and dispatch the appropriate equipment—in this case, an ambulance, engine company, medic unit and a heavy rescue squad.

"One of them boys was thrown clean from the vehicle," Griffin said.

"Okay, Mr. Smith, help is on the way," Esther said. "I need you to answer some questions for me, okay?"

"Oh, them poor boys. Their poor mamas."

"Mr. Smith, you say there are two people involved?"

"Yes, ma'am, the driver and the passenger. The passenger was thrown out on impact."

"Is the passenger breathing?"

"No, no, ma'am, he ain't. Ah, shit, I . . . I can see his brains, ma'am." He started to cry.

Esther looked at her upper left-hand screen. Fire and rescue dispatched at 13:02. WCSD dispatched 13:02. WCSD marked responding at 13:03.

"Griffin, hang with me, sir. Don't look at it. Don't look at the awfulness."

"But he's dead."

"I know. That's terrible. Tell me about the driver."

Esther's computer screen flashed another incoming emergency call, this one from the other end of the county. Alicia Blakely took it.

"We should say a prayer for that boy," Griffin said.

"He's already in the Lord's arms, Griffin. You know that. He's already in the place that we pray one day to go."

"Yes, ma'am, I suppose you're right."

Esther felt a tiny spark of happiness when the computer showed Ambulance 4 responding to Hadden's Hill Road at 13:05. Some of the volunteers must have been hanging around the firehouse when the call came in.

Alicia's call posted as a structure fire, requiring a standard response of two engine companies, a ladder truck or heavy rescue and an ambulance.

"What about the driver, Griffin?" Esther asked. "Tell me about him. How badly is he hurt?"

Sounds of movement. "It . . . it's hard to tell. He's breathing."

"That's good. That's great, actually. Is his seatbelt on?"

"Yes, ma'am. And his face is beat up pretty bad, but I bet you that's from the air bag."

"Is he conscious? The driver?"

Another incoming call, this one from only two miles away from Griffin. Katie Howe took it.

Away from the phone, Esther heard Griffin say. "Hey. Hey, buddy. Hey, you awake? Can you hear me?" Then, into the phone, "No, I think he's unconscious."

"What about obvious injuries?"

"No. Well, nothing I can see from outside the vehicle. Just the bruising on his face."

"I don't suppose you have any medical training, do you?" Esther asked.

"No, ma'am, I do not."

"All right, then, Griffin, I'm going to ask you to do the hardest thing there is to do."

"What's that?"

"I'm going to ask you to do nothing more. I want you to find a safe spot along the side of the road, away from the immediate accident scene, and just chill out until help arrives."

Katie's call posted as a structure fire.

"How long will that be?"

She looked at the computer again, did the math. As she was running the calculations, Engine 4 and Rescue 4 diverted to the structure fire, leaving Wagon and Ambulance 4 to tend to Griffin's auto accident.

"Police, fire and rescue are all on their way," Esther said. "Figure seven, maybe ten minutes before they get there."

"That's a long time," Griffin said.

"I know it'll sure seem like it. But I'll be right here. I'll stay on the phone with you."

"So I don't go crazy and run off?"

"Nope," Esther said. "So I know that my new friend Griffin Smith stays safe and sound until help arrives."

Another incoming call.

"What you just went through is tough. And it'll be tough again tomorrow, maybe when you think about it. If you need to talk and maybe you're not sure others want to hear what you want to share, you give me a call. Just call the non-emergency number for the fire department and ask for Esther. Everybody knows how to find me."

Griffin didn't respond, but he didn't hang up, either. After a few minutes, she could hear the sounds of sirens building in the distance, and she watched the statuses on her screen change from responding to on scene.

"Hey, Griffin, you still there?"

"Yes, ma'am."

"Okay, buddy, well, this is it for us for now. You remember what I told you, okay?"

"Yes, ma'am, I'll remember. And Esther?"

"Don't say it, Griffin. No need. You're welcome. I meant every word." She pressed the dump button before it got weird.

Esther picked up the emergency line that had been ringing unanswered for fifty-four seconds. "Nine-one-one, what is your emergency?"

"Help me," a voice said. "My house is on fire." He recited an address and hung up. Something wasn't right. The voice sounded... fake. The address was within a mile of the first structure fire that was dispatched. If Esther tapped out this one, she would end up dividing that response team.

"Wagon Two to Control," said a voice over the air.

Craig Tierny keyed his mic. "Wagon Two."

Another incoming call.

"I've got it!" Esther shouted as she raced to press the connect button.

"Control, be advised, we are on the scene at the dispatched location, and the homeowner advises he never called."

Esther said, "Nine-one-one, what is your emergency?"

"Help me. There's an intruder in my home." The same voice as before gave out a different address.

Over the radio: "Engine Four to Control. Be advised, we are on the scene of the reported house fire and there is nothing here. Homeowner did not make a call."

Another incoming call.

Another incoming call.

Katie Howe shouted, "Esther, what's happening?"

Esther stood at her station. "Everybody, stop!"

More calls coming in.

"Is everybody getting the same electronic, computer-sounding voice?"

A general murmur of agreement rumbled through the EOC.

"I think this is some sort of cyber attack," Esther said.

"What do we do?" somebody asked.

"I make a phone call to my boss is what I do. In the meantime, keep answering calls, and use your best judgment."

Scotty Tagget let out a war whoop as he watched the statistics roll on his computer screen, and he listened to the confusion on the fire and police dispatch channels.

"Yes!" he yelled, punctuating the word with a fist pump. "Omar, Ervin. You wanted to know if I could do it. Well, there it is. There's the evidence. Not to toot my own horn, but I am a freaking genius!"

Wellington County Sheriff Ervin Morrissey rested hands on his Sam Browne belt as he leaned in closer to Scotty's computer screen. The lighting sucked in this glorified barn that Omar Farook called a command center. "What am I looking at, exactly?"

"This is the diversion Omar was asking for. The diversion of all diversions. I've designed a program that will flood the emergency call center with random fake emergencies. The system has all the addresses in the county—taken from the tax records, along with the names of property owners—plus their phone numbers of record. I've given the system thirty different emergencies to choose from randomly. When I push the go button the system matches an address to an emergency, spoofs the phone number and calls nine-one-one."

"Then what?"

Scotty recoiled in his seat. "Seriously? That's not obvious? They dispatch resources to emergencies and then we flood the zone. I can program this to do as many as seventy-two calls per minute. They can't possibly keep up."

"I don't get it," the sheriff said. "What do we gain from that?"

"The dispatchers stop taking calls." This voice came from behind, and it belonged to Omar Farook, the man in charge of all things related to the Event, and the man paying literally millions of dollars to make it happen. "We train them to stop taking calls when that's what we need them to do." He looked to Scotty. "How long has it been running?"

Scotty looked at the timer. "Seven minutes."

"Turn it off," Farook instructed. "That is enough for now. That is proof of concept."

Disappointed, Scotty turned back to his keyboard and tapped the appropriate keys. "Okay, done," he said.

"How did last night's rehearsal go?" Morrissey asked.

"Quite well," Farook said. "We have a talented team who could go tomorrow if we had to, but we will wait for the assigned date. We need to wait for the exact layout, which I'm told is forthcoming. Eliminating the guesswork will make the plan much stronger."

"Always does, I suppose," Morrissey said. "Speed is going to be important. Maximum damage in the shortest period of time."

"You're telling me things I already know."

"Your boy Willy K still out on his vendetta hunt?"

Farook glared at him. "Do you have a reason for being here?"

"Yeah, I do. I left a Pelican case of batteries for Willy K. He's going to modify them for me. He knows what to do."

"What kind of modifications?"

It was Morrissey's turn to shoot the dangerous glare. "The kind that you need to ask Willy K about if you really want to know."

As Scotty watched the exchange between the two men, he did his best to remain invisible. Whenever they were together, he was half surprised that they didn't go to guns. Willy K surprised him that way, too. It was like the whole leadership team hated each other. The rank-and-file members of Farook's army—his American Jihad—didn't get along all that well, either, but you expected that when you brought a bunch of snake-eating mercenaries together in the same place.

Hell, Scotty didn't like most people, either.

Leading a bunch of mercs wasn't an easy task, for sure. It was like leading unleashed egos. Strong, unified leadership was essential with groups like this, but Farook's leadership team all seemed to be pulling in different directions. Maybe because Omar Farook saw this as some kind of divine mission when everybody else just saw it as a paycheck and said all the right things to make sure the six-figure checks ended up in their accounts.

Or, maybe it was the nature of the target package this time. That's what really wore on Scotty.

It stole a special chunk of your soul to intentionally kill a bunch of kids, no matter how big the payday.

CHAPTER TWO

Jonathan Grave hated boats but loved the water. He was an excellent swimmer because Uncle Sam once required it of him, but swimming for recreation ranked right up there with putting a fork in his eye. But the view of water—in this case, the Rappahannock River along the shore of Fisherman's Cove, Virginia—and the sight and sound of the water soothed him.

Back when he was maybe ten years old, he'd discovered an outcropping of rocks above a feeder creek about half a mile from town. Nearly invisible through the trees, that vantage point provided a breathtaking view of what he called the ass end of sunset. Facing east, as the sun sank low in the afternoon, the angle of the light on the water and the flora made problems seem easier to manage. Mama Alexander—his surrogate mother after his real mother passed away—named the spot Jonny's Point. As a boy, it's where he did his deepest thinking. As a teenager, it's where he took dates, knowing that there'd be a ninety-eight percent chance of action. Nowadays, it was just about the peace.

This afternoon, he shared the spot with his longtime friend and occasional lover, Gail Bonneville. A lawyer by trade, and a retired FBI agent and former sheriff of a small town in Indiana, she was one of the best shooters Jonathan had ever known—earning herself the call sign Gunslinger, which she hated. Gail seemed to regret every pull of the trigger, even when the result was to rid the world of another bad guy.

They sat side by side in low-slung folding beach chairs, sharing a bottle of sauvignon blanc as they watched the scenery mostly in silence. The private investigation firm he owned, Security Solutions, Inc., often took on the kinds of cases that generated lots of noise. Sitting here in the quiet with a close friend made it all—

"You know, you're quite a contradiction, Digger," Gail said.

He suppressed a sigh. Not everyone appreciated silence. "Yeah? Is that a good thing or a bad thing?" Movement in the underbrush on the other side of the creek bed, maybe a hundred yards away, caught his attention. He leaned forward in his seat, as if cutting a few inches off the viewing distance would make a difference.

"Neither good nor bad," Gail said. "You don't often show your nature-loving side. I have to say that I like—"

"There's somebody in the forest over there," Jonathan interrupted.

Gail huffed at the interruption then followed his eyeline and scowled. "I don't see anybody. What are they doing?"

"I don't know. I only saw one, but I don't like the way he was moving."

Gail leaned forward, too. "Do you see him now?"

"No."

"Maybe he's a hiker," Gail said. "A fellow nature lover."

"Maybe." But he didn't like what he saw. The guy had been walking with an odd, hunched-over gait, as if he were trying to go unnoticed. People who wanted to remain unnoticed were up to no good in Jonathan's world.

"Whoever it is, they have every right to be there," Gail said. "You don't have to be at war in your mind every day."

That's exactly where he was. He'd created too many enemies. Every mystery was a threat until proven otherwise. He considered that to be the secret sauce to survival.

"There he is again," Jonathan said, resisting the urge to point and give away the fact that he'd seen the guy. "This time, it's not an image of the guy, but do you see how the bushes are moving right above that big deadfall on the creek bed?"

"It could be a breeze."

"Breezes move everything, not just one section of bushes." It occurred to him that the guy's position would be an excellent spot to set up a sniper's nest.

"Do you want to go check him out?" Gail asked.

"Part of me does. It doesn't have to be confrontational. We could—"

Jonathan caught a flash of white light from the bushes over there, as if the woods were winking at him. It could have been a flashbulb, but intuitively, he knew better. It took all of a quarter of a second for him to realize that it was a lens flare from a rifle scope.

"Gun!" Jonathan yelled. He grabbed a fistful of Gail's blouse, right where the buttons were, and he yanked her off her chair and onto the hard rock.

"What the hell, Dig—"

Before she could finish her sentence, Jonathan heard the whiz and crack of passing bullets that tore into the chairs they'd just vacated, followed immediately by the booming reports of the muzzle blasts. The first two shots came as a quick pair, a double-tap. There was a brief silence, during which Jonathan, acting on instinct, grabbed Gail in a bear hug and rolled to his right. When he was on his back, he heaved Gail over the edge of the rock face onto the mulchy ground below.

More shots came from the woods, the bullets tearing into the rocks and shattering on impact, sending hot fragments of copper and lead in every direction.

Movement was key. The attack wasn't yet five seconds long, and Jonathan felt confident that the shooter wasn't experienced enough to lead his targets. He kept shooting at where Jonathan and Gail were, rather than where they were going to be.

The rate of fire doubled, tearing up the world as the guy did a mag dump on the targets he couldn't hit.

He heard Gail make a barking sound as she hit the ground below, and then he heaved himself over to the same spot. He'd just gone airborne when something white hot pierced the right side of his neck, just below his ear. When he landed on the soft ground, the shooting stopped.

"You're hit," Gail said, reaching for his neck.

He could feel the trickle of blood tracking down to the collar of his T-shirt and then beyond to flow down his chest.

But the headline was that he could feel. That meant he was alive and that his spinal cord was intact. He reached to the wound and his fingers found the jagged edge of a piece of metal sticking out of the flesh.

"It's a fragment," he said. "Can't have gone too deep because I'm still here."

"Let me take it out for you," Gail said.

"No, leave it in place. I don't think I'm in mortal danger, but the metal has to be tamponading the flow of blood at least a little."

"We've got to get you to a hospital," Gail said.

"Bullshit. Sonofabitch was trying to kill us. I'm returning the favor."

"We're a bit outgunned for that, don't you think?"

"I've got my Colt and two spare mags." Jonathan always had his Colt 1911 .45. His enormous coworker, Boxers, called the pistol Digger's little sister. He never let it out of his sight. "What've you got?"

"It's just an outing," Gail said. "I have my forty-three." The Glock 43 had a magazine capacity of six rounds, plus one in the chamber.

"Spare mags?"

"I didn't expect going to war." She sounded defensive.

"Not a problem," Jonathan said. "We've got twenty-one rounds between us. That's enough. Let's go."

"Suicide wasn't on my list for today, either."

"Okay," Jonathan said. "Let me have your gun so I can still have twenty-one rounds."

"You can't do this alone," Gail said. "You're wounded and you can't set up a crossfire."

"Right you are," Jonathan said. "So let's get going. There's only one path out of that end of the point that will lead to a road. If we hurry, maybe we can make it."

He didn't wait for an answer. Gail would come or she would stay. Either choice was legitimate under the circumstances, but he didn't have time to debate the point. He took off at a run, keeping low and watching the blood trail he was dropping onto the vegetation. It wasn't really a flow, but more like a fast trickle. He hoped maybe the trickle would stop on its own.

He fought his way through briars and sticker bushes to get to River Road, and then he turned right and started to run in earnest. He dared a glance behind him and was pleased to see that Gail had decided to come along.

He'd never measured the distance, but it felt like the trailhead would be about a quarter mile away. On a good day, he'd be able to close that distance in ninety seconds, but the hole in his neck, even though it was small, slowed him down. Every stride hurt.

Up ahead, he saw a black SUV pulled off to the right shoulder, just past the access to the trailhead. That would be their ambush point.

As Gail caught up, Jonathan motioned for her to take her place just inside the tree line on the left side of the road while he ran beyond the SUV to take cover in the trees on the same side of the road as the target vehicle.

If the shooter was any good at his craft, Jonathan knew exactly what was going through his mind now. He'd missed his targets, and now he was the one being hunted. All of his choices at this point sucked. The shooter could assume that his targets had run away—the smart thing for any target to do—in which case, the police would soon be on the way. He couldn't afford to stay where he was.

Unless his targets hadn't run away, and were lying in wait for him, waiting for him to make a move, in which case moving could prove to be exactly the wrong thing to do.

Ultimately, he had no choice. He had to move *somewhere*. Problem was, this part of Virginia, around Fisherman's Cove, had miles of nowhere, and very little somewhere. That's why Jonathan liked it so much.

The smart money said he'd return to his ride. And Jonathan had infinite patience when it came to waiting for people who had tried to kill him. He drew his Colt and thumbed off the safety.

Turned out Jonathan didn't have to wait long at all. After ten minutes, he heard movement on the trail. It sounded hurried yet cautious. In this head, he imagined a nervous shooter praying for this afternoon to end.

A glance across the street brought relief that Gail was in place, exactly where she should be, just far enough into the trees to be invisible to anyone who wasn't looking for her. If she had to shoot, her distance to target would be about thirty yards—a challenging pistol shot for even a marksman of her abilities.

Jonathan figured his own distance to target to be ten to fifteen yards, depending on where his prey emerged from the woods.

His first clear glance at the sniper led him to believe he'd had military training. It was the way he advanced with his M4 carbine at high ready, his finger poised just outside the trigger guard. But the real giveaway was the way his left hand—his support hand—grasped the barrel shroud at arm's length in the tacti-cool over-hand grip that made for great photos, but that Jonathan found wasted too much energy. His own preference was to grasp the mag well to keep his arms tucked tight. But what did he know?

The shooter might have been a soldier, but he definitely was not a Special Forces operator. Even though he swept side-to-side for targets as he advanced, he was too focused on his sights. The deadliest part of the universe lay in wait in the periphery.

The guy never saw the man who was about to shoot him. There'd be no warning, no dramatic "Freeze or I'll shoot" or "Drop your weapon." This asshat had already declared his purpose and he'd earned what was coming.

Jonathan settled his front sight on the sniper's right elbow and pressed the trigger. The Colt barked and the shooter's trigger arm flapped away from the M4, the back of his hand slapping him in the shoulder.

The guy howled in pain—as well he should because that had to hurt like holy hell.

Moving fast, Jonathan re-engaged the safety, holstered the Colt and darted to the wounded man. The guy's eyes showed nothing but confusion as Jonathan threw an elbow blow into the spot where his jaw and his skull came together, just in front of the ear. The guy dropped as if he'd been unplugged.

As he waited for Gail to join him, Jonathan drew his pistol again and switched the magazine out for a fresh one from his belt. He believed that guns were happiest when their tummies were full. He returned the happy Colt to its holster.

Gail arrived at his side. "Now what?"

"Load his ass in the SUV and take him back to the firehouse," Jonathan said. His residence and office both resided in a lavish converted fire station which he'd bought when the fire department abandoned the place in favor of a glass and concrete monstrosity located on the highway on the outskirts of Fisherman's Cove.

"What about a hospital?"

"He'll live. He's got a boo-boo on his arm and a concussion. Not bad, considering what he was planning for us."

"And the police?"

"Oh, hell no. Not yet, anyway. I've got some questions to ask him—even if he says he wants a lawyer."

Jonathan unthreaded the guy from his rifle sling and checked him for more weapons. He found a Sig Sauer P320 in a holster under his shirt—the civilian version of the Army's new M17. He dropped the mags out of both, cleared their chambers and opened the back passenger side door. He tossed all the hardware over the back seat and into the cargo space.

"Give me a hand with him," Jonathan said. "You take the legs."

Jonathan grabbed their new friend under his armpits and hoisted him high enough to clear the edge of the seat. Then he pulled. The shooter was young and lean, maybe one hundred seventy-five pounds. Easy peasy. He climbed back outside through the driver's side, slammed the door and then opened the door to the front seat.

Gail closed the back door then climbed in to ride shotgun.

"This isn't right," she said. "He needs to see a doctor. Yeah, he did a bad thing, but that's no excuse—"

"Please stop talking," Jonathan said. "You're not going to win this one. There are a lot of moving parts to what this guy tried to do, not the least of which is how much does he know about what we do. If we call in Doug Kramer and his police force, they're going to take him into custody and out of our hands. If our friend in the back seat is smart, he'll utter the word *lawyer*, and all the talking will stop. We'll have no idea if there are others out there gunning for us, and if so, why. Plus, he started it."

Jonathan pressed the start button on the dash and the engine came to life. Now that everything was triggered by a fob these days, he didn't even have to search for a key.

As he slipped the transmission into drive, he pulled his cell phone from his pocket and punched a speed dial number.

A familiar voice answered after the second ring. "Speak." It was Brian Van de Muelebroecke—aka Boxers, call sign Big Guy. The way his voice echoed, Jonathan knew exactly where he was.

"Are you in your Fortress of Solitude?"

"I am. Getting high on the aroma of Hoppe's and gun oil. Please don't ruin my buzz." An enormous underground reinforced concrete bunker spanned the distance between Jonathan's firehouse and the basement of St. Katherine's Catholic Church next door. In it, Security Solutions stored its weapons, ammunition and explosives—all the things that made Big Guy happy. Personnel could access the space through either the basement of the firehouse or the basement of the church, but deliveries arrived via a reinforced steel roll-up door that couldn't be seen from the road.

"I don't know if I'm gonna ruin that buzz or make it buzzier," Jonathan said. "Got into a bit of a scuffle with a young man who thought I needed to be dead. I'm bringing him back to answer some questions, and I was hoping you could open the delivery door for me."

CHAPTER THREE

Kerry Smallwood had just handed his customer her extra-large nonfat decaf latte when he saw Senator Maxine Bridges enter the coffee shop and take her usual seat in the far left-hand corner, facing away from the door.

His boss, Anton Ford, leaned in close to his ear. "Uh-oh. Somebody's girlfriend is in the house." Anton was twenty-three and his status as general manager no doubt had something to do with the fact that his father owned the place.

Kerry shrugged away. "Cut it out," he said. "She might hear you."

"So? I'm pretty sure she was young once herself. A long time ago."

"Dammit, Anton, stop!"

"I'm having a hard time imagining her naked, though."

Kerry whisper-shouted, "*Shut up!*"

Anton laughed. "That is some family friend to have. With your grades and youthful stamina, she's not going to yank your Annapolis appointment because your knucklehead boss made her feel uncomfortable."

"Please, Anton? I'm begging you here."

"Fine. Go suck up to her."

"Does she look like she wants company to you?"

Anton scoffed. "Why would a senator come into a public coffee shop if she wanted to be left alone?"

"It's the way she's facing away from the door."

"She's a cougar, lying in wait for her boy toy." Anton made a growling sound. "Let me put it another way. Why would she come into *this* public coffee shop—the one with her cougar-y boy toy—if she wanted to be left alone?"

Kerry felt himself blushing. "I never should have told you."

Anton kept going. "Maybe she's facing away from the door because she doesn't want the world to see that she's all hot and wet over a teenager."

"You're disgusting."

"There's nothing wrong with learning from experienced instructors." Anton launched a big laugh and whacked Kerry in the balls with the back of his hand, drawing an *oof* and doubling him over at the waist.

"God, you're an asshole," Kerry grunted. Anton was a sack tapper. It was his thing. Never hard enough to injure but always delivered at an inappropriate time.

"Now, go forth and have a sexy chat. Drinks are on the house. What's her usual order?"

Kerry breathed through his mouth as he willed the ache to leave his gut. "Medium regular drip. Cream, no sugar."

"You're on the house, too," Anton said. "What do you want?"

"Seriously?"

"I can always change my mind."

"Okay, extra-large regular drip with cream and four sugars."

"Jesus, you'll be a diabetic before you're an ensign. Go have a seat. I'll bring the drinks."

Kerry tried not to walk funny as he crossed the floor to join Maxine Bridges. He stood at the chair opposite hers. "Good afternoon, Senator."

She looked up from her phone, on which she'd been typing intently with both thumbs. "My, but aren't we being formal?"

Kerry blushed.

The senator rolled her eyes. "Oh, for God's sake, have a seat."

He pulled out the chair and sat.

The senator leaned in close and lowered her voice. "Look, Kerry, I appreciate that you want to be discreet. I get that in your fantasies, you imagined losing your virginity to someone who looked way different than me—"

Reflexively, Kerry shot a panicked look around the room.

"Now, you're being insulting."

Kerry stammered, "I-I'm sorry. I didn't mean . . ." He didn't finish the sentence because he wasn't sure what he hadn't meant to do. The whole thing started as an interview for his Naval Academy appointment. She'd invited him to her house for tea. He didn't even like tea, but he knew that she and his dad had gone to high school together, and so why not? Then they started talking about the physical training requirements and she wanted to know how many push-ups he could do. And then, how many sit-ups. She made him demonstrate and when he got sweaty, she encouraged him to shower. Looking back on it, maybe he should have—

"Look, Kerry, I was there, remember? I was the other party in the room. I saw, felt and heard everything and all indications were that you had a very nice time. Am I wrong?"

Kerry couldn't make eye contact. "No, ma'am."

"Don't call me ma'am."

"No, then. You are not wrong."

"In fact, if I remember right, you had a very nice time at least twice. Or was it three times?"

Kerry wondered if the skin on his face would catch fire. "It was three times."

She laughed. "Appreciate your youth while you have it. There was nothing wrong with what we did. You're eighteen, right?"

He nodded.

"There you go. Legal. Hormonal. Don't let normal get weird." She reached across and squeezed his hand. "Okay?"

He forced a smile. "Okay."

As a shadow approached, she quickly let go. Anton. "Excuse

me," he said. "I have a medium drip, cream no sugar for the lady, and a liquid candy bar for the gentleman." He placed the coffees on the table and disappeared.

"That was Anton," Kerry said, answering the unasked question. "He's my boss. A bit of an asshole, but overall, okay."

"Get used to the type," the senator said. "They're everywhere."

"Can I call you Maxine?"

"No. Never in public." She reached out for his hand again, but this time he pulled it away. She reached into her purse and produced a pack of cigarettes and a skinny lighter. "Life is just damned complicated sometimes, isn't it? But you got your Academy appointment. You've got to feel good about that." She put the cigarette between her lips and lit it.

"I do. I'm really excited." He shot a look toward the front to see if Anton was looking. "Ma'am, um, Senator, you can't smoke in here."

"Are you going to stop me?"

Kerry blushed brighter. "Um, I'm supposed to."

"That's an answer for a question I didn't ask. You're *supposed* to, but will you? And if so, how?"

He answered with silence. He carefully took a sip of his coffee, halfway expecting it to have been rendered undrinkable as a practical joke, but it was actually just right. Another glance at Anton revealed a death glare.

"Don't worry about him," the senator said. "One of the privileges of national office is having people be afraid of you." She shifted her posture. "Did you get my email?"

Confused at first by the abrupt transition, Kerry got it after a second or two. "Oh, yeah." He stood to get better access to his pants pocket and reached in to retrieve a thumb drive he'd been carrying for two days. "Here."

Senator Bridges took it and placed it in her purse. "Is it the whole layout?" she asked. "Everything?"

"Just like you asked. In fact, Dad met with the planning staff for the final time three days ago to finalize everything. What you have is the locked-down, unchangeable version."

The senator smiled. "Now, Danny doesn't know anything about this, right?"

Danny was his dad. "Right. I've been moving like a spy to keep everything secret. I copied that drive I gave you while he was sleeping. It's a big file, though. To get the detail you told me you were looking for, it's going to be a huge print."

The senator nodded. "That's exactly what I was hoping for. I'm thinking three feet by five feet minimum. I want this to be a real tribute for all the work Danny has put into organizing the Planetariat. When I think that it's all volunteer work to benefit hundreds of kids from all corners of the country, he needs more than a simple trophy and a thank-you."

"He's gonna be thrilled. The Starlighters don't get a lot of respect. A gift like this from you is gonna be amazing. I don't know where he's gonna hang it, but I know he's gonna love it."

"It's a shame people are so cynical," the senator said. "They show hate toward things they don't understand. I get it, but it's a shame. What's not to like about an organization dedicated to steeping young men and boys in the wonders of science and astronomy?"

"Scouting for geeks," Kerry said, quoting the unofficial Starlighters motto.

"Exactly," she agreed. "I've told people for years that the difference between the two organizations is that when a Starlighter builds his campfire, he's as interested in the chemistry of combustion as he is in cooking the marshmallows."

Kerry chuckled. "Actually, I hate marshmallows."

"Sacrilege."

"The uniforms don't help our cause," Kerry said. They were quite suggestive of a certain television show whose five-year mission was to explore strange new worlds.

"You're right. Maybe when you make Fleet Commander one day you can make the appropriate changes."

Kerry winced. "Okay, and the titles of our rank structure work against us, too."

Senator Bridges took one last sip of her coffee and stood, leaving the cup half empty. "When you can, I'd love you to come to the house and cut my grass for me. Maybe do a little gardening. It'd be great to see those muscles gleaming with sweat." She winked.

For a few seconds, he couldn't speak. Then he asked, "Are you serious?"

She walked to the door and exited without answering.

CHAPTER FOUR

"Jesus, Boss," Boxers said. "How hard did you hit him?" The shooter was still *very* unconscious when they pulled him out of the vehicle in the privacy of the underground bunker.

"I think I lost my temper a little bit," Jonathan said.

Boxers smiled. "I'm proud of you. Put him on the ground over there."

"I'll get the trauma kit," Gail said.

"You're gonna waste expensive med supplies on this piece of shit?" Big Guy said.

"'Slinger is right," Jonathan said. "You know the rule: If it's ugly, cover it up. We're going to want Venice here when we start questioning him, and she will freak out if she sees the elbow wound. We need to dress it and bandage it."

The wound was an ugly thing, through and through, just above the elbow joint, with white bone exposed to the air. Among the three operators, Boxers had the best medic skills, so he took care of dressing and bandaging the mess.

While Boxers worked on the arm, Gail stripped the shooter of all his pocket junk.

"No way he keeps this arm," Big Guy said as he wrapped gauze around a wire mesh splint and fitted it.

The manipulation of the limb made the shooter stir. Then he

started to yell. As consciousness returned, he tried to sit up, and that didn't go well at all. He howled in pain.

"Shut up!" Boxers barked. "Quit doing stupid shit and it won't hurt as much."

The guy's face showed progressing comprehension, and with it came confusion and fear.

"His driver's license says his name is Richard Goldsbury," Gail said as she examined the shooter's wallet. "Same name for his concealed carry permit and two credit cards."

"Where am I?" Goldsbury asked.

Jonathan stepped into view and looked down at the guy. "Recognize this face?" he asked.

Goldsbury took a deep breath as his eyes widened. The movement brought a severe wince and a groan.

"Here's the difference between you and me," Jonathan said. "I hit what I shoot at."

"Stick it up your ass."

Boxers tapped the elbow with his boot, launching a screech. "Watch your manners."

Jonathan held out a hand. "Don't. We don't do that."

"What's this we shit?" Boxers said, but he took a step back.

"Mother Hen is on her way down," Gail said, looking at her phone. Mother Hen was the call sign for Venice Alexander—pronounced Ven-EE-chay because of a tantrum when she was a teenager. Like Gail, Venice hated her pseudonym. Said it made her sound old and fat. Too bad. She was neither of those, and Jonathan got to assign the names. Fact was, Mother Hen was a wizard with electrons. Among the titans of computer chicanery, FreakFace666—a pseudonym Venice had chosen for herself—was lauded as one of the world's great hacking geniuses.

"What are you going to do with me?" Goldsbury asked.

"Well, let's see," Jonathan said. "You just tried to kill me. I have a few questions about that. Seems reasonable, don't you think?"

"Hey, Scorpion?" Gail said. Jonathan got to pick his own call sign. "I think you want to see this."

They walked toward each other. She held a tiny box in her hand. If it were twice its real size, it would have looked like a jeweler's box for a ring.

"What is it?" Jonathan asked.

"I think I know, but I don't want to poison the well." She opened the box to reveal extensive padding in both the lid and the base protecting a glass ampule about the size of Jonathan's little fingernail. A bit of elastic ribbon secured it in place.

Jonathan knew exactly what it was, but he hadn't seen one in many years. "Holy shit, Richard. Why are you carrying a cyanide ampule?"

The assassin stared straight up at the ceiling.

The slap of flip-flops announced the approach of Venice Alexander. She carried a black and silver Briggs & Riley backpack slung over one shoulder, no doubt filled with computer equipment. As she joined the circle of coworkers and got a look at the man on the ground, she gasped.

"Oh, good Lord," she said. "What happened? Who is this?"

Jonathan explained, "Best we can figure out, his name is Richard Goldsbury and he just tried to kill Gunslinger and me out on Jonny's Point."

"What happened to his elbow?"

"I shot it."

"Why isn't he in a hospital?"

"He has to earn the privilege of medical attention," Jonathan said. He turned his attention to Goldsbury. "And you do that by answering our questions."

"Screw you."

Boxers moved a foot to kick him again but backed away from Jonathan's glare. Instead, Big Guy said, "There's time. If it gets too bad, I've got the tools to do the amputation here. It's just a shame we don't have any anesthetic."

Goldsbury tried hard not to show fear, but Jonathan could see that Boxers' words had broken through his shield.

"Could I have a chair, please?" Venice asked. She rarely came down here to the bunker and her body language showed that the sight and aroma of munitions made her nervous. The blood didn't help.

Boxers disappeared behind the stack of shelves closest to the wall and came back with four folding chairs. "We might as well all be comfortable," he said. Then, to Goldsbury, "Well, not everyone."

Jonathan opened a chair for Venice and she sat down. She put her backpack on the floor and opened the flap. She withdrew a laptop with enough dongles dangling to make it look like an electronic octopus. Next came a device about the size of a credit card, but thicker.

Venice pointed to Gail and the materials gathered at her feet. "Is that his pocket junk?"

"It is."

Venice reached out with the new device. "I'll trade you," she said. "Let me go through his stuff and you get a set of fingerprints for me."

Gail carried the pocket junk to Venice, and they made the switch. She started with the assassin's phone. She looked at it, pressed a button and handed it to Jonathan. "Scorpion, point this at his face to open it, will you?"

It wasn't like Venice to be this bossy, but Jonathan stayed out of her way and did exactly what she asked. He figured that she wanted to keep as far away from the wounded assassin as possible. Doing his best to stay out of Gail's way as she touched the print reader to the guy's fingers—he was surprisingly cooperative—Jonathan pointed the phone at Goldsbury's face and the device unlocked. Jonathan was a little ashamed that he hadn't already thought of that.

Venice thanked him for handing it over, and then plugged in one of the dongles to the bottom of the phone.

"You downloading the whole thing?" Jonathan asked.

"Even down to the photos," Venice said. After about a minute, her computer dinged and she unplugged the phone. "Here you go," she said, handing it to Jonathan. "I got everything and then I wiped it clean. You might want to take out the SIM card."

"Did the fingerprints transfer?" Gail asked.

Venice checked her screen. "They did." Then she closed the laptop, returned it to her backpack, dumped all the pocket detritus into the belly of the backpack and zipped the cover closed. "I'm done here," she said. "I'll see you in the War Room later, I'm sure." She stood and she left the bunker.

When Venice was gone, Jonathan returned his attention to Goldsbury. "Richard, I have only one question for you. Why did you try to kill us?"

Goldsbury managed a menacing smile. "Because you were next on the list."

Jonathan kept his poker face despite the chill between his shoulder blades. "Yeah? What list is that?"

"The one you're still on, Jonathan Grave, aka Scorpion." He shifted his gaze. "And Gail Bonneville, better known as Gunslinger." He looked to Boxers. "And Brian Van de-something unpronounceable. You prefer to be called Boxers and your call sign is Big Guy."

Jonathan glared, not knowing what to do. This was bad.

"And let's not forget Ms. Venice Alexander, aka Mother Hen. I believe she has a son named Roman. Am I close?"

Jonathan felt a rage building like a fire in his brain. He knew that Boxers and Gail were as astonished as he that this guy knew what he knew.

Boxers kicked Goldsbury in the elbow, launching a howl from the man.

"Oops," Big Guy said. "Muscle twitch. That must really hurt though."

Jonathan didn't approve, but in this case, he didn't disapprove either. He squatted down to one knee to get closer to the shooter. "Where did this list come from?"

Goldsbury's eyes were tightly closed, and he huffed to catch his breath from the pain.

Jonathan gave a loud sigh. "Think this through, Richard. We're not cops and we're not murderers. When we're done here, we're going to let you go. But you have to ask yourself if whoever you're protecting is worth the shit you might have to go through between now and then."

When he got control of his pain, he opened his eyes.

"Where did the list come from?"

"I have no idea."

Jonathan looked to Boxers and Goldsbury shouted, "No! Don't. A dossier was given to me by a guy named Willy K. He gave it to me as my assignment. I was one of a few over the past couple of weeks. Today was just your turn."

"Who gave it to Willy K?"

"I don't know. Why would I care?"

"How many others are on the list?" Gail asked.

"I don't know. I've never seen the whole thing. I just get my assignment and I take care of it."

"Are we the first of the list that you've *taken care of*?" Gail asked.

Goldsbury set his jaw.

"This Willy K," Jonathan said. "Who is he?"

The shooter closed his eyes and set his jaw tighter.

"He's done talking," Jonathan said. "Big Guy, secure his good arm, put a bag over his head and load him back into his vehicle."

"Be a pleasure," Boxers said.

Goldsbury's eyes opened again. "What are you going to do?" He didn't fight back as Boxers zip-tied his left wrist to his belt.

"Exactly what I said," Jonathan said. "We're going to let you go."

They drove for nearly two hours, Boxers behind the wheel, Jonathan riding shotgun. Gail didn't want to come along. No one said much. Goldsbury grunted at all the bumps in the road. He asked three times where they were taking him but stopped when he figured out there would be no answers.

Jonathan had never done anything like this before. He always considered himself to be on the side of the angels in the work he did—and that work frequently involved killing. But he was not a killer by trade. He was the guy who rescued innocent victims from the clutches of killers. In that process, bad guys often died. With the world relieved of the evil they perpetrated, he felt no remorse.

There was no good in this thing they were about to do.

As they drove deeper into the piney woods of rural Maryland, he began to have second thoughts even as he searched for the perfect spot for what was coming.

"Up there is good," Jonathan said, pointing through the windshield to a narrow path that cut through chest-high grass.

Boxers piloted the SUV about three hundred yards up the path before he stopped. "The ground is getting pretty soft," he said. "We don't want to get stuck."

"Here it is, then," Jonathan said. "Hey, Richard, you're home."

"Where? What are you going to do to me?"

Jonathan and Boxers went around to the back and opened up the tailgate. Goldsbury lay as they'd left him when they loaded him into the vehicle—more or less flat on his back but listing to his left to keep pressure off his ruined arm. His right hand was clearly unsavable now, the fingers showing a gray pallor that no bit of anatomy should ever see.

"Where are we?" Goldsbury asked. His voice sounded muffled behind the canvas bag that was lightly cinched around his neck.

Jonathan ignored him.

"Shoes and socks?" Big Guy asked.

Jonathan nodded.

"Shoes and socks!" Goldsbury shouted. "What the hell—"

"If you kick me," Boxers growled, "you'll be barefoot with your ankles zip-tied."

"I don't know what you're planning, but I want a doctor."

"I want world peace," Jonathan replied. "I think we're both going to be disappointed in the short term."

Goldsbury wore over-the-ankle tactical boots of a kind often used by American soldiers. Jonathan watched as Boxers cut the laces away with his Benchmade clip-on fighting knife.

Surprisingly, but to his benefit, Goldsbury didn't fight back as Big Guy rendered him barefoot.

"Time to get you out now," Jonathan said. "We'll try not to hurt you."

"Speak for yourself on that one," Boxers said, earning himself a glare.

"I'm speaking for both of us," Jonathan said.

They did indeed move carefully as they maneuvered him around until he was sitting upright and his feet were dangling off the edge. The transition from sitting to standing, though, was tough, eliciting an impressive string of profanity.

Once Goldsbury had settled himself, Jonathan grabbed him gently by his left biceps—his good arm. "Come with me," he said. "We need to move to the front of the vehicle so we don't run over you when we back out."

"You're going to leave me here?" Goldsbury's voice carried the hard edge of panic.

"You're alive," Jonathan said. "This is a way better choice than the choice you were leaving me." The gravel of the road was hard on the prisoner's feet as Jonathan walked him along the side of the SUV to a spot ten yards in front of the grill. "This will do it," Jonathan said and he let go of Goldsbury's arm and started back to the vehicle.

"Listen to this," Boxers said. "It's important." He heaved the boots and socks deep into the tall grass, one on the right side and one on the left. "Those are your boots. We're leaving them for you."

"Wait," Goldsbury said. He was crying now. "What about the hood? My hand's still tied to my belt! You can't leave me like this!"

Jonathan was first to the vehicle, with Boxers close behind. Big Guy settled in behind the wheel and pulled the transmission into reverse.

"You can't leave me like this!"

"Is this too much?" Jonathan asked.

"He tried to murder you, Boss. At least you're leaving him alive."

"He can't possibly survive."

"I'll drink to that," Big Guy said. "Actions have consequences. You gave him a chance. That's better than I woulda done."

Jonathan was relieved when they were back on the road and he didn't have to see what he had done.

CHAPTER FIVE

Jonathan and Boxers returned to the firehouse by midafternoon. They parked Goldsbury's SUV in the bunker, where it would remain until Jerry Devro returned from vacation. A longtime friend of Jonathan's, Jerry owned Devro Iron and Metal, and for a few hundred bucks, he'd ask no questions when Jonathan asked him to run the vehicle through his shredder.

At 3:00 p.m. sharp, Jonathan convened the team in the War Room to discuss what Venice had learned through her evaluation of Goldsbury's pocket junk. Jonathan met Gail at the door to the elaborate teak conference room that had more—and sometimes better—electronic equipment than the Pentagon.

"So?" Gail asked. "Goldsbury?"

"Are you sure you want to know?"

She took a few seconds to study his face. "No," she said. "I don't."

Jonathan appreciated the honesty. He stretched a hand toward the door. "After you."

The rest of the team was already in place. Essentially an elaborate conference room inside the section of Security Solutions' offices that employees called the Cave, the War Room was off limits to all but precious few employees. An armed guard stood at the door twenty-four/seven to prevent unwanted visitors or eavesdroppers from learning the nature of the business conducted by this corner of the company.

They sat in their unofficially assigned seats, with Venice at the command station at the long end opposite the 106-inch projection screen. Jonathan sat to her immediate right, Gail to her immediate left with Boxers sprawled in the massive chair specially designed to hold him.

"I have news," Venice announced.

"I figured you might," Jonathan said.

Venice pushed a button to dim the lights and brought up a picture of the assassin in a Marine Corps dress uniform, staring intently with the stars and stripes in the background.

"Your would-be killer is indeed named Richard Goldsbury. He turned twenty-seven last week. He joined the Marines right out of high school as an infantryman. He saw two deployments to Iraq and three to Afghanistan. That third trip to Afghanistan proved to be his undoing."

"What does that mean?" Jonathan asked.

"It means he punched out his commanding officer. That got him two years in prison—excuse me, the *brig*—and a dishonorable discharge."

"What did the CO do that deserved getting punched out?" Boxers asked.

"Unclear at this point," Venice said. "But the prosecution's evidence included letters he wrote to his parents bemoaning the uselessness of the missions."

"What about that makes him want to kill Gail and me?" Jonathan asked.

"Also unclear. But . . ." The screen changed to show a list of seventeen names, Jonathan Grave, Gail Bonneville and Brian Van de Muelebroecke among them.

"What the heck is that?" Gail asked.

"I believe this is the list that Mr. Goldsbury said he didn't have," Venice said. "I found it among his photos. I presume that means this is a screen shot of a different document."

"That means no metadata for the original, right?" Gail asked.

"Exactly," Venice said. "I can't trace back to see where it came from, but it's interesting. Of the names on the list, only John Avery, Ashley Monroe, Grant Anderson, Farrell Sulkey, Linda Taylor and you guys have asterisks."

"And they look hand-drawn," Jonathan said. "I wonder why there's a line drawn through the Sulkey guy."

"We're listed differently, too," Boxers said. "All of the others have a line to themselves, but the three of us are all on the same line."

"What do we know about the asterisk entries?" Jonathan asked.

"Nothing good," Venice said. She typed a little and an image appeared of a family in swimsuits, posing for a photo at the beach. Nice-looking family.

"Grant Anderson, from Fairfax, Virginia, was shot as he was getting out of his car in his driveway. It was a sniper shot. Newspapers say that it came from four hundred yards away. One bullet through his head. He died instantly."

"What do we know about him?" Jonathan asked.

"He was a CPA. Specialized in forensic accounting. John Avery is even more interesting. He was also sniped dead. According to his social media, he was an electronic hardware guy. Planting and detecting listening devices was his specialty."

"Do we know if they were shot with the same weapon?" Jonathan asked.

"No. But they were both shot with five-five-six millimeter bullets. No shell casings were recovered at the scene."

"That means he collected them," Gail said.

"Or, he used a bolt action," Boxers corrected.

Another picture appeared on the screen. This was the image of a thirty-four-year-old female above a news article about her death.

"Meet Ashley Monroe," Venice said. "She was crossing the parking lot of a grocery store in Vienna, Virginia, when she was shot from several hundred yards away. Police have been doing their best to tamp down panic that there might be a serial killer on the loose."

"Five-five-six again?" Gail asked.

"Yup. The article says she was involved with cybersecurity," Jonathan said. "What the hell does any of this have to do with us?"

"There's got to be a common denominator," Gail said.

"What about the other asterisks, Farrell Sulkey and Linda Taylor?" Jonathan asked.

"Nothing that made the news or has come up in the police databases. I do know that Sulkey is a photographer. As far as we know, they're both still alive."

"That line through Sulkey," Boxers said. "Do we think he got a reprieve?"

"I think I see what's going on," Gail said. "I think what we see is an entire hit list, and that Goldsbury was only responsible for taking out his part of it."

"Other shooters, you think?" Venice asked. "Let's see." She typed in one of the un-asterisked names. She scrolled for a few seconds. "Nope, nothing on her." She typed another name and right away recoiled from her screen.

Venice pressed a key and another article popped up on the screen, this one featuring the face of a guy with gray hair and a very charming smile. This looked like a professional portrait. "This is Clay Riley. He was murdered while smoking a cigar in his backyard. Give me a second." She typed aggressively, as if the keyboard had offended her.

"Okay, here it is. According to ICIS, Clay Riley was shot from a distance, but this bullet was three-hundred blackout, whatever that means." Pronounced EYE-sis, the Interstate Crime Information System was a means to track ongoing investigations in real time.

"It means a second shooter." Jonathan never understood the attraction to the .300 Blackout round. It always seemed to him to be a solution in search of a problem.

"Or just a different rifle," Gail said.

"No, you know that shooters are creatures of habit," Boxers said. "We find a platform we like and we stick to it."

"And the asterisks," Jonathan said. "That has to be more than a coincidence."

Venice clicked the image on the screen to something else.

"Wait," Boxers said. "Go back."

"To what?"

"The Riley guy."

Clay Riley's face returned.

"We know him," Boxers said. "I thought he looked familiar, and now I know why." He stood to walk closer to the screen. "About four, maybe five years ago, we were working that op to rescue twins from human traffickers in Baltimore. We needed confirmation that one of the detectives was a conspirator."

Jonathan snapped his fingers. "Got it. Wolverine put us in touch with him. I didn't remember his name, though. Now that I see it, I can't un-see it."

For more years than Jonathan cared to count, he'd enjoyed a lucrative, somewhat parasitic working relationship with Irene Rivers, director of the FBI, to whom he'd given the call sign Wolverine. He'd long admired her as the only honest political appointee in Washington and doubly admired her ability to stay ahead of the career swamp monsters who were unrelenting in their efforts to bring her down.

Not that long ago, in no small measure due to a wildly illegal mission Jonathan had conducted to bring war to a Mexican drug cartel on Mexican territory, Wolverine had sacrificed her career to topple the presidential administration of asshat Anthony Darmond. The depth and breadth of the scandal had been without precedent, leaving dozens of senior executive branch appointees unemployed, lawyered up, and facing minimum sentencing guidelines measured in dozens of years. The since-impeached president led the pack.

For her part, Wolverine had disappeared—shamed by Washington media as a traitor and pariah. Last Jonathan had heard, she'd relocated to family land somewhere in West by-God Virginia. They were never to speak to each other again, if only to limit the likelihood that any of the projects they'd worked on together might ever be made public.

"Is that the common denominator, do you think?" Gail asked. "That we were all part of Director Rivers's OTR operations?" Off The Record.

"I'm not sure we can draw any conclusions from a single data point," Jonathan said. "But it *is* a data point. You remember how untrustworthy her staff was. They leaked everything and derailed any plan they didn't agree with. That's why she worked with us, and I think it's naive to believe that we were the only ones."

"Want to reach out to Wolverine and run the names by her?" Venice asked.

"We can't," Jonathan said. "Not possible. After she tanked President Darmond and his crew, every swamp monster in DC is trying to find a way to get even. We have to assume that her phones are tapped and that she's under surveillance. Irene told me that her internal communications were being shared inside the Bureau and within the CIA and the other intelligence agencies with people who didn't have the right to the information they were being fed."

"What did these off the record contractors actually do?" Venice asked.

Jonathan scoffed. "I have no idea what the others were doing, but I can guess. I think Wolfie turned to outside expertise to keep track of the bad actors who were working against her."

Venice scowled. "Doesn't the Bureau have its own group to do that sort of thing?"

"Of course they do. But she didn't know who she could trust. That's how we ended up doing so much work for her."

"Her concerns turned out to be spot-on," Boxers said.

"Spot-on and then some," Jonathan agreed. "There at the end, she had enemies at every gate."

"You know," Boxers said, "even if everybody on the kill list was one of Wolfie's OTR operators, that doesn't get us any closer to who is doing the killing or why."

Big Guy was right. By taking care of Goldsbury, they'd bought time for themselves, but if their assumptions proved correct, there was another shooter out there, working for somebody, and for reasons unknown.

"We need to get to the root of this," Gail said. "If this is somehow a government program, we can eliminate every shooter, and another one will just pop up like whack-a-mole."

"This doesn't feel like an op sanctioned by Uncle Sam," Jonathan said. "Just the presence of a list of names tells me that this is something else."

"A personal vendetta, maybe?" Gail offered.

"That's possible," Boxers said. "I don't know what those other folks did, but Lord knows we ruffled our fair share of feathers."

"People kill for revenge and they kill to keep secrets," Jonathan said. "Killing an accountant for revenge seems like a stretch to me."

"Okay," Venice said. "How do we uncover the secrets that are worth killing for if we can't reach out to Wolverine?"

"I've got it," Jonathan said. The answer arrived from nowhere. "Paul Boersky."

Boxers scowled. "Why do I know that name?"

"Because he's Jesse Montgomery's uncle."

"You mean Torpedo?" Boxers asked with a smile. Jesse had earned his call sign Torpedo through his questionable skills as a boat driver. The team had worked with him and his father, Davey, more than once. "Hey, how come they're not on the hit list?"

"First of all because we don't really know what that list shows," Jonathan said, "and second of all, Irene didn't recruit Torpedo and Chief. I did. Boersky was Wolverine's right hand for decades. If he survived the DOJ temper tantrum, he might be in a position to verify whether or not Wolfie's OTR list included these names."

"How are you going to get in touch with him?" Gail asked. "If he was that close to Wolverine, then he might still be radioactive."

Jonathan turned to Venice. "Can you get me his cell number?"

She feigned insult. Twenty seconds later: "I just texted it to you. So, you're just going to ring him up?"

"Nope," Jonathan said, pulling his own phone from his pocket. "I'm going to let Dom do it."

Father Dominic D'Angelo was pastor of St. Kate's Catholic Church, and, as a licensed psychologist, he was the default therapist for the children who lived in Resurrection House, the residential school for the children of incarcerated parents, which sat on the other side of St. Kate's from the firehouse. He and Jonathan had known each other since they shared a freshman dorm room at the College of William and Mary in Virginia. They'd even followed each other to the Army recruiting office and beyond before Dom turned to the sound of a different trumpet call than the one Jonathan had followed.

Back when Irene Rivers was head of the FBI, all of her telephone calls were public record, making it impossible to reach out directly to Jonathan to ask for the kinds of favors she would need from him. A call to or from her priest, however, was shielded from public scrutiny. Dom became the conduit for communication between Jonathan and Irene. The priest would alert one party to the desire of the other to meet and then he would stay out of the way.

Jonathan punched Dom's speed dial. "I'm hoping that pastor privilege, or whatever it's called, is still in effect."

CHAPTER SIX

William Kearns, Willy K to pretty much everybody he knew, pulled his Toyota pickup to the curb in front of the 1940s bungalow that belonged to Senator Maxine Bridges. He parked at the retaining wall that kept the front yard from sloughing down into the street. All the houses here on Illinois Street in Arlington, Virginia, were tiny, charming and different. And despite their size, they no doubt commanded huge prices. This kind of convenience to Washington was worth a fortune. Anything to shorten the twice-daily nightmare that was the commute in from the burbs.

As he stepped out into the heat, he got his first glance at a shirtless teenager pushing a gas-powered lawn mower with the enthusiasm of a man on his way to death row. The kid's eyes seemed locked on a point just in front of the mower deck, and he seemed unbothered by the sweat that dripped from his nose and his chin.

Willy K climbed the spalling concrete steps that took him up to the yard, and then waited for the slave labor to cross the front walk with his mower before walking up to the front door.

The sight of Willy K seemed to startle the kid out of his mowing trance. He jumped and pulled an AirPod out of his ear. "Oh, I'm sorry," he said. "I didn't see you."

"You didn't come close to hitting me," Willy K said. "Don't worry about it. Sure looks like you're having fun."

The kid shrugged and wiped sweat away with the back of his hand. "It's probably good for me to be out and getting drenched in my own stink." He smiled. "I owe the senator a favor."

Oh, I bet you do, Willy K thought. Maxine Bridges had always liked her men to be boys. Just ask some of the Senate pages who worked in the days before the inside secret of page boffing came perilously close to becoming an outside secret.

As he approached the steps to the stoop, Maxine opened the door and then the screen. "Good afternoon, Willy," she said. "Thanks for coming."

They shook hands as he passed her at the doorjamb and stepped into the tiny foyer. Absent central air conditioning, the house depended on window units to stay cool, and because the foyer was windowless, it was hot as hell.

"I see you got a new boy toy," Willy K said as Maxine closed the door and led him to the tiny living room on the left of the center hall.

"For a virgin, he really knows what he's doing." She sat in the middle of a tiny love seat.

Willy K took the green brocade wing-back chair on the other side of the coffee table. "You took care of the virginity thing, I'm sure, Senator."

"I did, and he's a quick learner."

"What did you promise this one?"

"An appointment to Annapolis."

Willy K winced. "Oh, now that's a cruel trick. What happens when he finds out it's not real?"

"This one is real," she said. "Assuming he survives to accept it. I really like Kerry."

"What can you possibly find to talk about?"

Maxine offered a sideways smile. "When we're together, talking is not a priority."

Willy K didn't get it. That boy behind the mower was a good-looking, well-put-together kid. Maxine . . . wasn't. Well into her forties, she'd had so much work done that her face looked too tight for her skull. Her breasts were her main attraction, he supposed, but they had been too big before the most recent boob job.

"But talking *is* a priority here," she said. "I'd like a status report on your, um, special project."

"You mean my murder tour?" Willy K asked. "I don't imagine we're being recorded here."

Maxine set her jaw. "I don't like that kind of language."

Willy K laughed. "You order people to be . . . terminated? Does that word work for you?" She glared. "You order it, but you don't want to talk about it. My status report is that I'm working on it."

"Each contract needs to be completed before the Event," Maxine said, leaning in. "Time is running short."

"I've only got one left. Well, two since you gave me the guy in Harrisonburg. The photographer. What happened there? Why did you reassign the hit?"

"Does it matter?" Maxine asked. "The fee goes with the operation."

"Fair enough," Willy K said. "Rest assured that everything will be taken care of." He paused. "Now, why am I really here? You don't do personal audiences unless it's important."

"How are preparations going for the Event?" She kept her tone low and conspiratorial.

"Looks like they're going fine to me. We've got quality personnel. It helps to have that final layout. That makes the drills more realistic. But you have to realize that no plan survives the first encounter. We have no idea what the actual turnout will be, though I can guarantee a high death count. Dozens, probably. Maybe more. But if you want a real assessment, you should talk to Farook."

Maxine shook her head. "I don't like speaking with him. He

doesn't respect me, perhaps because I am a woman, and it's too much of a risk. I need to be at arm's length from everything. When the Event is over, I imagine that authorities will eventually link it to Omar Farook. The public is going to want to see blood, and I need to be on the side of the public. Omar understands this."

"Letting them use your farm for training is a shitty plan for staying off the radar."

"Thanks. Your opinion means so much to me."

"I mean, seriously. I don't really understand why you're doing this in the first place, but allowing the use of your farm—"

"Just stop," Maxine said. "The Event is not launching from my property, and Omar assures me that when all is done, there'll be nothing to trace it back to me. It would take a lot of evidence to justify a search warrant on property I own in North Carolina when I spend half my life here in DC."

"But why—"

"I have my reasons, Willy. How about we just leave it there?"

The *why* was fundamentally none of Willy K's business, and he understood that. For some reason, something inside of Senator Bridges had broken and made it seem okay to kill a bunch of young people—not as collateral damage, but as the primary targets. Yes, it was Omar Farook's plan and his money, but given all she had to lose, Willy K couldn't wrap his head around why she would be willing to take such a chance of being associated with the Event, even if at arm's length.

Willy K had given up on wallowing in the morality question of what he did for a living. His work was never personal. It was always about the paycheck—and this one was the one that would help him disappear off the grid forever. But Maxine Bridges had a lot to lose—she had *everything* to lose—if this thing went even a little bit sideways.

"All right," Willy K said. "I'll stop pressing for answers and concentrate on giving answers. What do you want to know?"

"When will you finish with your terminations?"

"Within the next few days," Willy K said. "It'll be done before you have to worry about it."

She seemed satisfied. "Now, walk me through the logistics of how the Event is going to work."

If the Catholic Church printed a fundraising calendar, Father Dominic D'Angelo would doubtless be on the cover. The man never aged. His dark brown eyes glowed with kindness, he was quick to smile, and there wasn't a single strand of gray in his black hair. Frankly, it kind of pissed Jonathan off.

Dom had made his phone call to Paul Boersky, and now sat in the War Room next to Jonathan. The priest looked nervous, like someone pulled into a board meeting to be reprimanded. He wasn't a regular in this part of the Security Solutions headquarters, but it wasn't his first time.

In fact, the first time involved shooting a guy.

"Boersky seemed almost grateful for the call," Dom reported. "Yes, all of those names on Goldsbury's list were contractors hired by Irene Rivers to perform various tasks."

"What kind of tasks?" Jonathan asked.

"Boersky said they were tasks that fell within their various areas of expertise. That's pretty much a quote. He had noticed the pattern of the murders, but he said he was not in a position to do anything about it. He was happy that I called."

"He's the FBI," Gail said. "Why can't he do anything?"

"I don't think you want him to," Dom said.

Jonathan agreed. "No one was supposed to know about Wolfie's list of OTRs. If that gets wide exposure, we could be looking at some bad days."

Dom looked to Venice. "Boersky said he was going to send you some files."

"And he did," Venice said, clearing her throat. "It took a few minutes to figure out what I was looking at, but then I was able to organize things. Here's a list of people that Wolverine ran investigations on."

The projected image showed a spreadsheet of names. A lot of names.

"How many enemies did Wolfie have?" Gail asked. "That's a who's who of the federal government."

That wasn't hyperbole. Irene Rivers had run some sort of investigation on every cabinet secretary and several hundred members of Congress.

"She never impressed me as being that paranoid," Boxers said.

"Paranoia and situational awareness are different things," Jonathan said. "You know how corrupt the Darmond crowd was. Christ, how many senior government pukes did we take down? I think she was wise to have these files—whatever these files were."

Venice said, "Father Dom, did Paul Boersky mention where he got these files? Are they, like, common knowledge?"

"We talked about that. To his knowledge, there was only one copy of this, and Irene entrusted it to him as she was on her way out."

"If there's only one copy, then how come somebody's hunting us down?" Boxers asked. "Somebody leaked something or stole something."

Dom answered with an extended shrug. "Ladies and gentlemen, I will take my leave. I have the sense that you are on the verge of discussing things I should not hear."

"Thanks, Dom," Jonathan said.

"One day," Dom said as he opened the door to exit, "I'm going to write my priestly memoir, and it will be unlike any other."

Gail pointed back to the screen. "It's not possible that every one of those people posed a threat to the country, is it?"

"There are threats," Boxers said, "and there are *threats*. With a list this vast, it's impossible to tell the severity or the scope."

"Remember, we're looking for a list of one. If we assume that one of these targets was scared enough or pissed off enough to order executions, then we need some kind of inside knowledge of what sins the OTRs were investigating. It's a big step to hire a killer."

"The way I see it," Big Guy said, "there's only two reasons to hire killers in this case. There's either revenge or fear. They're pissed off that they were spied on, or they need to shut up people who know stuff."

"It's got to be fear," Jonathan said. "Revenge would be for sins past and frankly doesn't fit with the Washington elite mindset. When the swamp rats are angry, they destroy their enemies through stories real and fake, leaked to the media. When they're scared, though, they're happy to kill to keep their secrets safe."

"There does seem to be an inordinate number of *suicides* among political aides," Boxers scoffed.

"That's the impossible part here," Gail said. "If we don't know the severity of the information Irene was gathering, how are we going to judge the likelihood that one of these targets—let alone *which* of these targets—is the one who ordered the killings?"

An idea bloomed in Jonathan's head. He pointed to the matrix on the screen. "Where up there does it tell us which of the OTR contractors worked on which targets?"

"Give me a minute," Venice said. Keys clacked under her fingers and the images on the screen danced and changed. "Those are two different databases," she said. "On the main spreadsheet, it looks like the contractors have code numbers. See there?" She moved her cursor to four-digit numbers in the far right-hand column. "The actual cross reference to the people who are so numbered are in this database." The screen jumped again to show a list of names.

"Stop," Jonathan said. He pointed at the screen again. "Right there. It shows one of our victims, Monroe, to be one-oh-seven-seven, right?"

"Right."

"Okay," Jonathan said. "Anderson and Avery are also going to have numbers. If you can tickle the electrons in your computer to find which of the targets on Wolfie's list had Monroe, Anderson, or Avery working on them to gather information, then we'll be a long way toward finding our bad guy. Right?"

"Follow the *who*, not the *why*," Boxers said.

"Wait," Gail said. "Are we assuming that the killer is a contractor hired by a government official?"

"At this point, I think we have to," Jonathan said. "It's what makes the most sense."

"Occam's razor," Boxers added.

"I just think that's a hell of a conclusion to jump to in the absence of real evidence."

Jonathan nodded to Venice. "Let's just see where the assumption takes us."

A minute and a half later, the screen shifted to show a mere 173 people.

"Holy shit," Jonathan said.

"Wait!" Gail said. "You did that wrong. You don't want to see which targets *any* of the OTR contractors worked on. You want to see which ones *all three* of them worked on. Right? Because you're operating on the assumption that all three were killed by the same gunman."

"That works for me," Venice said. More typing reduced the list to seventeen contractors, who together investigated twelve different targets.

"Are we projecting seventeen total murders?" Boxers scoffed. "That's gonna be one exhausted shooter. We don't have it yet."

"Some of those names aren't on Goldsbury's list," Venice said. She highlighted a name with her cursor. "This guy, Joseph Cranston. He worked the same targets as the dead contractors, but he's not on the list."

"Maybe he's already dead," Jonathan suggested.

Venice typed. "Nope. Alive and well and running a security firm in Provo, Utah."

"All right, then," Jonathan said. "Drop Mr. Cranston out of the mix and see what we're left with."

The projection screen danced again. Five contractor names remained, three of them already dead.

"And then there were two," Jonathan said. "I believe at least one of those remaining names belongs to the next victim. Work your magic and tell me everything you can find in thirty seconds about Farrell Sulkey and Linda Taylor."

Venice leaned into a second screen that the others in the room couldn't see. It didn't take long at all. "Sulkey is a photographer and Taylor is a geek. Specializes in artificial intelligence." More typing. Then a lot more typing. "Digger, we've got to talk about a raise. Linda Taylor makes nearly a million dollars off her AI consulting work."

"Is that a lot?" Jonathan asked.

"It is when you have no employees."

"Sounds to me like her clients might not be the kind a mother would be proud of," Boxers said.

Venice slapped the table, startling all of them. "I got it!" she proclaimed. "We're there. The only person that all five of these OTRs investigated was Senator Maxine Bridges of North Carolina."

The screen blinked again to display a lady in a business suit sporting a fake smile and posing in front of an American flag.

"Here she is," Venice said. "She's quite the busy beaver. Her committee assignments are Banking, Housing and Urban Affairs, Foreign Relations, Environment and Public Works, Homeland Security and Government Affairs and the Special Committee on Aging. For whatever Director Rivers was investigating there, she'd assigned Monroe, Anderson, Avery and Sulkey, and Taylor."

Boxers said, "So, a corrupt, murderous US senator. Who saw that coming?"

"What's the next step?" Gail asked.

"We have to let Sulkey and Taylor know, right?" Venice said.

"Um . . . yes?" Jonathan said. "But to what end? Just call them and tell them that someone *might* be trying to kill them? How does that work, exactly? And what are they supposed to do with that information?"

"They take more precautions," Venice said.

"For how long?" Gail asked.

Boxers added, "You get people spun up that their lives may be in danger and then don't give them an exit ramp, that's just a recipe for panic."

"So, you're suggesting we do nothing?" Venice looked aghast. "What was the point of this exercise?"

"No, I'm not suggesting we do nothing," Jonathan said. "I'm suggesting that we come at them with a solution as well as a problem."

"What solution would that be?"

"Their problem doesn't go away until the shooters go away. And the shooters don't go away until we figure out who they are and why they were hired in the first place."

"We need to interview the surviving contractors," Gail said. "We need to get them to tell us what they saw, heard or learned that was worth killing for."

"Then what?" Venice asked. "We'll have a pile of dirt gathered against a senator who is unlikely to step up and say, *Yeah, I'm the one who hired a hit man.*"

"She might if the evidence is compelling enough," Jonathan said. "We're not there yet, but who knows? Sooner or later, we're going to have to confront her."

"We need to alert the future victims first," Gail said.

"We need to split up," Jonathan said. "We'll interview the contractors—"

"While they're still alive," Boxers said.

"Always easiest. Where do they live?"

Venice scanned her screen. "Farrell Sulkey lives in Harrison-burg, Virginia, and Linda Taylor lives in Chevy Chase, Mary-land."

"I hate Maryland," Boxers said.

"You hate everything," Gail scoffed. "Fine, I'll take Linda Taylor."

"I'll babysit Big Guy," Jonathan said.

CHAPTER SEVEN

Jason Sulkey was in hell. It was three hundred degrees out here, with humidity you could see, and his dad somehow thought that a great gift for Jason's fourteenth birthday would be to give him a rifle and have him sit in a tree stand waiting for a pig to wander by so he could shoot it. Murder it, really, because they weren't going to harvest the meat. The order was to kill as many as you could see and let them rot and become vulture food.

Um, no.

The tree stand lasted in Jason's life for about ten minutes. Essentially a chair fastened to a tree about ten feet off the ground, the wooden slats pinched his legs (okay, maybe he should have listened when Dad told him to change into long pants) and the sightly forward pitch of the seat made him feel like he was about to fall. With a rifle in his hands. What could possibly go wrong?

Dad had always been Mr. Manly-Man—hunter, fisherman, company softball star—but since the divorce, with Mom having custody most of the time, he'd been progressively more obsessed with *manning up* Jason, who really wasn't very good at anything athletic. He could get a basketball through the hoop from pretty much anywhere on the court, but he couldn't dribble and move at the same time. He could catch a baseball okay (who the hell can't?) but he couldn't throw for shit. Don't even talk about batting.

Still, Dad took him to batting cages, and to the gym to shoot hoops, and even to the driving range, where Jason's shots posed a lethal hazard to anyone standing anywhere but downrange.

As far as he knew, the only physical activity at which Jason had even a lick of natural ability was with guns. Pistols, rifles, shotguns, it didn't matter. He could smoke the birds at skeet or sporting clays, and he could always make the steel ping at the pistol range. Rifles were easy, once you got the optics sighted in. Just settle the crosshairs on the spot you want to hit and ease the trigger straight back. Physics took care of the rest.

The problem with shooting some of Dad's arsenal was the weight of the larger caliber rifles. Dad was old-school, so he believed in firearms with wood furniture rather than some of the lighter composites. They were a tad too heavy for Jason to shoot reliably offhand, so he always had to use something to rest the barrel on to get a reliable shot.

For his birthday, then, Dad bought him a brand-new Ruger American Ranch rifle, chambered in 6.5 millimeter Creedmoor. The furniture was all made of a light composite material, and the 6.5 Creedmoor offered far less recoil while delivering enough punch to drop a deer.

But Jason didn't want to drop a deer. He wanted to poke holes in targets and pulverize clay pigeons. What had a deer ever done to him? Let alone a pig?

He guessed he understood his dad's confusion. If you want a hunting rifle, it must be to go hunting, right? The logic is clear. But the facts were wrong. Jason wasn't a tree-hugger or a vegan, but he wasn't an animal murderer either. He'd let others do the murdering while he filled his stomach with the spoils of their animal war.

Dad was settled in place a hundred yards or so to Jason's right, so he couldn't see that Jason now sat at the base of his tree, texting with his buddy Carmine about how hot, miserable and bored he was. He wondered how much he could sweat on his phone before the phone thought it had been dropped in the toilet and the electronics fried.

He was posing that exact question to Carmine when he heard the sound of an approaching truck.

"What the hell?" he muttered aloud. He rose up to his knees to peer above the bushes that blocked his view. They were too far into the property to hear road noise, so whoever this was had to have come through the gate. Sure enough, a green four-door sedan was making its way through the grass.

He said it again. "What the hell?"

Willy K enjoyed the irony that he was hunting humans during hunting season. The irony was even deeper since his next target was in fact wandering the woods hunting.

He'd have preferred to wait for another time—say, a time when his prey wasn't armed with a high-powered rifle—but in this particular game of poker, you had no choice but to play the hand you were dealt.

He'd be lying if he said he wasn't concerned. The first three targets in this contract had fallen awfully easily. While he didn't believe in luck, he did believe in Murphy's Law, and he always got nervous when things were going well. He'd spent a lifetime dealing with FUBAR—effed up beyond all recognition—and he was comfortable with it. This shit-going-right shit felt all wrong.

Come to think of it, he held the same attitude toward what most people called happiness. Love and smiles and laughter all just set you up for a longer fall when life's shitty realities came by and slapped you in the head.

He'd planned this hit to be just like the others—take the guy out at his home—but it went sideways when he saw that the driveway held the wrong car and garage was empty. A helpful babysitter had told him that Farrell Sulkey and his boy, Jason, were out hunting feral hogs and coyotes on a bunch of land the family owned just outside of Shenandoah National Park. She even gave him the address.

Clearly, whoever designed the modules for babysitter training needed to beef up their chapter on stranger danger.

Hunting a hunter did make him reconsider his armament. The carbine he'd used for the other hits was chambered in a .300 Blackout and it wasn't the right gun for this. First of all, carrying one of the scary black rifles that had been vilified by the media attracted unwanted attention from onlookers, so Willy K chose his old yet reliable Browning X-Bolt .308.

Plus, given the nature of Sulkey's intended prey, Willy K figured Sulkey would be carrying something high-powered. Once hogs rolled in the mud and baked in the sun for a while, they developed an armor coat that was bulletproof to smaller rounds.

A ninety-minute drive took Willy K to the end of a gravel driveway that he didn't see until he'd already passed it. He glanced in his rearview mirror to verify that no one would rear-end him and executed the kind of emergency spin you only get to do when you're out in the country. Screeching tires filled the air with the acrid stench of burning rubber that rooster-tailed out from under the chassis. He recovered the spin, slowed, and made the left-hand turn onto the gravel drive.

Twenty-five yards in, he encountered a steel cattle gate, hinged to a post on the left and padlocked to a post on the right.

Willy K stopped his car, threw the transmission into park and leaned back into his seat to think. What was the right call here? They'd placed giant rocks on either side of the gate, filling the space between the driveway and the trees, so driving around wasn't an option. He thumbed the button for the trunk release.

He kept his burglar tools in two canvas bags, a large one and a small one. He unzipped the big one, removed a pair of long-handled bolt cutters and walked them to the gate, where he made quick work of the bale on the lock. Now that he got a closer look, he saw that it was one of those cheap spring lock models that he could have opened in seconds with a pick.

The voice of an old forcible-entry instructor echoed in his

brain: *Try before you pry.* Yeah, well, next time. He opened the gate.

He returned the cutters to the bag, closed the trunk and drove through the opening he made. Having grown up as a country boy, he couldn't bring himself not to close a gate he'd opened, so he parked again, got out, closed the gate and returned to the driver's seat. He didn't bother with the ruined lock. What would be the point?

Through the gate now, he was facing a wide expanse of nothing, a beautiful, undeveloped landscape, to his eye equal parts field and forest. Assuming Sulkey was out here, how the hell was Willy K going to find him?

No sooner had he asked himself the question than the answer arrived in the form of a pair of matted vehicle tracks through the grass, not brand-new, but no more than a few hours old.

He mimicked a Munchkin voice when he said, "Follow the yellow brick road."

Dad was going to be *pissed.* He hated it when people broke onto the property. This was the first time they'd caught a trespasser in the act. This could be a good show.

Jason stood to his full height but stayed in the shadow of a tall tree.

Way down to Jason's right, he saw his father emerging from the thicket of trees that concealed his ground blind.

From what Jason could tell, the newcomer was looking for their pickup truck, which was parked way on the other side of a field, on the far side of another thicket of trees. Was he going to rob the truck? There was a lot of ammo in there. And a pistol.

His dad waved to get Jason's attention, then made a tamping motion in the air, telling him to stay put. With his rifle slung over his shoulder, Dad started walking toward the stranger's car.

Because of a thicket that grew between them, Jason didn't think Dad could see the trespasser removing a scoped rifle from the back seat of his car. The guy wasn't dressed for hunting. No camo gear, but rather just a pair of blue jeans with a windbreaker and a flannel shirt. He opened the bolt of his rifle, inserted a magazine, then chambered a round.

"Holy crap," Jason whispered. "He's a poacher."

Jason picked up his Ruger from the ground and brought it up to his shoulder to watch the guy through his scope. Technically, he was breaking the rule about not pointing a gun at anything you don't want to destroy, but he had no round in the chamber.

For the first time in all of this, Jason felt a hint of fear in the base of his spine. He wondered if he should yell out and warn his dad. But there was no need.

From fifty, seventy-five yards away, Dad shouted, "Hey! You! Can I help you?"

Dad had a voice that matched his size. When he wanted to sound intimidating, nobody could do it better.

The guy at the car didn't hesitate. At the sound of Dad's voice, he jerked his rifle up to his shoulder and fired a round straight at him. A half-second later, Jason heard a shot fired from his dad's location and a hole appeared in the fender of the poacher's car.

The poacher chambered another round, brought the rifle to his shoulder, but then didn't take the shot. Instead, he brought the weapon to his chest and started off in Dad's direction.

"Dad! Oh, shit!" Terrified, Jason settled his crosshairs on the poacher's chest and pressed the trigger.

Nothing happened.

"Dammit!" His breech was empty. Jason worked the bolt. A cartridge slid into place.

The poacher was running toward Dad, toward the thicket. In another couple of seconds, Jason wouldn't be able to see him anymore because of the lines of sight.

Jason double checked that the safety was off and he raised the rifle to his shoulder again. This time, it was a hurried shot, before the guy could disappear, and he yanked the trigger pretty hard.

He lost his sight picture on the recoil, but when he recovered it, the poacher was gone. Probably because Jason had hit him.

Probably.

Shit, shit, shit. Had Dad been hit? What if he'd been killed?

Jason found himself running before he even thought about it. Running toward his father. Dad would know what to do. "Dad!" he yelled. "Are you okay?"

No reply.

"Dad!" Holding the rifle with both hands across his chest, he pumped his legs as hard as he could to propel himself across the grass and through the underbrush. "Dad!"

He wished he'd brought some kind of two-way radio. He wished they had decent cell service. He wished they'd stayed home.

Somebody moaned from the bushes, from where Dad would be if he was hiding. He stopped and listened.

"Jase, I'm over here. Stop making so much noise."

Oh, thank God. He wasn't hurt after all. "Where are you?"

"Walk five paces and look to your right." Dad's voice sounded different.

"Right here," Dad said. His voice came with a liquid gurgle— a sound he'd never heard before.

His dad had run and stumbled to the base of a scraggly cedar tree, where he'd collapsed. He sat on the ground with his legs forming the numeral 4 and his back supported by the tree trunk. He was leaning severely to his right side, where Jason could see a hole in the fabric of his camouflage T-shirt, just below his shoulder. He didn't see much blood around the wound, but bloody spit bubbles had formed around the corners of Dad's mouth.

And there was that gurgling.

"You need to get out of here, Jason. That man's not a poacher, he's a murderer."

"You don't look so good," Jason said. "I don't see a lot of blood, but I think you're bleeding pretty bad."

"You need to run, son. He's going to—"

Time to *man up.* "Is your trauma kit back in the blind in your backpack?" Dad was a be-prepared guy.

"You don't have time for that," Dad said. "And you don't know how to use a trauma kit."

"You can talk me through it."

"I don't know what that asshole is up to or why he's shooting at me, but he's not going to stop. You need to run to—"

"I shot him, Dad," Jason said. As he spoke the words, he felt guilty. He felt sick.

"Where?"

"Back there."

"No," Dad said, frustration evident. "Where on his body? Where did you hit him?"

"I aimed for his chest."

"Is that where you hit him?"

"I think so."

"Is he dead?"

"Yes. He dropped right where he was when I shot him. He went right to the ground."

"Are you sure?"

CHAPTER EIGHT

Linda Taylor lived like the millionaire she was. Chevy Chase was the land of old money in Washington. Not Georgetown money like in Kalorama, where once-poor former presidents could afford to live after leaving office, but *influence* money. The power brokers who lived in this neighborhood still conducted business on golf courses and the nineteenth hole.

The Taylors' whitewashed red brick home sat atop a hill five blocks away from Chevy Chase Circle, barely over the Maryland line. Larger than her neighbors' houses on either side, the boxwoods lining the walkway to the front door were perfectly trimmed—not a single errant sprig rose out of the flat surfaces.

Gail found a spot for her Ford Excursion along a curb a block and a half away, triple-checking for signs announcing any of the parking traps that the area was known for. Finding none, she locked the door, made sure that her blazer covered the holstered Glock on her hip, and walked back to the Taylor place.

A press of the doorbell button produced a Big Ben chime on the other side of the elaborate door. She was not at all surprised when a uniformed housekeeper answered—though a little surprised that he was male. Maybe twenty-five years old, he had an East African complexion and a very broad, white smile.

"Good afternoon," the man said.

"Good afternoon," Gail said. "I need to speak with Linda Taylor. Is she here?"

The housekeeper's smile remained fixed. "Who may I say is calling?"

"My name is Gerarda Culp." It was an alias she used frequently, and it was tied to ersatz FBI credentials that she hesitated to use, especially with Irene Rivers no longer at the top of the food chain at the Bureau.

"May I say what this is in regard to?"

After a beat, Gail said, "No. But it's important."

"I have to tell her something," the man said.

Gail understood that the guy had a job to do. She had to offer him something. "All right. Tell her it's about some work she did for a government office on Pennsylvania Avenue."

The housekeeper seemed unsure. "Is that all?"

"That should be enough. In fact, if she questions, tell her I *said* that that should be enough."

"I-I don't understand."

Gail forced a smile. "Please?"

The housekeeper continued to stare.

"Sometime today," Gail said. "Now, actually."

The housekeeper stepped aside and motioned Gail in with a circular waving motion of his arm. "Yes. Certainly, certainly. Please wait in the foyer and I will alert her that you are here." He hurried down the center hall and button-hooked to the right to go up the stairs.

Alert seemed like an odd verb under the circumstances, but she chalked it up to language differences. The interior of the home struck Gail as aspirational plantation. The smoky-green wainscoted walls featured portraits of men and women in colonial attire, and one in a Union officer's uniform. They all looked to be original oil paintings and showed the appropriate aging. When this visit was over, Gail thought maybe she'd have to do some research into the Taylor family tree.

She only had to wait a minute or two before she heard the

sound of high heels on the wooden steps. A woman in her forties, with brunette hair that was a week or so late for its appointment with her colorist, made the turn from the base of the stairs and approached Gail with her hand outstretched. Trim and attractive, she wore a blue blazer over jeans and a red sweater.

"Hello, I am Linda Taylor. Jeffrey said you needed to speak with me."

They shook hands. "Gerarda Culp. Sorry for the mystery. I promise that I mean no harm. It's extremely important, however, that you and I chat."

"About what?"

Gail scanned the various empty rooms surrounding the foyer. "Someplace private?"

Linda hesitated.

"It's about the off-the-record work you did for Irene Rivers when she was FBI director."

Linda's shoulders sagged a little.

"I believe your life may be in danger."

That did it. Linda indicated the room to the right of the foyer with her open palm. "Please. Let's go into the parlor."

Unsure of the differences between a parlor and a living room, Gail led the way into a small, charming, elegant and *very* femininely decorated room. Four Queen Anne style upholstered chairs had been arranged around a circular ebony-inlaid cherry coffee table.

"Sit where you'd like. Can I have Jeffrey offer you anything?"

Gail took the seat that faced the foyer doorway. "No, I'm fine, thank you."

Linda sat to her right, facing the front window. "You said I'm in danger?"

"Potentially, yes," Gail said. "And I'll get to that. But first I need to ask you some questions." She pulled a slim reporter's notebook from the inside pocket of her blazer and clicked a ballpoint.

"Are you *armed*?" Linda asked with a slight gasp. Apparently, she'd glimpsed the Glock on Gail's belt.

"My life is equally in danger," Gail explained. "What was the nature of the work you did for Director Rivers?"

"I don't want a gun in this house."

"Then the faster we get through these questions, the faster both the gun and I will leave. Now, please focus. What sort of work did you do?"

Linda's face lost some color. "I-I, uh." She would have been a terrible poker player.

"I'm sorry to be so blunt, Ms. Taylor, but the work you did is the root of why you are in danger. Director Rivers left a lot of upset people in her wake when she left, and many of her darkest, most closely kept secrets have come to life. I believe that you are among those secrets."

"I think I need to call my lawyer." Linda stood.

Gail stayed seated, held up her hands to calm her. "No, you really don't," she said. "Please have a seat and listen to me for a few minutes. You don't have to say a thing. If you don't speak, there's no need for your attorney. And when you've heard everything I have to tell you, I don't think you'll want one. Is that fair?"

Linda looked every bit as confused as she should have. As she sat back down, Gail rose from her chair and pointed to the double doors that led to the foyer. "May I close those, please?"

Linda nodded. She might have said, "Yes," but no sound came out.

Gail checked to see if Jeffrey was eavesdropping before she pulled the doors closed and was pleased to find the foyer empty.

Returning to her seat, Gail leaned back and crossed her legs, hoping to project calm comfort. "Here it is. I was likewise one of Director Rivers's off-the-record contractors. You and I are both members of a club whose membership list was never to be released. Somehow, though, it *was* released, and so far, at least three of her OTR contractors have been killed. We have reason to believe that you are on the assassin's list of targets."

"*We* have reason to believe?" Linda asked. "Who is *we*?"

"I'm part of a larger team," Gail said.

"A larger team that does what?"

Gail knew she was walking the razor edge of dangerous territory. She'd opened this door. She couldn't very well close it without saying something by way of explanation. "A team that does things like finding and stopping assassins," she said.

"So, you're *counter-assassins*." Linda used finger quotes.

Gail grew serious. "Be careful with your language, Linda. I'm here as a favor to you, hoping to stop the killer before he gets to your name."

Linda's shoulders sank, reminding Gail in an odd way of an embarrassed turtle.

"I-I'm sorry," Linda said. "That was shitty of me. When I get nervous, I get snarky. I didn't mean—"

"You make your living in the artificial intelligence space," Gail said, interrupting. "Is that the nature of the work you did for Director Rivers?"

Linda was still hesitant, still circumspect about coming clean. She started to say something but then stopped herself.

"I can't help you unless you help me," Gail said. "It's really that simple. And really that hard."

"That's . . . sort of what I did for Irene," she said. "I was what I think Richard Nixon called a plumber. I worked at fixing leaks. Irene's office could not—or, as it turned out, chose not to—keep secrets, especially when they potentially embarrassed the director, or if they involved ongoing efforts to seek out corruption within the government. She hired me, among others, to use my technical skills to track down those who were disloyal to her and to point them out."

Gail waited for more. When it didn't come, she prompted, "And then what?"

"And then I deposited my check."

Gail's bullshit bell pealed. "What about retaliation?"

Linda looked away. "I don't know what you're talking about."

"Yes, you do. Some friendly advice: Never play poker for big money. You don't bluff well."

Linda shifted in her chair, placed her forearms on her knees, then sat back again. "Look, she said we would have immunity for all of this."

"I'm not a prosecutor, Linda." Gail couldn't keep the exasperation out of her voice this time. "Nobody gives a shit about your immunity. Jesus, people are dying—perhaps you among them. Get with the program."

After a big breath, Linda settled herself and leaned back into her chair. "Sometimes, we would plant very real-looking false items in people's files and emails as a way to either get them disciplined, or I presume, as a way for Director Rivers to be able to leverage their cooperation."

"What kind of false items are we talking about?"

"You know, emails that they never wrote, deep fake pictures of them doing things or hanging out with people. Irene always assured me that these were things that they had actually done, but for which her evidence wasn't strong enough to take official action."

It was Gail's turn to stare. She didn't know if she was impressed or appalled. "Give me an example."

Linda tilted her head up, as if searching the ceiling for the perfect choice. "Well, in one case, it was a senior DOJ staffer who was taking bribes to tamper with evidence. I created the email string between him and the moneyman setting up all the conditions. I even engineered the metadata to show that he'd tried to delete the conversation after he'd written it."

"What happened to the staffer?"

Linda shrugged. "I don't know. I don't think Irene cared. She got him to ask for a transfer far away from her, and I think that was enough. Then there was that member of the House two years or so ago, who was thrown out for his sexual advances on the underage pages."

"I remember that," Gail said. "From Ohio, right?"

"Right. Well, those security pictures you saw on the news of him *in flagrante* with the pixelated page may or may not have been created by me. It was enough to get him thrown out of Congress, but true to her word, Irene refused to use those photos as evidence in a criminal trial so he was never indicted."

As Gail let the information settle into her brain, she pulled the pen and notepad from her blazer pocket again.

"Are those the people you think are trying to kill me?"

"I don't know," Gail said. "And to be clear, I don't have affirmative evidence that *anyone* is actually trying to kill you."

"Then why are you here?"

"Because our circumstantial evidence is very strong. Your name is on a list of names of people who are being murdered. All the names on the list are people who worked on the same target individual as you did. It feels like a connection. So here we go: Do the names Ashley Monroe, Grant Anderson or John Avery mean anything to you?"

"No."

"Please don't answer so quickly," Gail admonished. "Give it some thought. Those are the names of the OTR contractors who have been killed in the last two weeks." She repeated the names slowly.

"No, they don't ring any bells. But that's not surprising, really, because we all worked independently. To tell the truth, until my conversation with you today, I thought I was the only one that Irene had leaned on for outside help. She always made me feel so important."

"We felt the same way," Gail confessed. "And we didn't know anything about other contractors until just yesterday. I wasn't *surprised* that there were more, but I wasn't aware."

"Exactly," Linda said. "Not surprised."

"Let's talk about Maxine Bridges," Gail said.

"The senator?"

"Right. Was she on your operations list at one point?"

Linda grew uncomfortable again, leaning back in her chair.

"Yes, she was," she said. "That one was strange. The director asked me to make sure that every email the senator got—whether through her official Senate address or from her personal account—was also routed to her.'"

"To Director Rivers."

"Right. And she also had me plant a camera in the senator's office and in her home. That was the first bit of real burglary I'd ever done. The only one, actually."

"Do you have any idea what she was looking for?"

"I have an idea," Linda said, "but I don't have facts to back it up. I think Director Rivers thought that maybe Senator Bridges was a spy."

Gail recoiled from the word. "A spy? Seriously?"

"Or something like that," Linda said. "I didn't read much of what we intercepted, but I know there were a lot of communications from the Middle East."

"That doesn't make her a spy," Gail said.

Linda shrugged. "You asked me, I told you. Do what you want with the information." Linda's eyes grew wide and she snapped her fingers. "Oh, and I'm pretty sure she hired some kind of private investigator to follow the senator."

Gail couldn't make the pieces come together in her mind. "I don't get it. Why would she use private contractors when she's got the whole FBI to do her bidding?"

"That one's easy," Linda said. "When she wasn't being a spy, Senator Bridges was an obstructionist against many of the director's plans to combat inner city crime, and as a senior member of the Judiciary Committee, her resistance was a real problem. It became clear to Director Rivers that someone in her office was leaking the content of secret meetings—strategy meetings—directly to the senator. She hired me to find out who was doing it."

"And?"

"It wasn't pretty. Things were every bit as bad in Director Rivers's shop toward the end as she said it was in her testimony. The agents under her watch—particularly the younger, most ambitious ones—had come to see their mission as less about the pursuit of justice than it was about the furthering of their careers. They knew that the president didn't like Irene Rivers, so they did whatever they could to get in her way and make her look bad."

"So there was more than one leaker?"

"There was a whole nest of them."

"What happened to them?" Gail asked.

"It looks to me like they won," Linda said.

Gail tapped her lower lip with tented fingers as she considered what Linda was saying. "What was Irene's reaction when you told her about the leaks?"

"I remember that so vividly," Linda said. "At first, she was mad—which was understandable, right? Because that's what I would have been. But that only lasted for a few seconds before she became really very sad. She said that the Bureau had become something she didn't recognize anymore. She said she didn't like not being able to trust the people she needed to trust."

Linda cocked her head and tapped the table with the tip of her middle finger. "Okay, your turn," she said. "You must think that Senator Bridges is somehow linked to the murders. Where's the connection?"

"I don't know," Gail confessed. "All I know is that from what we can tell, Maxine Bridges is the common denominator for OTR work performed by you, Ashley Monroe, Grant Anderson, and John Avery. She is also the *only* common denominator for you and one other contractor that is also on the list."

"I can tell you for sure that I didn't work with anyone else," Linda said. "I didn't have to. It wasn't that kind of operation. I didn't need partners."

It hadn't occurred to Gail that perhaps multiple operations had been launched against Senator Bridges, with each op utilizing a different team. She used her arms to press herself to a standing position.

Linda followed.

"I think that's all I need for now," she said.

Linda reached out with both hands. "Wait. What am I supposed to do now?"

Irene shrugged. "I honestly don't know. Be very careful, I guess. Watch out for strangers, try to vary your routine from day to day—you know, don't leave the house at the identical time, drive different routes at different times, that sort of thing."

"For how long?"

"Until the problem is fixed," Gail said.

"And you said that's what you do."

Gail smiled.

"Don't you think I should call the police?"

"Call them if you want," Gail said, "but what do you intend to tell them? That a stranger told you that a member of the US Senate *might* be trying to kill you for the illegal things you did at the behest of the ousted director of the FBI?"

She let the words settle.

"My advice," Gail said, "is to let it ride and trust me and my team to uphold our end of what needs to be done. I promise we won't leave you hanging. When it's settled, we'll let you know."

"And it's your plan to stop the killer who's trying to kill me?"

"Yes."

"How?"

Gail smiled and headed for the door. "I'll let myself out."

CHAPTER NINE

Willy K cursed himself for being so stupid. He'd let his guard down. He'd made too much noise on his approach, and he'd *assumed*—how many people had that word killed over the years?—that the father and his son would be hunting from the same spot. It had never occurred to him that the kid might shoot from a second angle.

Sulkey's mistake was to give a warning. If he'd just taken his shot from the trees, then Willy K wouldn't be around to be thinking these bad thoughts about himself.

After Sulkey's shot, he thought maybe he was going to have himself a gunfight—the most miserable kind there was, a close-range bolt action slugfest. That would be World War One shit.

But the second shooter surprised the shit out of him. No warning there, by God. The first Willy K knew about the shooter was the hammer blow to the inside of his thigh that felt like a white-hot ice pick slamming through his flesh at a thousand miles per hour.

In all his years of shooting people, Willy K had himself never been shot, and the level of pain was beyond anything he'd imagined. The impact blasted the air out of his lungs. Like, *holy shit*!

Now, as he lay on the ground, he was distantly aware of the

long blades of grass that were irritating his nostrils with every breath.

He never even saw the sonofabitch who shot him. But whoever it was—it had to be Sulkey's kid, right?—he was going to go to bed dead tonight.

First, he had to take inventory. He hadn't looked at his wound yet, but if it was where he thought it was, it was in femoral artery territory, and that was the kind of leg shot that might as well have been a bullet through the heart. That he was thinking these thoughts was a good sign. It meant that he hadn't bled out.

He also hadn't moved yet.

Daring to move only his right leg—the one he was sure had been hit—he kept the rest of his body still as he tried to bend his knee and bring his thigh within range of his hand.

"Jesus God that hurts!" he grunted aloud. The whole lower half of his body erupted in a lightning storm of agony.

Get over yourself, pussy.

There weren't a lot of possible outcomes at this point. He could lie here until he healed, he could lie here until he died, or he could find a way to get his ass off the ground and bring the fight back to the assholes who had put him here.

But that meant moving.

Shit.

What felt like a minute and a half probably didn't take longer than thirty seconds, but that didn't matter when your body was screaming for your brain to put you to sleep again. Finally, he got his thigh to hand height and it was time to find out what he might not want to know.

Intellectually, he knew that the bullet hole couldn't possibly have been as large as it felt—roughly the diameter of a sewer lid—but even after having inflicted so many such wounds on others, he felt surprised—and maybe a little cheated—that it was barely the diameter of his fingertip.

How was it possible for that much pain to emanate from such a tiny insult?

He explored the wound oh so gently with his fingertip, mostly to assess the level of bleeding. His thigh was wet and slippery, but he felt no pulsing spurting of blood. That was the best possible news. That extended his options. That meant that he would live to see the next confrontation. The one that would leave the son-ofabitch who did this to him deader than John F. Kennedy.

The relentless ticking of the clock wore heavily on Willy K. He knew that he'd shot Sulkey, but he also knew that he hadn't killed him. At least not right away. He also knew that the second shooter was as healthy as he was when he woke up this morning.

What was he up to? Was he waiting for Willy K to raise his head so he could blow it off and complete the task he'd started? That's what Willy K would do if he were in that position.

The longer he lay here being a pussy, the higher the likelihood that the asshole amateurs would take him out.

The thought of going to hell didn't bother Willy K all that much. But the thought of the other residents of hell spending eternity making fun of him for being stupid was more than he could endure.

He needed to stand. That was the key to everything. That meant he needed to make the commitment. He was almost certain that the bullet had missed his femur—even as it had come terrifyingly close to his nut sack. If he was wrong, he'd know the instant he tried to put weight on it.

There was no way to stand without putting weight on your femur.

Favoring his left leg, he lifted himself to his left knee, leaving the right leg dangling for as long as he could.

So far, so good.

Setting the safety on his Browning, he planted the buttstock into the grass and climbed it like a pole. The right leg screamed, but he did not. Something to be proud of—baby steps. He oh, so slowly let his right leg bend and then he set that knee on the ground as well.

Oh, Christ on a crutch, that hurt! But the leg held his weight. If the femur had been hit, it would have folded on him.

This was great news. He wasn't bleeding to death, and his thigh bone wasn't broken. That meant he was structurally sound. The rest was just about pain.

Hell, pain was just a feeling.

Though, muscles had jobs to do, too. And his right adductor was not in the mood. His left leg did all the work to get him standing, and then a second test seemed to light him up from knees to nipples. But the leg held strong. Okay, if not strong, at least it didn't collapse under his weight.

Now that you're standing, you're a target, moron.

Sometimes, that little voice in his head did him a real solid. This was one of those times. Willy K needed to stop feeling sorry for himself and get on with the business of killing. Only now it would be two for the price of one. It *was* only two, right? He'd fallen for that once before. It was always possible that there'd be a third. Hell, the way his luck was going, he could be facing down a whole hunt club.

Bring it on. He'd take whatever was coming one shot at a time.

He started following the tracks he'd noticed the first time. They led more or less to the spot where Sulkey had stood when he shouted his warning.

Willy K might not have killed him, but he knew he'd delivered a solid first shot. If Sulkey had crawled away, he hadn't crawled far.

He'd still be somewhere in the vicinity of the pathway through the grass.

The second shooter was the wild card. Willy K was certain that the second shooter remained unwounded, and that made him a dangerous threat.

With his prized Browning now across his chest, Willy K started out on his new mission. Each limp of a step made him look like a fool, the pain causing him to flap his elbows in an effort to limit the pressure on his wounded leg. The pain never eased, but it never worsened, either. When this was over, he'd have to find a doctor to give it a look.

But there's an upside to pain, too, if you looked at it the right way. Each step, each lightning bolt of agony focused him on his commitment to kill the sonofabitch who did this to him.

"I'm not telling you again," Dad said. "You need to leave me. Save yourself."

"I can't do that," Jason said.

"You have no choice, Jase."

Jason wanted to run, to get the hell out of there. He saw the pain his dad was in, and he didn't want any part of that for himself. He said that the poacher was dead, but in reality, he had no idea. If he was dead, then they were borrowing trouble.

But if he *wasn't* dead and he was still on the hunt . . .

"Why is this happening, Dad?"

He seemed to be drifting away. "I don't know."

Jason needed to do *something*. Otherwise, Dad would die.

"Okay, Dad, listen to me. I'm going to go get the car. I think the poacher is dead. I'm *sure* he's dead. I'll get the car, and we can drive you to a hospital."

A slight smile creased Dad's lips. "You don't know how to drive."

"I'll figure it out." Time to *man up*. "I'll get the car, get you in it, and then we'll get out of here."

Jason felt like he should do something before leaving Dad alone—maybe kiss him on the cheek or something, but Sulkeys weren't kissers. They weren't huggers either. To do it now felt like it would be a curse. "I'll be back," he said.

Dad nodded, but he didn't seem able to form words.

Jason didn't have time to dick around here. He needed to move. He didn't pay that much attention during the lame first aid classes they taught in Boy Scouts, but he remembered that time mattered.

He remembered something about a thing called a golden hour. When dealing with trauma, if you haven't been treated within sixty minutes, you were pretty much screwed.

He turned and bolted out of the thicket to get the car.

Willy K had never moved this slowly, or with this much pain. After each step, he had to pause for a few seconds to recover his breathing and draw up the will to take another step.

Maybe this revenge thing wasn't all that important after all. Sulkey was surely dead.

Right?

Willy K was nearly certain he'd delivered a kill shot. Not a clean one, obviously, but a fatal wound.

Nearly certain.

Shit.

He was a professional, goddammit. In what universe was *nearly certain* an acceptable standard?

Maxine Bridges had ordered this package of hits for a reason, and she'd made it very clear that this was an all or nothing deal. That part, he sort of understood. She had tracks to cover, and she was convinced this was an important step.

But god*damn* this hurt.

Movement along the tree line straight ahead and a little to the left startled him. A guy—a boy in T-shirt and shorts—burst out of the trees with a rifle in his hands.

Jason knew he was in trouble the instant he cleared the tree line. Something had changed. The angle was different, of course, because he'd moved a hundred yards closer to his dad and he'd never looked back at the field after he'd shot the poacher, but he was almost certain that the poacher wasn't where he used to be—where he was supposed to be.

He'd moved.

"Shit!" He was standing *right there* in the middle of the field. In the open. With a rifle in his hands.

Jason dropped to his knees, vaguely aware that it was probably exactly the wrong thing to do. Deer that stopped when they were scared became venison. That's why instincts tell them to run.

The poacher had seen him. Jason could tell by the way his body weight shifted. His body wasn't right, though, and there was blood. A lot of it.

So, Jason had hit him but hadn't killed him.

There's no more dangerous animal than a wounded animal.

This dangerous animal was bringing his rifle to his shoulder.

"No!" Jason yelled. "Don't!"

The poacher didn't hear or didn't care.

Jason wanted to run but he didn't know where. And what would be the point? Shit on a stick, he didn't want to kill pigs, but now he had to kill a human.

He found himself crying, and the tears blurred his vision. He swiped them away with the heel of his hand and he brought his brand-new Ruger up to his shoulder. He knew what he had to do.

In his head, he tried to pretend that he was on the range and that this target was no different than the silhouette targets he shot all the time. It's amazing all the stuff that flies through your mind in nanoseconds when you're stressed.

His form was perfect.

Shoulder press.

Cheek weld.

Finger on the trigger—just the pad before the first knuckle. Feel the trigger safety give way.

Sight picture acquired.

He pressed straight to the back of the trigger guard. Follow-through meant everything.

Nothing. Not even a click.

Shit, shit, goddammit. Did he forget to disengage the safety? No. He'd forgotten to chamber a round after his last shot.

No time.

Jason rolled to his left, pressed himself into the grass and crawled like an alligator back toward the trees. He'd hooked his rifle's sling in the crook of his elbow. Once he got to cover and he had two seconds to spare—

A searing hot sledgehammer crushed his ass, causing him to yell out in a visceral howl.

Half an instant later, he heard the gunshot.

"Mother . . ." Willy K cursed. Remember that shit about being a professional? Well, the first part of that was being able to hit your goddamn target.

A good shot required a good stance—a good platform—and his leg wound simply wouldn't allow it. He got a shot off, but he knew the instant the trigger broke that he missed his mark. He might have caught a chunk, but he didn't log a kill.

His ears were still ringing from the gunshot when he heard the scream.

Yeah, he'd caught a chunk.

"Oh, God, I'm shot." Jason said it aloud. "I'm dead."

Except he wasn't dead. He was every bit as alive as the poacher. Who was also shot.

Jason needed a place to hide. Like right *now*. If he was hidden, he'd have time to chamber another round and take another shot.

But he didn't have that kind of time. The poacher knew where he was. In one more gunshot, it would be over.

Screw it. Screw the pain. He had to run. The cover of trees was only fifteen, twenty feet away.

Tick-tock.

His ass muscles screamed at him as he drew his legs up and he launched himself at the trees. He couldn't launch straight, though. His left leg was working better than the other one, so he heaved far to the right.

A rifle shot split the air. The bullet sounded like an angry yellow jacket as it whizzed past his left ear.

* * *

"God *damn* it!" Willy K was not given to verbal outbursts, but Jesus God this was ridiculous. He hadn't missed a kill shot in more years than he could count. He hadn't missed *completely* since the beginning of time. That kid dove off to the side like he knew a bullet was on the way.

Putting all his weight on his good side, Willy K worked the bolt and chambered another round. If he'd done the math right in his head, his magazine was empty now. No way was he hobbling back to the car to get more ammo. This cartridge would have to be the one that got the job done.

This kid—the luckiest kid in the world—was about to meet Saint Peter.

A whole tree now stood between Jason and the poacher. He didn't know trees well enough to know what kind this was, but it was tall and thick.

His ass *really* hurt. He was pretty sure that it was just his right cheek, but his whole leg felt the hot waterfall of blood that coursed all the way down to soak his sock.

If Jason could stop this guy—if he could *kill* this guy once and for all—he and Dad could survive. No one had ever died of an ass-cheek wound, had they?

The poacher needed to die.

Jason needed to make him die.

Keeping all of his weight on his left leg, he rose to his full height, his back pressed against the tree trunk.

He held the Ruger vertically in front of him, muzzle straight up. He lifted the handle and pulled back the bolt, sending the spent shell-casing spinning into the woods where it landed with a soft thud on the mulchy forest floor.

When he pushed the bolt forward, it moved easily. He felt the next round seat itself in the chamber and he pressed the handle home.

This was it. The moment for Jason to save the day. He checked the safety one more time, saw the red dot. *Red means dead.*

Because he was right-handed, he spun to his left, hoping to expose only his rifle as he kept his body covered by the tree.

The Ruger was ready, pressed into his shoulder.

The poacher was waiting, not ten feet away.

They fired at the same time.

CHAPTER TEN

Kerry Smallwood parked his ten-year-old Jeep Sahara in the sunshine against the split rail fence, as close to the gate as he could. He chose the sunlight rather than shade because the Planetariat was slated to last for five days, and to park under a tree for that long was to invite ten thousand bird turds to cover your vehicle.

He grabbed his backpack and other gear out of the back and wrapped his keys around his finger so they could be stored in the key box in the administrative tent along with the keys from other troopers who were old enough to drive. The theory behind the key box was twofold: officially, it allowed vehicles to be moved in the event of an emergency. Unofficially, it kept untethered teenagers from shirking their duties and paying visits to establishments that neither their parents nor their pastors would approve of.

His dad had arrived two days ago to start the stuff he had to do to get the Planetariat up and running. Apparently, it was a big deal to house, feed, and take care of the personal hygiene needs of over three hundred boys who belonged to other people. Who knew?

And like Senator Bridges said, to do all that work for free was truly service above and beyond.

Kerry still couldn't believe he'd had sex with her. He wanted to feel ashamed for it because of the ridiculous age difference, but good God, that stuff she did with her mouth—well, he didn't think that actually happened outside of porn videos. She seemed to enjoy it, too.

What he *really* wished was that he wasn't too embarrassed to tell his friends about it. A) They'd never believe it, or B) if they did believe it, they'd think it was disgusting that he lost his virginity to an old lady just so he could get an appointment to the Naval Academy. The fact that that's not what actually happened wouldn't matter because it sure as hell *appeared* like that's what happened, and in cases like this, appearances trumped reality.

The appointment and the sex were two separate transactions. And if it embarrassed him so much, how come he couldn't stop thinking about it?

One of the things he hoped most would come out of these days working with troopers here at the Planetariat would be to refocus his brain on something other than that night. Just inside the gate, he hooked a turn to the left and walked through the door of the administration tent, where his dad was busy unpacking boxes and arranging things. Every bit of twenty feet in diameter, the peaked roof gave the place the vibe of *military meets Harry Potter meets Ottoman Empire*. This was the brain of the Planetariat, the place from which Danny Smallwood ran everything with the assistance of a handful of adjutants—trusted troopers who, even at their young ages, possessed good communication and administration skills. Kerry thought of adjutants as the future accountants of America.

Danny wore the summer work uniform of the Starlighters Fleet Command—black shorts with a red stripe on the outside seam, black tennis shoes and socks, and a red Polo shirt with the five stars of his rank stitched high on his left breast.

"Hey, Dad. I'm here. Need any help?"

"It's Fleet Admiral Smallwood for the next five days," Danny corrected. "And you are Commodore Smallwood. Might as well start getting used to it. Next time I see you, I expect to see a uniform. As to your question, have you got an extra day you can tack onto the calendar between today and tomorrow?"

"I left it at home. I wish you'd told me you needed it." Kerry hung his keys on a peg in the box marked CAR KEYS. His dad loved to label things.

"I always sensed that I was a failure as a parent. Now I know. Go square your stuff away. I believe you'll find a happy surprise waiting for you at your campsite."

"When do your adjutants arrive?"

"Whenever their parents get around to dropping them off, I imagine. Commodore, you are dismissed."

"Aye."

Just outside the door, he added a pirate-worthy *aargh*. As his life sailed closer to the real Navy, he grew progressively more uncomfortable with the pretend naval trappings of the Starlighters. As a little kid steeped in all things related to space travel, he'd loved being known among his dweeby peers as *Ensign* Smallwood, notwithstanding the fact that it was the lowest possible rank in the organization.

Now, to be *Commodore* Smallwood, the highest possible rank before the adult, fleet-level ranks, was a big deal. He'd worked hard to achieve it, and he wanted to feel proud of it. But times had changed, and the uniforms frankly felt more like costumes than statements of achievement. And that was on him, he knew. That was him being snotty.

It was the attitude he needed to lose.

A four-by-five-foot board with campsite assignments by trooper name in alphabetical order blocked the view from about ten feet inside the front gate. As command staff, Kerry had the advantage of being here a day early, so he'd be able to set his stuff up in relative peace. Come tomorrow, when the rest of the troopers arrived to set up, this place was going to look like ants on spilled soda. It was a Prime Directive of the Planetariat that each trooper must set up and be responsible for his own living and sleeping area. Kerry had learned the hard way over the years that by lending a helping hand early, squadron-level leaders could spare themselves a lot of heartache and lost clothing.

There was no limit to what new troopers were capable of losing or forgetting. If past was precedent, he'd have to deal with missing tent poles and spikes, totally improper clothing—either too hot or too cold—forgotten toothbrushes, and underwear. How bad a parent would one have to be to send their son away for a week without underwear or a toothbrush?

Kerry found his assigned spot easily—B-47.

Each site was marked with a labeled wooden stake that had been driven into the dirt. He found a note on his, written in precise block letters.

KERRY,
AFTER YOU GET YOUR TENT SET UP AND YOUR
GEAR SQUARED AWAY, COME SEE ME AT THE
RIFLE RANGE.
    G.S. SCHULTZ

Kerry had crossed paths with Mr. Schultz a couple of times, and always in a setting like this. He came off as stern, not mean, a stickler for the rules, and not particularly interested in having a good time. He didn't know what Mr. Schultz actually did in real life, but he would have made a good calculus teacher.

Kerry made quick work of changing into his uniform—same uniform as his dad's but with one star instead of five—and setting up his campsite. He made his way to the rifle range, as ordered. They'd set it up at the base of a natural berm. A grassy hill that sloped up at about forty-five degrees would serve as the backstop behind the target stands, in front of which, by maybe twenty feet, they'd set up two long tables under rectangular canvas pole tents to provide shade. Kerry noted the stack of folding card-table chairs that hadn't yet been set up. All but one of the seven target stands were empty, with the other displaying a fresh, unmarked orange and black splatter target.

An old-guy tent sat off to the side and behind the tables— tall enough for real chairs and square, with flaps pulled back. Mr. Schultz's pickup truck sat off to the side. There were no signs of life.

"Mr. Schultz?" he called. "It's Kerry Smallwood."

"Over here, General." Schultz was a contractor, not a Starlighter, and the tent was for daytime shade, not for nighttime residence.

Kerry hadn't seen the box trailer attached to the back of the pickup truck. Mr. Schultz emerged from it, squinting against the sun, his T-shirt soaked with sweat. He had a rifle in his right hand, held by its forestock, and what looked like a fifty-round box of .22 ammo in his left.

"Just getting in?" Schultz asked.

"Hasn't been a half hour since I parked the car."

Schultz pointed to the tables with his forehead. "Let's go to the shooting stations."

Once they got there, Schultz put the rifle and the ammo on the table and offered his hand. "Nice to see you again."

"Same, sir."

"Your dad tells me you're headed to Annapolis."

"In a few weeks, yes, sir."

"He also said you're good with guns. Said you would be a good choice for my assistant."

Maybe it was because of the glare of the sun, but Mr. Schultz had done nothing but scowl since they'd first made eye contact. "I'd like to think so," Kerry said.

"What are the four cardinal rules of gun safety?" Schultz challenged. He held up his forefinger, ready to count.

"Treat every gun as if it were loaded, even when you're sure that it is not loaded."

A second finger.

"Never point the muzzle of a gun at anything that you're not willing to destroy."

A third finger. And a shadow of a smile.

Kerry decided to throw caution to the wind and go for a laugh. "Keep your booger hook off the bang switch until your target is acquired."

There it was. The stern mask broke with a real smile and a chuckle. "Try that one more time for the official record."

"Keep your finger off the trigger until the target is acquired."

"Very good. And number four." With the finger.

"Always know what's behind your target before you shoot."

"Put a star on that young man's forehead," Schultz said. He pointed to the rifle on the table. "Are you familiar with that weapon?"

"Yes sir, that's a Ruger 10/22."

"Is it loaded?"

"Always." Kerry wasn't born yesterday. He knew a trap when he heard it.

"No, I mean is it *really* loaded?"

"Of course."

"Are there bullets actually in the gun?"

"I assume there are."

"Do me a favor and solve that mystery for us."

Kerry took two strides to the table, lifted the rifle by its grip, just behind the trigger guard, and pressed the lever to release the rotary box magazine from the bottom. A quick glance showed that it was empty. Then, keeping the muzzle pointed downrange, he cycled the bolt three times then locked it back in the open position, revealing an empty chamber, and placed the weapon back on the table.

He stepped back to stand next to Schultz, who gave him a quizzical look. "Well? Is it loaded?"

Kerry grinned. "Yes, it is," he said. "Because all guns are loaded. That one just happens to have no bullets in it."

Schultz's smile broadened. "You are clearly your father's son. Now, do me a favor and load that magazine. Give me the tightest group of ten that you can manage."

"What about eyes and ears?" Kerry asked.

That got the biggest grin yet. "Ah, good for you," Mr. Schultz said. "You're a natural." He lifted a towel from the table to reveal two sets of earphone-style hearing protectors and two pairs of safety glasses.

Kerry donned both, then opened the box of CCI Mini-Mag .22 caliber cartridges that was little bigger than a box of strike-anywhere matches. The lead-tipped cartridges dangled in perfectly straight lines from a plastic jig inside the box, five to a row. In a move he'd done countless times, Kerry exposed two rows of five, and dumped ten bullets first into his palm, and then onto the table.

Picking up the magazine, he loaded the rounds one at a time until all ten were pressed home and the mag was full.

He looked back to Mr. Schultz. "Permission to go hot?"

"Permission granted."

Kerry yelled, "Range is hot!" Then he pressed the magazine home into the underside of the breech, released the bolt, checked to make sure the safety was off, and brought the stock up into his shoulder.

The Ruger 10/22 was the perfect rifle for young shooters. Essentially without recoil, it tested a marksman's skills of sight acquisition and trigger control. Keeping both eyes open, Kerry settled the front sight on the center ring of the target then pressed the trigger. The rifle fired and he was rewarded with a strike just to the right of his intended mark.

He suspected the sights were off, but that didn't matter for this exercise, because his instructions were to shoot a tight group, not a high score. He kept the same aim point for nine more rounds in as many seconds, and when he was done, you could have covered all the holes with a single nickel.

After the tenth round, Kerry locked the bolt back, dropped the magazine, set the safety, and set the empty mag and the rifle back onto the table.

"Do we have empty chamber flags?" he asked.

Mr. Schultz clapped him on the shoulder. "Yessir, young Mr. Smallwood, you'll do just fine as my assistant instructor."

CHAPTER ELEVEN

Farrell Sulkey's neighborhood was the very definition of non-descript. No doubt developed in the 1980s, every house was two-story and featured the same combinations of brick fronts and vinyl siding, and two-car garages. Each sat on what Jonathan figured to be a fifth of an acre. The only true variations were the presence or absence of a front porch. The Sulkey residence had one.

He rode in the shotgun seat of the Batmobile, the customized, heavily armored Chevrolet Suburban that offered protections and armaments that rivaled the highest levels offered to government officials. Boxers drove.

"I would eat shredded glass and set my face on fire if I had to live here," Boxers said.

Jonathan snorted a laugh. "Now, there's an image. Where did that come from?"

"What do these people do?"

"What everybody else does," Jonathan said. "They go to work and they come home to their families. Just like you. Except for the family part."

Big Guy had never been married so far as Jonathan knew. Jonathan had been married once, but that turned out with terrible results for both husband and wife. Theirs were not relationship-friendly lifestyles.

"At least I live in the city," Boxers said. "There's something to do."

"You hate people," Jonathan reminded. He pointed to a driveway up ahead.

"That doesn't mean I don't want them around me."

"Box, I can't count the times that you literally have said to me, *I don't like having people around me.*"

"Now you're just being a pain in the ass," Boxers said. He pulled into the driveway. "Are we playing cops?"

"Let's try not to flash the badges unless we have to," Jonathan said. "And try to look smaller than you are."

"That's a brave ask from a cute little fella like yourself."

They left the Suburban and walked to the house together. By habit, neither stood directly in front of the door—in the *cone of death*—but rather off to the side as Jonathan pushed the button for the doorbell. It was old-school, just a *ding-dong*. No chorus from "Greensleeves" or chimes from Big Ben.

After only a few seconds, he heard the chain slide and the knob turn. The door opened to reveal a very tired-looking young lady with a blonde ponytail that appeared to have been shredded from its rubber band binder. Wisps of hair floated around her scalp like an aura.

"Please don't make any noise," she said. "Please, please, *please.*" Then she glanced up at Big Guy. "Holy shit. Oh, sorry."

"He gets that a lot," Jonathan scoffed. "My name's Neil. This is my partner, Xavier. We're here to speak to Mr. Farrell Sulkey."

"He's a popular guy today."

"Excuse me?"

"A guy was here a couple of hours ago asking to see him, too."

"And?"

"And I told him what I'm going to tell you. He's not here. He went hunting with his son."

Jonathan and Boxers exchanged glances. "I'm sorry," Jonathan said. "I'm confused. Are you his . . . daughter?" No way was she old enough to be his wife.

The young lady laughed, covered her mouth as she did. "No, no sir. I'm Lori Madison. I'm the babysitter. This is Farrell's weekend with his boys, but the little one is too young to go hunting yet. So, Farrell and Jase are out shooting pigs and I'm here taking care of Rascal."

"A pet?" Boxers asked.

Lori looked confused. "Huh? Oh, no. Rascal's a five-year-old. Real name's Regent. And he's *finally* taking a nap."

Boxers made a sound that made Jonathan stifle a smile— something close to a growl but not quite. Big Guy didn't like a number of aspects of modern naming conventions for children. Even Jonathan thought Regent was a bit over the top.

"Mr. Sulkey is divorced, then?" Jonathan asked.

"Oh, very," Lori scoffed. She lowered her voice to a whisper. "I know it's none of my business, but sometimes you can't help but overhear. They can get *ugly* with each other."

"Any idea how long they've been divorced?" Jonathan asked.

"Not really. Years. Like I said, Rascal's five, so I'm gonna guess less than that." Lori scowled and cocked her head. "Should I be telling you these things?"

"What do you know about Mr. Sulkey's work?" Boxers asked. "We know he's a photographer, but what kinds of things does he photograph?"

"Oh, he takes beautiful shots," Lori gushed. "He did one of my mom's friends' weddings. They came out beautiful. You know, sometimes those pix are just people and places? Well, Farrell— nobody calls him Mr. Sulkey—does lots of things with backgrounds and focuses and stuff. Really artistic."

Jonathan pressed in closer to the door. "Do you mind if we step inside? It's hot out here."

Lori looked unsure. "Um, I don't—"

"I promise we'll be quiet. We won't want to wake the little one."

She hemmed for a couple of seconds, then stepped aside to let them pass.

"Thank you," Jonathan said. Boxers followed silently. They stood on a parquet tile foyer that led directly to a surprisingly bright and open center hall with an Ikea living room on one side and an Ikea dining room on the other. Artwork filled the wall space, each piece a photograph.

Lori closed the door but stayed next to it, her hand on the knob.

"Did Mr. Sul . . . excuse me. Did Farrell take all of these photos?" Jonathan asked.

"Yes, he did. Well, I don't know about all of them, but most of them."

They projected an artistry beyond that of most commercial photographers. Jonathan didn't have the vocabulary to describe it in a way other than more *in depth*. The black and whites seemed sharper, crisper. The colors more intense.

"What do you know about his customer base?" Boxers asked.

Jonathan cringed. He liked to interview people as a single and Big Guy knew that. He'd ask for help if he needed it.

"I'm sorry, who are you again?" Lori asked.

And that was why Jonathan liked to be the lone talker.

He tried to get in front of it. "I understand how a photographer gets a wedding gig," he said. "Or, at least I think I do. Someone calls and says, *Hey, I'm getting married. Can you be our photographer?* But how does one sell beautiful stuff just for the sake of its beauty?"

It wasn't at all the question he wanted to ask, and he didn't give a flying fig about the answer, but he didn't want her getting wrapped around the axle about the intrusive customer question.

"Oh, I don't know," Lori said. "We never talk about that. We don't talk about much, actually. I'm just, you know, the babysitter." She squared off and crossed her arms, her back against the closed door. "You still haven't told me who you are." She said it with a smile, as if being faced with a prank.

"We're friends here to help Farrell," Jonathan said. "He's in some danger and we're trying to help get him out of it."

Lori gasped and brought a hand to her mouth. "What kind of danger?"

"The dangerous kind. The lethal kind."

As her shoulders sagged, so did her knees and she turned pale.

"Oh, shit," Jonathan said. "Big Guy—"

"Got her." Boxers grabbed the sides of her shoulders with his massive hands and guided her to the nearest chair in the living room, under a photograph of a covered bridge transversing autumn leaves. "Here you go, have a seat."

Jonathan kneeled on the carpet in front of her. "I'm sorry. I didn't mean to scare you so badly. I just—"

"It's not you," Lori said. "It's the other guy. The one who came here this morning."

Jonathan glanced at Big Guy and got the same look of dread that he was feeling. "Tell me more," he said.

"It was just like this. Well, he didn't come inside, but he wanted to know where Farrell was and I told him."

"That he went hunting?"

"Right."

"Did you tell him where they went? I mean, specifically?" Jonathan asked.

It startled him to hear her reply with a complete street address.

"What is that? What kind of place?"

Lori had started to tremble. "Am I in trouble? Did I put them in danger?"

"You're certainly not in trouble," Jonathan said, "and I don't know about the danger part yet."

"Jason is with him."

"That's his son? You called him Jase before?"

"Uh-huh. He just turned fourteen."

Boxers growled again. This could be bad.

"The place," Jonathan reminded. "The address. What's there?"

"I-I've never been there, but it's the same place they always hunt. I think it's family land."

"A little over an hour from here, Boss," Boxers said, looking up from his phone.

"This guy," Jonathan said. "What did he say? What did he want to know?"

"Is he the source of the danger?"

"Lori, the only way this works is if the questions flow in one direction. What did he say or ask?"

"He said he needed to speak with Farrell."

"And?" Jesus, it was like pulling teeth to get answers.

"And I told him he was about an hour late, that he'd gone hunting with Jase. The guy said it was really important that they talk, so I gave him the address and he left."

"How long ago was that?"

"Maybe two hours ago?"

Shit. If the assassin drove straight through, there'd be no way to intercept him before he arrived at the hunting camp.

"What's Farrell's phone number?" Jonathan asked, pulling a burner out of his pocket.

"Why? What do you think is happening?"

Patience. "Maybe nothing. I'll know after I call."

She gave him the number.

Jonathan dialed, waited as it rang to voicemail and hung up. He didn't leave a message because there was nothing to say.

"Oh, God," Lori gasped. "He didn't answer? Does that mean something's wrong?"

"Um, we gotta go, Boss," Boxers said.

"It could also mean they don't have cell coverage," Jonathan said. "Or they silence their phones when they're sitting in a blind— which is exactly what I do." It was important not to jump to conclusions at times like this. Confirmation bias was a real thing. Just because all the facts *appear* to lead to a certain conclusion doesn't mean that appearances aren't deceiving.

In this case, though, Jonathan was having a hard time coming up with a scenario that wasn't catastrophic.

Boxers was right. They needed to go. But first, he had one favor

to do for Venice. He withdrew his own phone from his pocket—
not the burner—and logged in. "Lori, I need something from you.
Well, two things. The first is the passcode to the Wi-Fi here." He
looked at the available networks. "I presume it's *photodream*?"

"Right," Lori said. "Why do you need that?"

Jonathan just waited for it.

"Okay," she said, before reciting a series of digits from memory.

Jonathan didn't need any of that for himself. He needed it so
that Venice could more easily break into their network storage
and maybe find a photograph that would explain at least some of
what was going on. After he hit send on the message, he turned
and took a knee in front of Lori again.

"Here's the second thing," he said. "I want you to listen to me,
okay?"

She nodded.

"Do you live on your own or with your folks?"

"I live with my mom."

"What does she do for a living?"

"She's a waitress. Sometimes she helps with a friend's house
cleaning business. Why?"

"How close does she live to here?"

"You're scaring me." Tears balanced on her eyelid as her lip
trembled.

"I don't mean to, but I really need you to answer."

A shrug caused the tears to overflow. "Five or six miles. Just
over ten minutes."

"Okay. Good," Jonathan said. "I can't tell you to do anything
here, but I really think that you should pack up Rascal and your
stuff and head back to your place for a while."

"I-I don't understand."

Jonathan reached out and she took his hands. They stood together. "I think you sort of do," he said. "You've done nothing
wrong, but I think that the man you spoke to this morning might
spell trouble. What can you tell me about him?"

"I'd never met him before."

"What did he look like?"

Her lip quivered even more.

"Please don't do that," Jonathan said. "Not now. My partner and I are going to try to save a couple of lives, but we can't really get started in a meaningful way until we get through this part. I need a description."

"I don't *know*. He was . . . ordinary."

"What color was his hair? Or was he bald?"

"H-he was wearing a baseball cap."

"What was on the cap? Was there a logo?"

Her eyes flashed bright. "Yes! It was a VT Virginia Tech logo. Gold letters, maroon cap."

"Perfect," Jonathan said. "What was he wearing?"

She looked toward the ceiling. "Um, jeans and shirt. A flannel shirt. Plaid, mostly blue."

"Excellent."

"And he was wearing sunglasses. Those wrap-around kind."

Jonathan took that to mean Oakleys or knockoffs thereof. "Was he armed?"

"What, with like a gun? No!"

"How tall?"

"Average," Lori said. "I know that's annoying, but how tall is anybody? Not short, but not as tall as either of you. *For sure* not as tall as him."

"You seem to be on a roll with your memory," Jonathan said. "Anything else?"

Lori scowled. A thought clearly passed in front of her eyes but she didn't engage.

"Say it," Jonathan urged.

"Well, he seemed . . . nice. He said it was really important and I just believed him."

Jonathan put his hands on her shoulders. He meant it as a re-assuring gesture, but it made her jump. "This brings us to why you need to take yourself and Rascal to your mom's house," he said. "Assuming the first visitor was trouble—which he might not be, but I really think he is—he's very dangerous, and you don't want to be here."

A new terror washed over Lori's face. "He saw me. We spoke to each other."

"Did you tell him your name?" Jonathan asked.

The fear deepened. "Maybe. I don't remember."

"Don't worry about it," Jonathan said. "He has no interest in you. If it's who we think he is, he only cares about Farrell Sulkey." More than that, Jonathan suspected that the killer or his employer cared even more about some of the photographs inside the house. "This just isn't the place to be for a while. Like I said, it's your decision, but that's my advice."

"Should I be calling the police?"

"No," Jonathan said. "I'll take care of that."

"How long should I plan to keep Rascal?"

"Overnight. Is there a place for him to sleep?"

"Oh, my mom loves the Sulkey boys," Lori said. "There's a bed for Rascal if he wants it, but he'll probably just curl up with her."

"Okay, then go get him, put him in the car and take him to your place."

"C-Can you follow me?" Lori asked. "You know, in case he comes after me?"

"We need to go help Farrell and Jase," Jonathan said. "Honestly, you have nothing to worry about right now."

"But what if—"

Jonathan held up a finger. "Give me your phone," he said.

Lori looked horrified.

Jonathan laughed. "I'm not going to break it, I promise you. Now, please."

Moving hesitantly, she pulled her phone from her pocket. "Want me to unlock it?"

"That would be helpful."

"I really don't understand why—"

Jonathan opened her Contacts folder and typed in *Neil Bonner* and a phone number. "This is my number," he said. "If there's any problem, you feel free to call me."

He handed it over and she took it back. "A problem? Who are you?"

"We're problem solvers," Jonathan said.

"I-I don't know what that means."

Jonathan winked. "I think you probably do, actually. Don't think so hard."

The number he gave her wasn't real. If she called it, she would connect with Venice in Fisherman's Cove, who would activate a noisemaking device that would make it sound as if she were working in a busy office. She would of course advise her—as she would advise any caller to the fake number—that Neil Bonner was unavailable, but would be happy to return her call if she left a message.

"But trust me," Jonathan said. "You'd best get going."

After another few seconds of hesitation, Lori turned and headed back toward the bedrooms.

"We'll let ourselves out," Jonathan said.

As they walked back to the Batmobile, Boxers said, "I can hear you thinking. You don't think the good guys have a chance in hell either, do you?"

"There's always a chance, Big Guy."

CHAPTER TWELVE

"Cease fire!" Kerry commanded. "All troopers cease fire!"

This was a squadron of young ones, ensigns all of them, except for the fourteen-year-old lieutenant who led them down to the firing range and would lead them back when their session was over. Kerry enjoyed this age group, when everything was so exciting. But they also had the attention spans of gnats, and when dealing with firearms, bad things could happen very quickly.

He surveyed all ten shooting stations and noted ten rifles brought to low ready position.

"Safeties on!"

Small hands moved in unison to reward Commodore Smallwood with a satisfying flurry of soft clicks.

"Remove your magazines." This was the tricky part, just because it required two hands. "Mr. Allison, your finger is too close to the trigger. Mr. Simpson, lower your muzzle."

When the magazines were removed from the mag well, the standing order was for the trooper to hold it up by his left ear, where Kerry could see it. When he saw ten magazines, he said, "Very well, gentlemen, put the mags on the table, clear your actions, lock back your bolts and prepare for inspection."

The boys all performed the task perfectly, and when the breeches were locked open, they laid their rifles on the table pointed downrange and took one step back to snap to attention.

"The firing range is now cold!" Kerry yelled.

The boys echoed, "Cold range!"

Kerry saw at a glance that everything was fine, but he nonetheless made a show of spending twenty seconds or so at each shooter's station to examine the firearm and congratulate the shooter.

When they were done, Kerry released that group to retrieve their paper targets from the stands, then authorized the next group of shooters to go downrange to staple their targets into place.

From his peripheral vision, Kerry saw Mr. Schultz approaching from his tent, both arms waving over his head. "Hold up, General!" he called. "Hold up, hold up."

The more he got to know Schultz, the more he understood the man to be a certified asshole. General instead of commodore. Yuckety yuck yuck. The clearest lesson Kerry had learned was that being Schultz's assistant instructor meant running the whole program while he spent the entire day in the shade.

Kerry would have met him halfway, but when guns and bullets were both exposed, he never turned his back on the firing line.

"You are officially relieved of duty," Schultz said as he arrived at Kerry's side. The guy had already worked up a sweat.

"What? What'd I do?"

"Not permanently, numb nuts. Your imperial poobah father wants to see you in the administration tent."

Kerry felt his anger swell. He knew the young troopers could hear Schultz's words and were absorbing the disrespect the man projected. Kerry owed it to his troopers not to let it go unanswered. He turned and took a step toward Schultz, halving the distance between them.

In a shout projected from his diaphragm he said, "Mr. Schultz, you will show respect, or you will leave these premises. The camp commander is Fleet Admiral Smallwood and I am Commodore Smallwood, and you will refer to us appropriately."

Schultz moved backward a step, as if blown backward by the sound pressure. "You can't talk to me that way."

Kerry turned back to the firing line. "Lieutenant Hornby."

A fourteen-year-old redhead at the shooting table snapped to attention. "Sir."

"I need to report to the admin tent. You are in charge. The range will remain cold."

"But we still have a half hour left."

Schultz showed his palms. "Don't be an asshole, Kerry. These kids—"

"Lieutenant Hornby, do you understand your order?"

"Yes, sir."

"Good. Assemble your troopers and move them in good order to the pool for ninety minutes of free swim." That launched a cheer from the entire crowd of boys. Free swim meant exactly that—unregulated time at the pool. It was among the most cherished commodities at the Planetariat.

To Schultz, Kerry said, "We'll see if we still have a shooting program tomorrow."

"I don't need this shit, you know," Schultz said. "How about I just pack up and leave?"

"That works for me, too," Kerry said. "Or, you could just show a little respect."

With that, Kerry turned and started his long walk up the hill, his heart pounding. He hated confrontations like that. He hated even more that sometimes they were essential. He just hoped he didn't look like an ass in front of the other troopers. He'd know soon enough after word spread about what happened.

Kerry opened the door to the domed admin tent and pulled up short two steps in when he saw three cops gathered around his dad.

"What happened?" Kerry asked.

Danny smiled. "Nothing. Though I can see how you might assume otherwise." He put his hand on the shoulder of the tallest of the three cops. "Sheriff Morrissey, this is my son and second-in-command, Kerry Smallwood. Kerry, Sheriff Morrissey."

Kerry stepped forward and shook the sheriff's hand.

Morrissey said, "These are Deputies Sherping and Caruso." Any jurisdiction would have been proud to have the deputies as models for their department brochure. Muscular, solid jaws, high-and-tight haircuts.

Kerry shook their hands as well, then looked to his dad for an explanation.

"A panicky parent made some phone calls," Danny said. "They didn't think we had enough security for the Planetariat. So, yada yada . . ." He nodded to Morrissey.

"I found money for some overtime, and deputies willing to work for it," Morrissey said.

Kerry was still confused.

"What?" Danny asked.

"Why am I here?"

"So you know," Danny said. "You're going to see cops with guns wandering the campground, and I wanted you to be prepared with answers."

"Is there some specific threat we're worried about?" Kerry asked.

"*We're* not worried about anything," the sheriff said.

"There'll be two deputies on duty here from seven p.m. to seven a.m.," Danny said.

"Because terrorists only attack at night," Kerry said with a grin.

"Because helicopter parents are afraid of the dark," said Deputy Caruso.

Kerry had a disturbing thought. "You're not gonna be wandering around, shining flashlights into tents and stuff, are you?"

"I expect we'll be sitting right there at the front gate," Deputy Sherping said. "I have no desire to ruin anyone's camping experience."

"Cool," Kerry said. "You start tonight?"

"Right."

After another round of shaking hands, the cops left.

"That's it," Danny said. "I just wanted you to know and to introduce you. You can go back to what you were doing." He snapped his fingers and touched his forehead—his tell that he'd forgotten to say something. "I meant to tell you that tomorrow during the concert, I'm going to be in town for a bit. Just for ninety minutes, maybe two hours. That'll put you in charge for that time."

Kerry shrugged. "Okay. What's in town?"

Danny glanced at the three adjutants who were pretending not to listen. "Some personal business." Translation: *I'll tell you later.*

The door burst open to reveal a red-faced Mr. Schultz. "Good," he said. "I've got you both."

"Oh yeah," Kerry said. "I meant to tell you that Mr. Schultz is being a dick."

CHAPTER THIRTEEN

"Stop here," Jonathan said, and Boxers brought the Batmobile to a halt. The gate across the gravel driveway lay half open, and even from ten yards away, the blood trail was obvious.

"We're late," Boxers said.

"No surprise there," Jonathan said. "Blood still looks wet, so maybe we're only a *little* late. Let's load up. Vests and long guns."

"Who are we gonna shoot?" Boxers asked. "The blood's on the gate. You think he *arrived* bleeding? Dude's in the wind, man."

Jonathan opened his door. "Vests and long guns."

Among the hard-learned lessons in Jonathan's life was, it's always foolish to enter the scene of a gunfight unarmed. He didn't expect the scene to still be hot, which was all the more reason to bring firepower. Millions of warriors had lost their lives over the centuries by underestimating the level of danger that surrounded them.

The Batmobile was a rolling arsenal, with fake floor panels concealing a wide assortment of firearms, ammunition, explosives, initiators, and all kinds of kit. It was not a vehicle to take to an international border crossing, but it was well enough insulated to survive a routine police check and an examination by a munitions-sniffing canine.

Jonathan had long ago settled on the M27 as his long gun of

choice. A modified and customized Heckler & Koch 416, the Marines adopted it a while back to replace their venerable M249 light machine gun as its squad automatic weapon. Jonathan further modified his personal M27 with advanced optics, a carbon fiber barrel to prevent overheating and reduce weight and a suppressor. Chambered in 5.56 millimeter, engineers designed the M27 to spit out eight hundred rounds per minute, but for most of Jonathan's applications, one bullet at a time worked just fine.

Boxers preferred the H&K 417 as his rifle of choice. Similarly kitted out with all the advanced toys, Jonathan referred to the 417 as Big Guy's portable cannon. Chambered in 7.62 millimeter, the much larger rifle fired a much heavier bullet that made a much bigger hole.

As always, they both wore cotton and leather shooters' gloves. While their fingerprints and faces were invisible to any database, thanks to the efforts of Venice and her hacking skills, it never made sense to leave prints where they needn't be. And here, it was clear that they were entering what would soon be a crime scene, once somebody got around to reporting it.

Jonathan walked to the gate and opened it all the way while Boxers piloted the Suburban through the opening. The blood was indeed still wet, meaning that whoever it belonged to had passed this spot no later than maybe twenty minutes ago, at most.

Jonathan climbed back into the cab.

"Want to just follow the tracks?" Boxers asked. With the rest of the field standing untouched, the tire tracks through the grass were as distinct as if they'd been left in snow.

"Onward," Jonathan said. This was his kind of property—rolling hills populated by old-growth trees and wild grasses. It reminded him of his own two-hundred-acre spread sixty or seventy miles south of here around Charlottesville.

"There's a vehicle up there," Boxers said, pointing through the windshield. "Looks like there was another one nearby."

"Drive up and join it," Jonathan said. "Stay out of the missing car's imprint. Our tire prints are already going to confound the homicide team when they get here. No sense screwing up the investigation into the other tracks."

Yes, he'd heard himself projecting failure, the assumption that the murderer had been here and done his job. As a rule, he prided himself on his ability to provide benefit of doubt at times like this, but optimism only went so far.

Once his feet were on the ground, he pressed the bolt release on his M27 to chamber a round and he verified with a touch of his thumb that the fire selector switch was set to safe. Standing tall, he held his rifle at a relaxed low ready, the web of his thumb resting on the pistol grip, finger alongside the trigger guard. Big Guy stayed to Jonathan's left and a little behind, allowing them each to have a clear field of fire if things went to shit.

They approached the empty vehicle with purpose, scanning all compass points for unexpected threats while simultaneously scanning the ground for clues as to what happened here. Most obvious to Jonathan was the lack of blood spatter out here in the field. In his mind, that meant that somebody got hurt, drove himself to the closed gate, where he had to get out and open it before driving on to wherever his next destination was.

"Holy shit," Boxers said, pointing ahead to the area imprinted by the missing car. "Looks like somebody slaughtered pigs."

A wee bit hyperbolic in his description, Big Guy wasn't all that far off the mark. Somebody had spewed a lot of blood around here. Not an arterial spray—a conclusion backed up by the lack of a corpse—but it was a significant bleed. The kind that would need a doctor.

And at that thought, he realized that they might have just stumbled onto their first big break. He pulled his phone from his pocket and punched the speed dial for Venice.

"Hello, Scorpion. How may I be of service?"

"Hey, I need you to check area hospitals and see if any of them have dealt with big bleeders."

"Can you give me more than that?"

"I think there might have been a shootout and one of the parties was alive enough at the end to drive himself somewhere. Judging from the amount of blood on the grass, the only smart place to go would be a hospital."

"Gotcha," Venice said. "I'll let you know."

He clicked off.

"Looky here, Boss," Boxers said. He stood at the right front fender of the remaining car, a green Crown Victoria. "There's a bullet through the engine. Judging from the hole, I'd say three-oh-eight or bigger. Somebody definitely engaged in a gunfight out here. I don't know how they did with each other, but one of them definitely killed a car."

Bloodstains crusted part of that door panel as well.

Jonathan pointed toward the tree line. "Blood trail goes that way." He brought his rifle higher and switched the safety off.

"This blood is recent," Big Guy said.

It's always unnerving to approach the unknown when the only certainty would be the discovery of violence. In a perfect world, the good guys would be alive, and the bad guy would be dead, but Jonathan didn't see how that was possible in a world where the bad guy always got the first shot.

He girded himself for the worst. In his mind, the bad guy was not only alive, but he was healthy and was lying in wait.

He and Boxers approached in silence. They'd done this countless times before. They were looking for anything out of the ordinary, anything that might indicate the presence of a shooter, living or dead. They followed on either side of the blood trail, not wanting to foul it, but as they closed the distance, Jonathan noticed that there were actually *two* blood trails, one less aggressive than the other. That one highlighted a path of matted grass that lay down the opposite way from the first.

Their bleeder was bleeding on the way in and on the way out.

Halfway across the field, something winked at Jonathan from

the grass to his right. He stopped and stooped to get a closer look. "I've got a spent casing," he said without touching it. "Looks like a three-oh-eight."

"Took a shot and rechambered," Big Guy said. "Must have been quite a scene."

Jonathan and Boxers weren't cops. They weren't about collecting evidence, but they *were* about piecing together a coherent narrative of what transpired out here so they could figure out what the next step might be.

Nearly at the tree line now, they discovered a big indent in the grass and more blood. "Somebody went to ground here," Jonathan said.

"After getting hit or before, do you suppose?" Boxers wondered.

They were close. Jonathan could smell the blood now. He could smell the violence. He believed that confrontations like this somehow left an imprint on the universe that could be sensed by others for years or even centuries to come. Those feelings were part of what he called his Spidey sense, and it was pinging like a church bell right now.

Somebody moaned. From beyond the tree line.

"Big Guy?"

"Yep, I heard it, too."

Jonathan brought his rifle to high ready and pressed the buttstock deep into his shoulder. If a fight was coming, it would start in the next few seconds.

Jonathan saw the boy's booted left foot first. It rested atop a deadfall he'd apparently tripped over before falling over onto his back into a thicket of scrub growth and sticker bushes. "Got a victim," he announced.

Jonathan swung his slung rifle around to his back and crawled over the fallen tree to kneel next to the supine kid. Blood was leaking from under his T-shirt at an alarming rate. "A child. I'm pretty sure he's been shot," he said. "Upper right quadrant, I think."

"Need help?" Boxers asked.

"Not yet. This isn't our guy. This might be Sulkey's son, but it's not Sulkey. See if you can find him and keep an eye out for the shooter in case he's still around."

Wincing against the sharp assault of the wicked spines of the sticker bushes, Jonathan kneeled next to the boy's shoulders, placed two fingers on his Adam's apple and then slid his fingertips into the carotid groove to find a pulse.

"Hey, Jase, are you with me?" He thought that's what Lori said his name was.

The kid had a pulse, stronger than Jonathan would have expected, given the blood loss. He needed a doctor a long time ago.

Jonathan needed to see what wounds he was dealing with. Jason had clearly also been hit somewhere in his lower body, but all else being equal, chest wounds were almost always more—

He moaned again. Except, it wasn't really a moan so much as it was part of a pattern of agonal breathing. It didn't seem purposeful.

"Come on, kid, don't die on me," Jonathan said.

He pulled his razor-honed KA-BAR knife from its sheath on the left shoulder of his vest, slipped the blade under Jason's T-shirt at the waist and cut the fabric away. As he pulled at the cotton he inadvertently lifted the boy an inch off the ground. He could hear and feel bones moving under his flesh in ways that bones should never move.

This time, the moan was intentional, and it was more of a scream. Jason's eyes lolled open but had no real focus.

A pain response was good. It meant he still had viable brain activity.

Speed mattered now. The entrance wound appeared tiny, about an inch below his right clavicle, equidistant between his shoulder and sternum.

Jonathan re-sheathed the knife, reached behind the boy's shoulder and found the exit wound he'd been expecting. There was no such thing as a good place to be shot in the chest, but if such a place existed, this might be it. His shoulder blade was shattered for sure, and maybe a couple of ribs, but for all the blood on the ground, his color wasn't all that bad, and the bullet holes weren't blowing bubbles—a good indicator that the bullet had missed his lung.

His earbud transceiver popped in his left ear. "Scorpion, Big Guy. Sulkey's toast."

Jonathan switched his radio from PTT—push to talk—to VOX—voice activated. "Copy. Mother Hen, Scorpion. You on the channel?"

While he waited for her response, he pulled a Velcro tab on a pocket in his vest to gain access to his field trauma kit. "Big Guy, bring the Batmobile to me."

"What's going on?"

"Expedite. Mother Hen?" All he could do for this kid here in the field was slow the bleeding, and modern technology had a solution for that, provided he wasn't already too late.

"Scorpion, Mother Hen. I'm here."

While Jonathan spoke, he unrolled the trauma kit, ignoring everything but the packets of QuikClot gauze dressings. "I'm pinging my location, are you receiving it?"

"Affirmative."

"All right. I've got a PC needing treatment, child of our original PC." Venice would recognize PC as *precious cargo*. "Approximately fourteen years old, GSW through and through. Lots of blood loss but still alive. I need the location of the nearest black site trauma doc."

The world of espionage and counterespionage was a dangerous one, and when its professionals were wounded on the job, the smart move was rarely to go to a public hospital, where every medical provider was a mandatory reporter of assaults and bullet wounds. The government had long taken care of its own, but in more recent times, with the proliferation of private security contractors, and diminishing opportunities for physicians to make money in a progressively more regulated environment, some of the best trauma specialists in the country had signed very lucrative, very secret pacts to serve the segment of society that survived by remaining invisible.

"That really our job, Boss?" Boxers asked in his ear. "There's this thing called nine-one-one."

Jonathan tore open the first packet of QuikClot, rolled the gauze into a tight tube and pressed it into the wound channel carved by the bullet as it pierced the boy's chest, eliciting another howl, but not triggering him back to consciousness.

"Nobody needs the public scrutiny," Jonathan said. "Not the kid who's being hunted by a killer and certainly not us."

"Is your plan to lay him out on the cargo bed?" Big Guy asked. Jonathan could tell from the effort in his tone that he was working while he was talking.

"That's pretty much it," he confirmed. "Scoop and swoop."

"Doctor James Penny," Venice said over the radio. "Board certified cardio-thoracic surgeon has a safe house clinic about twelve miles from you. The key code is in the database. I'll send that and the address to you and then text him."

In a more perfect world, Jonathan would have donned a pair of gloves for this procedure, but infection was a tomorrow problem for this kid, not a right now problem. If he could get the bleeding stopped—and he was progressively more hopeful by the second— this kid would have a good shot at seeing at least another sunset. Another sun*rise* would be at the hands of someone else.

With the first wad of QuikClot stuffed into the front side of the wound, Jonathan rolled the kid partially to his left side and shoved a second wad in through the exit wound. The boy yelled, and Jonathan tried not to think about how agonizing it must be as his fingers advanced the gauze past dislodged bits of shattered bone and torn tissue.

Jonathan heard the massive Suburban that was the Batmobile stop on the far side of the tree line, just beyond his line of sight.

"I'm here, Boss," Boxers said over the air. "Need anything other than the stretcher?"

"Just a stretcher, time and smooth roads."

The folding combat stretcher was standard kit in the Batmobile, built into a cabinet near the right rear wheel well. Made of lightweight aircraft aluminum, when folded up it was barely bigger than a golfer's umbrella, but when deployed it was easily stout enough to carry anyone from the Security Solutions team, with the exception, perhaps, of Boxers, but nobody would be able to carry him anyway. Certainly, it was enough for this skinny kid.

"What about the leg wound?" Big Guy asked as he kneeled next to Jonathan.

"The bleeding seems to have slowed, and I don't want to take the time with it now. Maybe once we're rolling."

Working together, they rolled the boy as a unit onto his left side, pressed the stretcher against his back while it was vertical, and then lowered him as a unit back to the ground, now with the ballistic nylon between his back and the forest floor.

"Are you sure you've thought this through, Boss?" Boxers asked. "We're taking custody of a bleeding minor who could die on us just as easily as he could live. That's a lot of explaining to do."

"He's not going to die on my watch," Jonathan said.

"I appreciate your commitment, but there's some biology in play here and it gets a vote, too."

"I'll ignore what it has to say. Even if this boy thinks he's dead halfway to the med site, he will still be alive. Am I clear?"

"Crystal."

"What the hell is the alternative, Big Guy? Leave him here with no chance of survival?"

"I was thinking more in terms of an ambulance, but I'm not fighting you. Let's get him on the road and into better hands than ours."

Two minutes later, the stretcher lay in the cargo bed of the Batmobile, secured to the floor by nylon cargo tie-downs. Jonathan climbed into the back with him while Big Guy closed the back lid and made his way back to the driver's seat.

"Scorpion, Mother Hen. I have good news," Venice said in his ear. "Doctor Penny's schedule turned in our favor. He had a cancelation and he'll be meeting you at the med site. You'll probably get there more or less at the same time."

"Copy that," Jonathan said. "Good news indeed. Any news about another gunshot victim needing assistance? I'm certain from the evidence on the ground that our shooter came out of this confrontation shot."

"I've been monitoring ICIS and the local police, fire and EMS dispatch sites, and I've come up with nothing so far. You'll be the first to know."

The ride out of the field in the back of the Suburban was tough, with lots of ridges and potholes causing the vehicle to rock and the boy to moan. His condition seemed to have stabilized at bad-but-not-getting-worse. Since they'd loaded him, his color hadn't worsened, and Jonathan didn't see any more blood loss. That didn't mean he wasn't bleeding out into his chest cavity, but if that were the case, it made sense to Jonathan that he'd have died a while ago.

After a final bump that took them back onto the paved road, the ride smoothed out.

"Howya doin' back there?" Boxers asked from the front.

"No change," Jonathan said. "Take your time and obey the law. This is exactly the wrong time to get pulled over." No amount of talking would be able to explain this scene.

"My chest hurts."

The sound of the raspy young voice startled Jonathan. The boy hadn't moved and his eyes were still closed. Jonathan put his hand on the boy's head. "Are you awake, son?"

The boy made a raspy noise and licked his lips. "Hurts. I got shot."

"Don't move anything," Jonathan said. "You're right, you did get shot. You've got broken bones in your chest, and you do not want to move." In his experience, everyone—even children—appreciated hearing the truth when it came to impending pain. Better to be forewarned than to be told everything will be fine only to then get a nasty surprise.

"Dad?"

Jonathan didn't know if that was an inquiry or a case of mistaken identity, but either way, it was a direction he didn't want to go.

"Your name is Jase, right? Jason?"

The boy nodded and then his features folded into a mask of pain. He grunted.

"Tell me what you remember, Jason."

In his ear, he heard Boxers ask, "Mother Hen, are you getting this?"

"Affirmative," she said.

"Me and Dad were hunting. Then a guy..." Jason's eyes opened. An interesting shade of green that seemed more appropriate to a cat than a human. "Where's Dad?"

"Tell me about the guy," Jonathan said. He didn't want to talk about Farrell Sulkey because as soon as Jason found out the truth, the conversation would be about nothing but emotion. But Jonathan wasn't going to lie to him and tell him that his father *wasn't* dead. He hoped to skate without addressing it at all.

"I don't know," Jason said. "I thought he was, you know, poaching. Then he shot..." His eyelids squeezed tight and tears tracked out of the corners, down toward his ears. "Dad's dead, isn't he?"

Jonathan pressed his lips together, felt the pressure of emotion behind his eyes. "Yeah, he is. I'm sorry."

Jason kept his eyes closed as he wrestled with whatever images he was wrestling with. "The guy just . . . shot him. Like, no warning or anything. I should have made sure he was dead."

Those words took Jonathan by surprise. "I don't understand. Made sure who was dead?"

"The poacher. After I shot him and he fell, I assumed he was dead, but he wasn't. He came back. I didn't expect that. Didn't expect to shoot each other again."

"You shot him *twice*?"

"I think so. I'm not sure. We fired at the same time. I don't know how I could have missed."

"We're three minutes out," Boxers' voice said in Jonathan's ear.

"We're almost at the doctor," Jonathan said. "Do you have any idea who might be trying to kill your father?"

Jason's eyes focused at a spot beyond the Suburban's roof. "I don't believe he's gone. That it happened."

For an instant, Jonathan thought the boy was grieving, but then he realized he was sharing news. "That what happened?"

Jason shifted just his eyes to look at Jonathan. "I think he knew something was going to happen. He seemed . . . worried."

"Did he tell you that he was worried, or were you just reading his mood?"

Jason winced against a wave of pain. After it passed, he was silent long enough to make Jonathan wonder if he'd forgotten the question.

"No, he didn't tell me he was worried, but I could tell. He spent a lot more time on his phone than normal, and he looked nervous. A couple of nights ago, he started talking about what I needed to do if something happened to him."

"What kind of something?"

"I thought maybe he was sick, but he didn't say. He said if anything happened to him, I was supposed to . . ." He stopped himself.

"What?"

"How do I know if I can trust you?"

"I'd like to think that being the guys who are saving your life would put a check in the *good guy* column."

The boy closed his eyes. "This is so screwed up. God, what's going to happen?"

Jonathan couldn't imagine the firestorm of thoughts and emotions that must be swirling through Jason's head. He needed surgery and psychological counseling and grief counseling and there wasn't time for any of that.

"What did your father tell you to do if anything happened, Jason?"

"We're here!" Boxers announced.

"Sixty seconds more," Jonathan said. "Concentrate, son. What did—"

"There's a safe in the basement," Jason said. "It's in the floor, under a drill press. If something happened, I was supposed to go into that safe, pull out everything and burn it."

"What's in there?"

"I don't know. He told me not to look at it, just to take the folders and disks to the fireplace and burn everything."

A face appeared at the back window of the Suburban, and it was soon joined by Boxers' face. The door lifted.

"I'm Doctor Penny," the stranger said.

Jonathan held up a hand for silence. "What's the combination, Jason? To the safe?"

"If we're going to save this boy's life, we need to get to work now," Penny said.

"We?" Jonathan said. "There are others?"

"I brought my team. Now, please get out of my way."

"Doc, I need what Jason's about to give me," Jonathan said. "The combination, Jason. What is it?"

"This can wait," Penny insisted and he reached past Jonathan to grab the end of the stretcher.

Boxers wrapped his fist around the doctor's arm. "Don't make me call a doc for the doc," Big Guy said.

Penny opened his mouth to argue, but then wisely backed down.

"Come on, Jason. Please," Jonathan said. "I really need—"

"Left seven," Jason said. "Right twenty-three. Left fourteen. Right forty-four."

"Did you get that, Mother Hen?" Jonathan asked. "Seven, twenty-three, fourteen, forty-four."

"Affirmative," Venice said. "I got it."

"Is that the same Mother Hen who reached out to me?" Penny asked.

"The one and only," Jonathan said.

CHAPTER FOURTEEN

Dr. Anson Wines, MD, watched as the digital clock over the automatic doors switched from 16:58 to 16:59. It had been an inordinately slow Saturday at Mountain Valley Urgent Care, most of the business front-loaded to the morning, immediately after opening. Mornings always dawned with a parking lot full of anxious parents whose children woke up sick in the middle of the night, and anxious husbands and wives, whose spouses' real and imagined maladies had robbed them of restful sleep.

A couple of the kids turned out to be mildly dehydrated from tummy issues, and one woman needed transport to the hospital for atrial fibrillation that wasn't responding to drugs the way Anson would have liked, but for the most part, it was a day of writing prescriptions and making referrals. Good thing, too, because he'd been working the place alone today since the assigned nurse called in with a stomach bug. That left just him and Francine, the front desk clerk who handled the insurance stuff but didn't know which end of a hypodermic needle was the sharp one.

If he could make it to 5:00—17:00—without those doors opening again, he could shut the place down and go home to Sally and the kids. And a beer. He'd already sent Francine home as an offering to the workplace gods to give him a break.

Alas, workplace gods are assholes.

Brigham Greene, a tweaker and frequent flyer here at the Urgent Care clinic, approached the glass doors from the parking lot waving his arms the way he always did—he believed it was necessary to do that to get the motion sensor to work. It made him look like a moron, and when the waiting room was full, the inherent desperation in the movement freaked people out.

Anson did not need Brigham Greene in his life right now. Certainly, not as the last patient of the day, and by-God certainly not after regular business hours. The ironic reality of Brigham was that he was the healthiest brain-fried tweaker Anson had ever dealt with.

"Doc!" Brigham called as he nearly stumbled over the threshold. "Doc!"

"We're closed, Brigham. And I'm right here. Whatever you need you can go down to the emergency room and get."

"It's not like that, Doc. You need to get a stretcher out to the parking lot. There's a guy out there hurt bad." He grabbed a fistful of the sleeve of Anson's lab coat and pulled. "Really, you got to see him."

"What's wrong with him?"

"I ain't the doctor. That's your job."

Anson hated that the tweaker had scored a point. He shook his arm free from Brigham's grasp. "Don't touch me," he said. "And for sure don't pull on me."

"You need to hurry. And bring—"

"A stretcher. Yeah, I heard you. And I'm not doing that." Instead, Anson snagged the handle of one of the wheelchairs that always rested in the airlock, and he took it with him into the parking lot. Other than Anson's own Prius, only one car occupied a parking space. "Is he in there?"

"Yeah. You've got to hurry."

None of this was feeling right, if Anson was being completely honest with himself. How did Brigham happen to be in the Urgent Care parking lot at just the right time to see some allegedly injured person? For that matter, when did Brigham start giving a shit about anyone on the planet other than himself? Why would this seriously injured driver drive all the way to a remote corner of the parking lot instead of driving up closer to the doors?

Why was there blood on the driver's door?

Why was the window down on such a chilly day?

Why was the guy behind the steering wheel pointing a gun at Anson's chest?

"You the Doc Anson my friend Brigham has been going on about?" asked the stranger with the pistol. Anson was no expert, but he knew enough about guns to recognize the pistol as a striker-fired semiautomatic. He couldn't judge the caliber, but the muzzle looked like a manhole cover from here.

"I-I'm sorry, Doc," Brigham stammered. "He made me come and get you."

"Only after I paid you a hundred bucks," the stranger said. Then, to Anson, "I need a doc, Doc."

Anson tried to focus on the patient and ignore the gun. "What happened?"

"I got shot."

"Where?" Anson noted the amount of blood crusted on the man's jeans and flannel shirt.

"In the leg. And in the gut, but the gut wound isn't much."

A leg wound and a gut wound meant that this guy was pretty immobile. Anson worked the angles in his head. If he cut quick to his right and took off running, he could put the clinic building between him and the gunman before the gunman could even react. One thing for sure that was not going to happen was that he was not going to lean inside that window to help the guy.

He made his decision. He had to move quickly. Spinning on his heel, he turned to run and—

"Don't make me shoot you, Doc." Brigham had a gun, too. And it was pointed at Anson's chest.

"What the hell, Brigham?"

"I'm sorry, Doc," Brigham said. "I really am. You've always

been good to me. But it wasn't a hundred dollars he gave me, it was *five* hundred dollars, and where else am I gonna get that kinda money all at once?" He looked sad.

"Would you really shoot me, Brigham?"

"If you tried to run away, I'd have to because if I didn't, Willy here would shoot *me*. He swore to it, and I believe him."

"I don't got all day," Willy said. "What's your decision? You want to live or die?"

Anson felt his shoulders sag as he turned to face wounded Willy again. "How long ago did this happen?"

"A couple, three hours ago."

"Did you ever lose consciousness?"

Willy's eyes grew hard, suspicious. He didn't want to answer.

"Look, Willy, you've played your hand, all right? And you've played it well. I'm here and trying to help. Answer or don't answer but ask yourself how a doctor can better help a patient. Would it be with or without information?" Anson surprised himself with that speech. He didn't sound nearly as terrified as he felt. "The question was—"

"I remember the question. Yes, I think I lost consciousness after each time I got hit. It was the shock of it."

"Did you see the gun that shot you?"

More hesitation.

"Oh, for Christ's sake. This isn't idle chitchat. This stuff makes a difference. Were you shot with a rifle or a pistol?"

"Are we gonna chat out here in the parking lot, or are you gonna take me inside at some point?"

Anson sighed. It sounded like a growl. "Moving a GSW victim is risky," he said, meaning gunshot wound. "Bullets tear through tissue and cause a lot of damage. If we twist or move you the wrong way, we could knock a clot free, and your blood pressure would tank, and you'd pass out. I can't get answers from someone who's passed out, but you're upright and cogent now. The severity of the potential consequences of a bullet wound have everything to do with the size and velocity of the projectile. So, let's try this again. Rifle or pistol?"

Willy's eyes said that he did not appreciate being spoken to this way. "Rifle, both times. Don't hold me to it, but I'm going to guess six-five Creedmoor."

Questions flooded Anson's mind. Who the hell gets into a gun battle with hunting rifles, and how the hell does such a thing even happen? But those questions were out of bounds. They had nothing to do with quality of care.

"When was the last time you tried to stand?" Anson asked.

"I last sat about forty-five minutes ago."

It wasn't exactly the answer Anson was seeking, but he didn't want to push the gunman too hard.

"All right," Anson said. "Here's what you're going to do and what we're going to do together. You're going to put that pistol someplace that is not pointed at my face. This is likely to hurt and I don't need your reflexes or flashes of anger making orphans out of my children."

He waited. "That's the first step. Hard stop. We don't begin to move you until that gun is put away."

Willy took a few seconds to think through his options. "Brigham, you remember what I told you, right? What your job is?"

"If Doc hurts you on purpose, I'm supposed to shoot him."

"Where are you supposed to shoot him?"

"In the knee the first time."

Anson felt something dissolve in his gut. Was it truly that easy to corrupt someone you've known for years? Someone you'd tried to help?

"I'm really sorry, Doc," Brigham said.

"Willy, this is *going* to hurt," Anson said. "How are you going to know what's intentional on my part and what's not?"

Willy made a show of shoving his pistol into a holster on his hip. "I guess we're all just going to have to trust the process," he said. "Now that I know that you know what's at stake, I'm comfortable that you'll be careful."

Anson found himself frozen, staring.

"You should probably open the door," Willy said. "That would be a good first step."

Yeah, boy howdy did it hurt! In the time Willy K had been in the car—the Sulkeys' car at that because his own had been shot to death in the middle of the field—his whole body had tightened up. The transfer to the wheelchair hurt like a sonofabitch, and once seated, the straps on the chair hit him in all the wrong places, lighting up both his leg and his belly.

Brigham kept his eyes cast everywhere except in Willy K's direction, for fear, he figured, that he would be given the order to shoot his doctor friend.

Once they were through the glass doors, Willy K ordered Doc Anson to lock them closed and roll him out of sight.

"All right, Doc, what do we do first?"

"Let's get you in a room and you take your clothes off. I can't treat wounds I can't see."

Willy K understood the point. He'd watched the docs treat dozens of wounded soldiers over in the Sandbox. After Doc Anson wheeled him into an operatory, the medico turned and started to leave.

"Whoa," Willy K said. "Where do you think you're going?"

"To give you some privacy."

"To run away, is what you mean. No, no, no. You stay where I can see you." He craned his neck to see past the doc. "Brigham! Where'd you go?"

Brigham slid into view from the other side of the privacy curtain where he'd been hiding. "I'm right here."

"You're supposed to be watching this guy," Willy K said. "He just tried to run off and you were nowhere to be found."

"I didn't try to run anywhere!" Doc Anson protested.

And Willy K knew that. He just wanted to make the point. "Now, Brigham, you do what you're supposed to do while I get these clothes off." Moving gingerly, Willy K pulled his pistol from its holster and placed it on the elevated stainless steel tray that stood guard next to the cot. He didn't need the firearm dropping to the floor as soon as he unfastened his trousers.

He removed his cowboy boots by stepping on the opposite heels, and once in his stocking feet, lowered his pants gently down to the floor, handling them by the waistband, and wincing as the coagulated fabric pulled away from his skin. He marched free of them.

His jacket was next, followed by his shirt. Within three minutes, he was standing there next to the cot in his socks and briefs.

"Are you going to let me come in close to take a look?" Doc Anson asked.

Willy K replied, "Nobody likes a smartass."

"Then get up on the table and let's get to work," Doc Anson said. "Brigham, put that gun away before you hurt yourself. And you, Willy, if you're going to shoot me, get on with it. Otherwise, I am a physician, and I will treat you like any other patient."

"No anesthesia," Willy K said.

"Again, as with any other patient, if you don't want anesthesia, you won't get anesthesia. But that's going to mean extra pain. That's the trade-off."

Willy K appreciated the candor. And he believed that the doctor would treat him well.

Over the next forty-five minutes, an X-ray confirmed that a bullet fragment had lodged in his femur and that he needed surgery to remove it. Until he had the surgery, his leg would hurt like hell, and he would always be on the razor's edge of developing an infection which, if it spread to the bone itself, could cause serious problems, perhaps resulting in amputation, or even death by septic shock.

But none of that would happen today. Instead, he accepted a shot of antibiotics and a fistful of pills that were better sized for a horse than a human.

His belly wound turned out to be more consequential than he had expected, but still not a huge issue. The bullet had missed all major arteries and organs, but it had clipped the underside of a rib in his back. The same antibiotics should protect him from infection in both wounds—to the degree that they would protect him at all.

When all imagery and diagnoses were completed, the doctor cleaned him up and bandaged him. Through it all, Brigham stood close by but out of the way. He no longer looked like he was going to pass out from the medical equipment and procedures.

"You can get dressed now," Doc Anson said as he was finishing up. "But it's a mistake to put off surgery for too long on that leg."

Willy K slid gently off the cot till his feet were on the floor, and then he held onto the edge for a few seconds to make sure he was steady on his feet. "I appreciate your concern, Doc, but you know as well as me that you can't just get bullet wounds operated on without alerting a lot of people I don't need to have all up in my business."

"And use that cane I gave you. The less stress you put on your femur, the less likely you are to irritate the wound and trigger infection." It was a geezer cane, the kind with four landing pads.

The bending and stepping that were necessary to put his clothes back on all required more effort, more concentration than they should. "Damn, that hurts."

"And it's going to for quite some time."

Willy K pulled his trousers up and fastened them. "I get it," he said. "And I really do appreciate all of your help." He adjusted the holster just so on his belt, then reached to the pistol that still lay on the tray. "Sometimes, I hate myself for what I have to do."

Doc Anson barely had time to express surprise before Willy K shot him in the forehead. Ten feet away, Brigham jumped a foot and struggled to pull the pistol he'd been given out of his pocket.

Willy K shot him in his left knee.

Brigham howled in agony as he dropped to the tile floor. He'd only just hit when Willy K shot him in the right elbow.

"Dude!" Brigham yelled. "Why, man? I did everything you asked. Oh, shit! I did everything, man!"

The next bullet took out Brigham's right knee.

Willy K grunted as he stooped to the writhing, howling wounded man and retrieved the pistol from his pocket. "This is what you were willing to do to your friend," he said. "That makes you a disgusting human being. Enjoy life in a wheelchair."

With considerable effort, Willy K pushed himself all the way to his feet and walked through the Urgent Care building to let himself out the back door. Last thing before stepping out into the humid air, he killed the power first to the phone system, and then to the whole building.

The staff would be met with quite a surprise when they reported to work in the morning.

As he limped around the building to return to the Sulkeys' car, he had to stop to fish the burner flip phone out of his pocket with his cane hand. He pressed the digit 1 and waited while the speed dial toned.

When the call connected, a recording said, "Go." Then the beep.

"Solomon, this is K. We've got a major complication. I'm coming in, but this can't wait. Get back to me asap." Then he clicked off. They needed to find a way to erase whatever videos might have been recorded of him in the hospital.

CHAPTER FIFTEEN

Darkness had set in deep by the time Jonathan and Boxers pulled into the Walmart parking lot in Harrisonburg to pick up Gail before returning to the Sulkey house. Young Jason was in good hands as far as Jonathan could tell, and he considered the boy to no longer be his responsibility. With Farrell Sulkey dead and the son wounded and in the care of a covert treatment facility, he was grateful not to be a part of crafting the multilayer lie that would have to be constructed for the cover story to work.

"I left Linda Taylor thinking that she wasn't in any real danger," Gail said after climbing inside. "It sounds like I need to give her an update."

"Your call, of course," Jonathan said, "but it always comes down to what are you going to say. It's like the rest of the Sulkey family. I don't know if they're in direct danger or not, but this shooter—whoever he is—isn't a close-up wet worker. You can be as paranoid and careful as you want, but there's no hiding from a capable sniper."

"I think we can be pretty sure that our killer is moving slower than he used to," Boxers said. "With all that blood on the scene, he's gonna have to hole up somewhere for at least a little while."

"Could be exactly the break we need," Jonathan said.

"Shot by a little boy, right?" Gail asked. "Isn't that what you told me?"

"I wouldn't call him a little boy exactly," Jonathan said. "But certainly a youngster."

The transceiver bud in Jonathan's ear popped to life. "Scorpion, Scorpion, Mother Hen." Venice sounded spun up.

Jonathan switched to VOX. "Go ahead. We're just arriving on scene."

"I think your shooter surfaced," Venice said. "Emergency services around Harrisonburg are lit up about a double shooting at an urgent care center. A wounded man arrived at closing time, forced a doctor to treat him and then killed the doctor and shot another man."

"Shot but didn't kill?" Didn't sound like a professional killer.

"It's terrible," Venice said. "The killer shot the man in the elbows and knees, specifically to cripple him for life. That's what he told the police."

"What a sick asshole," Boxers said.

"Any idea on who the shooter was?"

"I have a picture, but I haven't run it yet. As soon as I saw the reports, I hacked into the Urgent Care's security system and grabbed some video. But you want to hear something really creepy and really interesting?"

She actually waited for an answer. "Why, yes, Mother Hen," Jonathan said, "I would love to hear something really creepy and really interesting."

"You don't have to be such a smart aleck," Venice said. "While I was in the process of copying the file, someone else broke in and deleted it."

The occupants of the Batmobile all scowled in unison. "Tell us what you're not telling us. What's the significance?"

"I think it's the bad guys, covering their tracks," she said. "Deleting the evidence before the police can get their hands on it."

"What makes you think it wasn't the police?" Gail asked.

"The police wouldn't delete it," Venice said. "They'd make

copies, download it, preserve it. Deleting destroys it. Plus, their warrant hasn't yet been granted."

"This means we're up against an organized enemy," Jonathan said.

"Didn't we already think that?" Boxers asked.

"This isn't easy stuff," Venice said. "It takes a level of expertise that—forgive me, all of you—rises above that of the average door-kicking shooter."

"Wow," Boxers said.

"That really hurts, Mother Hen," Jonathan added.

"As truth so often does," Venice fired back. "Now some good news. Since the bad guy hacker did his work at the same time I was doing mine, I think I might have been able to capture enough of his electronic footprint to figure out some details about who or where he is."

Amazing.

"Wait," Gail said. "Is that a two-way street? Could he have collected that same data about you?"

Hesitation. "Yes, but less likely. We only occupied the same space for maybe twenty seconds, and he'd have had to know to look for me. Copying isn't as obvious an activity as deleting."

"Unless maybe the reason you're deleting is a fear of being copied," Boxers said.

"I think we're okay," Venice said, but Jonathan heard the doubt in her tone.

They turned into the Sulkeys' neighborhood. "Want me to park in the driveway or down the block?" Boxers asked.

"Down the block," Jonathan said. The way the day had been going, he felt it wise to presume the worst, and they didn't need a bunch of doorbell cameras associating the Batmobile with the home of a murder victim.

"I don't like the fact that our shooter is as mobile as he is," Jonathan said to the team. "I don't like that he's still in the fight and he's got support behind him to help cover his trail. Mother

Hen, has there been any radio traffic about the PC's murder in the woods?"

"Negative. You shouldn't have to worry about a police presence where you're going."

"Good to know," Jonathan said. Sooner or later, Farrell Sulkey's body was going to be found, or Jason Sulkey was going to phone his mom, and as soon as the world knew that there'd been a murder, this home would become a crime scene and the focus of a lot of attention. Jonathan wanted to get in and out before any of that became an issue.

As they cruised past the front of the Sulkey residence, Jonathan's stomach fluttered. A light was on in the front room. And then another came on.

"Oh, that's not good," Boxers said.

Jonathan took a few seconds to catch Venice up on what they were seeing. "Somebody's got the same intel we have," he said.

"But they're in the wrong spot, right?" Gail said. "The important stuff is in the basement."

"That's what Jason said."

"What's the plan?" Boxers asked.

"We're going to join them," Jonathan said. "Beat them to the punch."

Boxers said, "Mother Hen, find me a close, out of the way parking spot, please." They all knew without asking that Venice was tracking their every movement on her screen.

"Big Guy, you're in luck," Venice said. "There's a park on the next block, almost directly opposite where you are now. The target house backs up to it."

Jonathan gave Big Guy the nod. Boxers reached into the center console, removed an old-school two-tube night vision array, and set it on his head. With the headlights off, they hooked a U-turn and started for the park.

"We need to assume the worst about these guys," Jonathan said. "Let's go in heavy. Long guns, vests, and NVGs." Night vision goggles.

The sign at the park's open entry gate read, EAGLE'S NEST PARK. The gate looked like it hadn't been closed in decades. Built without streetlights, the entire neighborhood felt dark, but back here, among the trees, the darkness had weight.

"I bet a few bambinos have been conceived in here," Boxers said.

"Not if they ever watched a serial killer movie," Gail said. "Freddy Krueger would love it here."

Jonathan pointed ahead through the windshield. "Park as close to the trees as you can." Behind him, he could hear Gail retrieving weapons and gear from the compartments in the floor and wall panels.

Two minutes after they'd parked, they were ready to go. Jonathan and Gail each carried an M27 as their long gun and Boxers, as usual, carried the HK417. With NVGs up and on, navigating the lush underbrush of the woods posed no greater challenge in the dark than it would have at midday.

"Who do you think these guys are going to turn out to be?" Gail asked over the air. Their radios were all set to VOX.

"No idea," Jonathan said. "My gut tells me they're the people who hired the killer."

"Maybe they're more killers," Boxers said.

"Who would they be here to kill if the house is empty?" Gail asked.

"Stop," Jonathan commanded. "Suppose they're here to kill us?"

"Come again?" Boxers asked.

"I know about the papers in the basement because Jason Sulkey told me about them. I think our intent to come here for them was pretty clear. Suppose he shared the same info with someone else who turned out to be a bad guy?"

"Doesn't that feel like a stretch?" Gail asked.

"Maybe. But remember, we were part of Wolfie's OTR operators. This could be a convenient way to check a bunch of boxes at once. They get the papers that seem to be so damned important, and they kill us in the process."

Boxers said, "I vote we don't let them do that."

"Second from me," Gail said.

"None of this changes what we're here to do," Jonathan said. "But it's an interesting thought."

They started forward again. "They could also be feds here to clean up whatever mess they're killing for," Gail suggested.

That would be the worst outcome, Jonathan thought. They were about to surprise some people who were likely to be armed. If a gunfight ensued, he'd hate like hell to explain how they'd shot it out with a bunch of federal agents.

The back of the Sulkey house featured a deck that spanned nearly the entire width of the structure. Only four feet above the ground, lattice work around the perimeter of the deck shielded from view what Jonathan imagined were windows into the basement. On the far left, a set of concrete steps descended below ground to what he imagined had to be a door.

He pointed toward the door with a bladed hand. "That's our entry point."

"All of us through the same door?" Boxers asked.

"Affirmative," Jonathan said without further explanation. More often than not, an entrance like this would be made from two directions, but that was only when they were concerned that someone might get away. In this case, Jonathan couldn't have cared less if the bad guys got away—in fact, he kind of hoped they would. Plus, he knew that the safe was in the basement, and they knew that their unsubs were—or at least used to be—on the upper level.

First, they had to kill the power to the house. Night vision was one of their primary force multipliers.

Jonathan had noticed before that the electrical service from the pole out front entered the house on the red side—the right side, when looking from the front.

"Go pull the meter, Big Guy," Jonathan said. "It should be over there."

Boxers tossed off a faux salute and turned the corner. Thirty seconds later, a blue flash pulsed the darkness—a signal that Big Guy had successfully pulled the electrical meter—which was essentially a big fuse—out of its receptacle.

"I hate that job," Gail said. "Big sparks freak me out."

"Nah, they keep you young and handsome," Boxers quipped as he turned the corner coming back the other way.

Inside the house, the sound of voices got louder.

Jonathan led the way down the stairs, with Boxers close behind. Gail stayed up top, taking a knee and bringing her rifle up to her shoulder to scan for trouble. She would remain there the entire time they were on scene. It would be deadly to be caught unaware if the bad guys tried to block the main escape route.

Once at the base of the stairs, Jonathan grabbed the doorknob and tried to turn it. Occasionally, you lucked out and the door was unlocked. This was not one of those times.

They could gain access quickly or they could do it quietly, but they couldn't do both. Jonathan stepped aside. "Kick it, Big Guy."

"Seriously?"

"Tear the scab off. The guys upstairs must know somebody pulled the power. If they're run-of-the-mill burglars, they'll rabbit. If they're something else, we'll draw them down to declare their intentions."

A laugh rumbled out of Boxers' throat. "Look at you bein' all cowboy. I'm proud of you. Now, step out of the way, little man."

The two men traded places, and Jonathan climbed up two steps to give Boxers room to move. A massive kick with the sole of his boot just above the doorknob did the trick. The jamb splintered and glass shattered as the door panel exploded inward.

The instant the opening was made, Jonathan and Boxers squirted into the basement, Scorpion going low and right while Big Guy went high and left.

The noise ignited panic upstairs. Footsteps pounded on the

floors above their heads and people shouted. Jonathan made out three distinct adult male voices. All of them were speaking English, but he couldn't make out what they were saying.

"Stay alert out there, 'Slinger," Jonathan whispered. "We kicked a hornet's nest."

Jonathan and Boxers moved in unison to the base of the interior stairs. They stood to the side, out of any direct line of fire, and waited for the inevitable. Their infrared laser sights—invisible without night vision—danced tiny circles on the door panel, waiting for a target to shoot.

The footsteps above converged on the doorway to the stairs.

"You in the basement!" a voice yelled. "Show yourselves!"

"I don't know who you are," a second voice yelled, "but you do not want to tangle with us. Come up the stairs with your hands showing, and you'll be free to go."

Jonathan's mind flooded with important data. If the other intruders were cops, they would have identified themselves as such. If they were skilled operators, they'd have managed to open the door to confront their enemy. None of that had happened.

"I know you're down there!" the voice said. "I know *somebody's* down there. Don't make me come and hunt you."

The bud in Jonathan's left ear popped. Gail said, "Contact. Contact. Black side. We've got an armed unsub—

"Freeze!" she yelled. Jonathan could hear the real-life voice and the transmission in his ear. "Show me your hands! No!"

Three suppressed gunshots rattled the night beyond the exterior basement door. Through it all, Jonathan's eyes never wandered from the interior basement door at the top of the stairs.

Gunslinger reported, "Tango down."

In that instant, the door at the top of the stairs burst open, revealing two men dressed in black, crouched in shooting positions on either side of the door. They probably thought they were invisible. They each held a pistol. Their muzzles flashed hot as they fired into the darkness.

They were nowhere close to hitting their targets, but they'd made the critical error of opening fire. The shooter on the right—Jonathan's target—made the even more critical error of leaning into the beam of the laser sight. Jonathan shot him in the left eye, launching a mist of brain and bone that appeared green in light of his NVGs. He fell forward and slid on his belly halfway down the stairs.

Boxers' suppressed HK417 thumped at the same time, but Jonathan didn't see what became of his target.

"Did you get him?" Jonathan asked.

"I'll pretend you're just kidding," Boxers replied.

"Two tangos down in the basement. 'Slinger, are you okay?"

"I'm fine," she said. "Feeling a little vulnerable, though. We've made a lot of noise."

She was right. If neighbors started to call the authorities, this would quickly become the designated last place in the world to be.

"'Slinger and Big Guy, grab IDs, get pictures of their faces. I'm going to the safe."

"Do you need the combination again?" Mother Hen asked.

"Not yet."

The drill press occupied a corner of the basement on the far side of the interior stairs, and it was a monster. Jonathan figured it would have to weigh seven or eight hundred pounds. How the hell was he going to move that out of the way to get to the safe in the floor?

He braced himself with his legs and wrapped both hands around the plate under the drill bit, preparing to topple the iron giant to the floor, or destroy his already tricky back in the process.

It moved easily, and it weighed nothing. The drill press was a fake, presumably designed to discourage people like Jonathan from ever trying to find the safe that was recessed into the concrete floor, just as Jason Sulkey had promised.

"I remember seven, twenty-three, fourteen, forty-four," Jonathan said. "Am I right?"

"Spot on."

Jonathan used his infrared flashlight to illuminate the face of the combination plate. The knob turned easily. He nailed each number on the first try, and as he settled on the final forty-four, he could feel the last pin tumbler fall into place. He turned the latch and lifted the heavy round door on its hinge up and out of the way, until it flopped face down on the concrete floor.

The interior of the safe measured maybe two feet by three and it was packed with all manner of computer disks and folders filled with what looked at first glance like papers, but on closer examination turned out to be printed photographs. With this kind of an installation, he was expecting to find money or jewelry or even firearms, but there was none of that.

"Time to wrap it up, team," Venice said over the radio. "Harrisonburg police just dispatched a shots fired call."

"'Slinger and Big Guy," Jonathan said. "Are you done?"

"Just finished," Boxers said.

"Affirmative."

"Okay, break off and make your way to the Batmobile. I've got to find a bag to put all this shit in." He kicked himself for not having brought a rucksack along. What the hell was he thinking? This was the problem with operations that evolved on the run.

"Look behind you, Boss," Boxers said. "You've got a thirty-gallon trash can."

Complete with a thirty-gallon trash bag.

"Got it," Jonathan said. "You two get going. We're best not to be seen together anyway."

"Don't get lost," Big Guy said. Protective by nature, Boxers didn't like leaving Jonathan alone.

Jonathan upended the trash can and spilled its contents onto the floor, grateful that they were dry. Stooping to his hands and knees, he put the file folders in the bag first and then backfilled with the smaller electronic stuff.

"Mother Hen, you're going to have a fun time with all this crap."

"Are you clear of the structure yet?" Venice asked. "Seven police units so far have marked responding to this call."

And he was done.

He picked up the trash bag, held it by its neck and spun it closed as he headed for the back door.

"Careful, Boss," Boxers said. "There are cop cars in the neighborhood."

Jonathan picked up his pace, and five seconds later felt comfortably invisible in the woods.

Behind him, on the far side of the Sulkey residence, two cruisers arrived in rapid succession and pulled into the driveway.

Jonathan started to run. These guys wouldn't swing into action right away—they'd have to survey the scene and assemble their manpower—but the activity would soon draw a lot of onlookers, and every new onlooker was a new opportunity to notice the black Suburban they'd never seen before driving through the streets.

"We're all aboard, Scorpion," Boxers said. "Are you strolling, or what?"

Running drew attention, too, especially at night, and doubly especially on the night when people had reported hearing gunfire.

"Load in the back door," Gail said. "More room to dump your stuff quickly."

The engine was humming, and Boxers had already pulled out of the parking space by the time Jonathan arrived. Gail had opened the passenger-side back door for him and sat on the driver's side waving him on with big motions of her hands.

He stopped at the door, tossed the trash bag in, followed by his rifle, after he'd shrugged out of its sling, and then he hopped in himself.

"Lights or no lights?" Boxers asked.

"Stay dark till we're clear of this block and then go legal."

"You got it, Kemosabe."

As Boxers piloted the Suburban out of the neighborhood, Jonathan worked with Gail in the back to get the long guns stowed and out of sight. Now, their biggest concern was a traffic stop.

Coughing up a cover story for why they were cruising the neighborhood was hard enough without having to explain the arsenal of weapons.

"Mother Hen, Scorpion. Any indication that our vehicle has been made?"

"Nothing yet," Venice reported, "but the call just went out about a triple homicide. Drive softly."

CHAPTER SIXTEEN

By morning, Venice had scanned and downloaded hundreds of photographs from the materials the team lifted from the safe in Sulkey's basement and had combined them into a slide show of sorts. By the time Jonathan walked into the War Room for the 8:00 a.m. meeting, he'd already downed two cups of coffee and was working on his third, this one in an insulated Yeti cup bearing the logo of the Army's Delta Force.

The others had already taken their seats around the teak conference table.

"Good of you to join us," Boxers quipped.

"One of the bennies of being the boss," Jonathan said. He glanced at the screen, which already featured the initial photo of the presentation. "First of all, thank you, Venice, for burning the midnight oil on this."

She didn't look up from her computer screen. "Deep dives are my happy place," she said.

"Before we get started," Jonathan said, "what's the fallout from last night's excitement?"

"About what you'd expect from a triple homicide in a small town," Venice said.

Jonathan looked to Gail as he took his seat. "You ran the IDs of the bad guys. What did you find out?"

Gail opened her tablet and pulled up a cheat sheet that he couldn't see. "Do you want to know their names?"

"Not unless I need to. Obviously, they were working together, so what do they have in common?"

"Two of them were twenty-seven years old and the third was twenty-nine. All of them were ex-military—two Army, one Marine—and they all shared scary stuff on social media. Lots of talk about hating what America has become, and lots about a coming day of reckoning."

"Cut from the same cloth as Goldsbury," Gail observed.

"Were they kind enough to give us a specific date for that reckoning?" Boxers asked. "I'd like to take that as a vacation day."

Gail smiled. "Nothing specific, nothing actionable. Just reads like empty talk. Breast beating."

"What about their work history?" Jonathan asked.

"All of them left the military at roughly the same time, about three years ago. Nothing exemplary, from what I can tell, nothing terrible. I don't know whether they served together. None of them have reported any W-2 or 1099 earnings since then."

"Uh-oh," Boxers said.

"Yeah." Jonathan saw it, too. "It's not hard evidence, but the combination of recent military service, angry posts and no job is a common footprint for crazy militias."

"Jihadists," Boxers said. "Not just from the Middle East anymore."

"Any history of dustups with the law?" Jonathan asked.

"I didn't find any criminal records for any of them," Gail said.

"Married? Kids?"

"Nope. But they do have one other point in common." The screen blinked to reveal an image—a surprisingly clear one given that it came from a security camera—of a young man in bloody clothes and holding a cane. He looked to be in a hospital setting and a man lay sprawled on the floor behind him.

"Is that our shooter?" Jonathan asked.

"This is William Kearns—Willy K to his comrades. Nearly identical background to the other two."

"Makes the militia thing seem even more likely," Gail said.

"Yes, it does," Jonathan agreed. "But what's their end game?" He tapped the table to get Venice's attention. "Let's talk about what these guys died for. The floor is yours, Mother Hen."

"Thank you. Seems that Wolverine kept Farrell Sulkey very busy. We're talking hundreds of photographs here of people on her list doing various things with various people. Nothing prurient, from what I've been able to tell. Mostly, it's just people chatting." As she spoke, the pictures on the screen changed, one after the other.

"Are there captions?" Jonathan asked. "Anything to help us know what's going on?"

"Not that I've found," Venice said.

Gail said, "I think what I find most interesting is the fact that these photos are still around. I imagine Wolfie expected to get the negatives, as it were."

"Breaking that kind of rule is a good way to get yourself killed," Boxers scoffed.

"How many times have you been through these?" Jonathan asked Venice.

"Half a dozen, maybe."

"And nothing jumps out as being worthy of murder?"

"No," she said. "Except . . ."

"Here it comes," Boxers said. Venice loved the big reveal.

The screen went blank for a few seconds while Venice's fingers hammered the keyboard, and when the screen came back on, it featured the official photograph of Senator Maxine Bridges of North Carolina.

"I presume you recognize this face?"

"Senator Bridges's official photograph again," Jonathan said. "Was Sulkey the photographer?"

"No. I just wanted you to get her face in your head." She

clicked her mouse, and the image changed to one of the senator in much more casual clothing—jeans and riding boots with a plaid shirt—involved in an intense conversation with a man in his thirties. He appeared to be in good shape and could have been of Greek, Italian, or Arab descent.

"Her lover?" Boxers guessed aloud.

"I have no idea," Venice confessed. "But there are dozens of pictures of the two of them, clearly taken on different days, even different times of year. Whatever this was about, it was important to Wolverine."

"Linda Taylor said that there was a suspicion that Senator Bridges was a spy," Gail said. "She talked about communications with Middle Easterners."

Venice sat taller. "Huh. That's interesting." She went back to her keyboard.

"What's interesting?" Jonathan asked.

Venice held up a finger for silence.

"Don't you love the suspense?" Boxers asked.

"No."

"I've got it," Venice exclaimed. "I've got the Mideast connection. I've been doing a deep dive on the senator since she floated up as our guilty party, and she's got a big secret to hide." The screen filled with the image of a teenager in a graduation gown and mortarboard.

Venice explained, "About six years ago, her only son, Samuel, was touring Pakistan on a junket with his mother when he was recruited and radicalized by jihadis. He'd just turned eighteen and refused to come back home. Maxine Bridges tried to force him to come with her, but the Pakistan government protected him. He changed his name to Samir Saka—it means nomad."

"You mean, she left him?" Gail asked, clearly appalled.

"What choice did she have?" Venice said.

"She's a friggin' US senator," Boxers said. "She was well-positioned to pull whatever strings she needed to pull."

"That's not the kind of publicity a politician wants if they want to get re-elected," Jonathan said. "So where are you going with this?"

The screen flashed and now showed the bloody aftermath of what had to be an explosion. Blood and body parts everywhere.

"Samuel-slash-Samir went deeply into the dark side," Venice said. "US intel linked him to four high-profile car bombings."

"Good Lord," Jonathan said.

"Samir ended up killing over two dozen people with his terrorism. Four years ago, we killed him in a drone attack."

"Oh, shit," Boxers said. "Collateral damage?"

"I don't think so," Venice said. "He was the target, along with the people he was working with."

"Are you saying that Uncle Sam killed a senator's son?" Jonathan asked. He wanted to make sure he was hearing it right.

"We smoked a bad guy," Boxers said. "What's the big deal?"

"It's a big deal if you're his mother," Gail said.

Jonathan scowled. "Why haven't I heard of this before? Killing a senator's kid should be worth a headline or two."

"You said it before," Venice said. "She kept it quiet, presumably to not torpedo her election."

"How did you dig this up?" Big Guy asked.

"It's mostly public knowledge," Venice said. "You just need to know where to look. But there's more, and I think this ties into the spying thing. She went off the deep end. Her social media posts turned very anti-American."

"While she was in the Senate?" Gail asked.

"She didn't post under her own name," Venice said. "But she used the same personal computer that she uses for everything else, so I was able to connect the dots."

"How anti-American are we talking?" Jonathan asked.

"One major string was all about how Nine-Eleven was only a good start. She referred to the United States as Murder Incorporated and posited that the only true patriots are the ones who want to see America burned to the ground and everybody living here to die violently."

"Okay, I think that qualifies as anti-American," Boxers said.

"Which brings me back to this photo," Venice said. The screen blinked to reveal one of the images of Maxine Bridges with her mysterious stranger. "I ran this guy through our facial recognition software and I couldn't get probabilities higher than eighty percent."

"This is the software you stole from Uncle Sam?" Jonathan asked.

"This is the software I received as a gift," Venice corrected. "It just happens to be the best FR software available anywhere. And that's the problem. How could I not get a hit?"

In the silence that followed, Jonathan said, "You know we have no way of knowing the answer, right?"

The image clicked to a tighter closeup on the stranger.

"Fooling facial recognition is harder than people think," Venice said. "For the effort to be successful, people first have to be aware of their position relative to the camera, and they have to have chosen that particular day and time to go covert. Here, this guy had no way to know he was being photographed in the first place, let alone know from what angle."

"Maye he's just not in the system," Gail suggested.

"I don't buy that," Venice said. "What is he? Mid-forties at least. Everybody that age is in the system."

"So, your answer is . . ." Jonathan had learned to help coordinate her reveals.

"Surgery," she said. The image changed yet again. "Do you see how his eyes are differently shaped? It's subtle, but it's there."

Jonathan pretended he did, but he really didn't.

"And his ears aren't symmetrical. His nose isn't right for the rest of his genetic footprint."

"Jeez, Ven," Jonathan said. "Can't that happen in nature?"

"Of course it can. But if it happened in nature, he'd be in the database where he is not."

Jonathan thought she had a good point—one for which he had no response.

"I have an idea," Gail said. "Let's reach out to Senator Bridges with a message that we know what she's doing, and that we need to meet."

"Why the hell would she agree to that?" Boxers asked.

"Fear," Jonathan said. He liked the idea. "These photos are important enough to hire a killer to protect the secret. Farrell Sulkey knew they were important enough that he should keep them."

"As a future insurance policy," Boxers guessed. "Or a future blackmailing scheme."

"Motivation doesn't matter," Jonathan said. "It's the fact that people are afraid that the images will be revealed."

"Assuming all of that is true," Boxers argued, "my question remains. Why wouldn't she tell us to shove our meeting up our ass?"

"Because we'll send pictures with the message," Venice said with a smile. "Along with a certain date when we will release them to the public if she doesn't meet with us."

"We're going to blackmail a sitting United States senator," Gail said. "What could possibly go wrong?"

"I like to think of it as giving a murderer something to think about," Jonathan said. "Ven, can you send this in a way that it's untraceable?"

"I will pretend you did not ask me that question," Venice said. "Where and when do you want to meet?"

"It'll need to be a public place," Gail said.

Mother Hen looked to Scorpion for verification. "Yeah," he said. "Keep it out of DC, but close in the suburbs."

"Alexandria, maybe?" Gail suggested.

"How about DCA?" Venice asked, referencing the code for Ronald Reagan Washington National Airport, just on the other side of the Potomac from the city. "Very public and very secure. The best of all worlds."

"Done," Jonathan said. "Set it up for tomorrow at noon."

"That sounds like a bad idea to me, Boss," Boxers said. "How are you going to have a discreet conversation—"

Jonathan held up a hand to interrupt. "You're right. It would be a terrible place to meet. But it's a place that she's familiar with. While she's all spun up and distracted, we'll meet her someplace else."

"Where?" Gail asked.

Jonathan winked. "At the spot where we can have the most impact."

CHAPTER SEVENTEEN

The message arrived on Senator Maxine Bridges's phone in the middle of a long-ago scheduled interview with CNN to discuss recent proposed legislation to provide additional aid to starving children in Central Africa. She'd just finished a well-practiced sound-bite-rich rant that excoriated the White House for turning a deaf ear to people of color.

She'd felt her phone buzz in her purse while she was speaking, so when the moment arrived that she could cheat a glance at the message, she took it. The instant she brought the screen to life, she felt her blood pressure bottom out. Her vision went a little fuzzy at the image of her speaking with Solomon Pritzker. She remembered the outfit she was wearing in the picture. They'd met at a winery in Middleburg, Virginia. It was the meeting when he'd first revealed his plan for terror at the Planetariat, but only after tightening the noose around her neck.

The text was even more chilling:

Tsk, tsk Maxine. We know that you've been killing people you're afraid of. We know that you're particularly afraid of the man in the photo. Today you killed the man who took this picture and so many others like it. You nearly killed his son. And when your minions came to steal the photos, they all died a bloody death.

That was the end of the first text, but there was a second text, time stamped only three minutes later.

Traitors die ugly, ugly deaths, Maxine. They are particularly vulnerable to unspeakable mistreatment while they are in prison. At 6pm tomorrow these pictures and the story behind them go public. Thus you begin your journey to the Big House.

She'd scrolled for more, but that's all there was.

"Are you all right, Senator?" the segment producer asked. "You don't look—"

"I'm fine," she snapped.

"I'm all set," the cameraman said. "Sorry about the delay."

Sean Halpert, the interviewer, asked, "Do you need a glass of water or anything, Senator?"

"No, let's get on with the interview. There's a constituent issue that I need to take care of when we're done." That last part was to give cover for her overly emotional reaction. The phone was still in her hand and she was placing it in her purse when it buzzed again. Her heart jumped, but she forced herself not to look.

Ten endless minutes later, the interview was finally over. She brushed away the efforts of production assistants to remove her microphone and the IFB in her ear. "I can do this myself," she said. "I've only done it about a thousand times."

She was ninety-five percent certain she heard one of the barely legal set workers call her a bitch. On a different day, she would have cared.

She couldn't bring herself to wait for the elevator ride down to the street and then the walk to the courtesy limo that would take her back to her office in the Russell Building. She needed to know what the rest of the message had to say, and she needed to know right now.

She returned to the greenroom—which was never green in any

studio she'd ever visited—and locked herself into the bathroom to review the rest.

It doesn't have to end that bad for you though. There's a way out of this. There's a way for your secret to be kept. Will it be expensive? Of course it will. But how do you put a price tag on your freedom and your reputation? How do you put a price tag on your life?

Again, the text ended. Whoever was sending these had a flair for drama and they knew how to build tension. They knew how to make a person feel sick with fear. The final message in the string bore a time stamp five minutes later than the previous one.

The solution for you is easy, Maxine. Show up at DCA tomorrow at noon. Enter at the departure level and stand near the stairs to the Metro. We'll find you. Keep your phone close. For security reasons, there might be a scavenger hunt to follow. But at the end, we'll show you how to slay the demons that threaten your life. For the record and for what it's worth, we're very disappointed that someone as stupid as you could be elected to the United States Senate. Hasta manana.

The remainder of the day had been one long panic attack. Once the courtesy limo delivered her to the entrance to the Russell Building, she considered going straight to her car, but the afternoon's calendar was full and included a meeting with party leadership at 5:00 p.m.

As soon as she could get the chance, she needed to get hold of Solomon Pritzker, not just to inform him of the texts she'd received, but also to seek his help in maybe getting some of his security people to station themselves around the airport to find and intercept the brazen thug who'd written them.

Finally, now, on her way home, alone in her own vehicle, she had a chance to make that call.

No answer. The phone rang ten times before she dumped it.

Maxine called back four more times, getting the same results. Finally, she abandoned the effort.

The closer she got to her home in Arlington, the deeper her anxiety set. The fact that those pictures were ever taken was proof positive that that bitch Irene Rivers knew *something* about the Planetariat plan, yet the fact that Maxine had not been arrested or even questioned by authorities had to mean that whatever she knew was not enough to take legal actions before she was tossed out of Washington.

The fact that the pictures still existed meant that Solomon Pritzker and William Kearns had reneged on their promises to make sure that all evidence would be destroyed.

As she pulled into her driveway and turned off the engine, she rested her forehead on the padded steering column. There was no way for this not to end in disaster.

No, that was not true. If she could get in touch with Solomon, he could put a security team on her to follow her and intervene with the blackmailer. That would undoubtedly mean violence, of course, but as long as it was performed out of her eyesight and earshot, she was fine with doing whatever had to be done to keep the secret.

She tried Solomon's number one more time. Still no answer.

"Shit." She pushed her door open and stepped out into the warm, humid night. Autumn couldn't come quickly enough.

Maxine needed a glass of wine. And she needed company. In the years since Samuel died, and his father before him, Maxine had rarely thought about bringing another man into her life. The virgin boys were exciting, sure—something about their awkwardness and excitement were energizing and entertaining, but there could be no serious engagement.

Maybe wine wouldn't do it for tonight. Maybe she needed a scotch.

As she made her way from the driveway to the kitchen door, she swore to herself yet again that she would clear all the crap out of the carport to make room for her vehicle before the arrival of the first snow.

The dead bolt turned easily when she inserted the key. She stepped inside the tiny kitchen of the tiny house and pressed the button to turn on the overhead light. Yes, the house was so old that push-button light switches still existed in several of the rooms. She hated the place, but she needed to rest her head somewhere when Congress was in session, and the thought of apartment living was beyond her tolerance.

She was just putting her purse on the kitchen table when a man in a balaclava stepped into the room from the center hallway.

Maxine jumped so hard and so high that she nearly lost her balance. A squeaky scream escaped her throat as she turned to run back out the door, but it was blocked by the largest person she'd ever seen. He, too, was faceless under a balaclava.

"You don't want to scream," the giant said. "That would be a very, very bad idea."

The first man—the smaller one—used the sole of his work boot to push a chair away from the table. "Have a seat, Maxine," he said.

"Who are you?"

"If I break your legs, you'll sit for sure," the giant said.

Maxine felt tears pressing behind her eyes, but she willed them away. Whoever these men were, they would not get the satisfaction of seeing her show weakness. She made a deliberate effort to straighten her spine, stand taller, and then sat in the proffered kitchen chair.

A third masked intruder—this one a woman—entered the kitchen from behind the first one and took the seat opposite Maxine. The lady terrorist didn't say a word. Instead, she just stared, her brown eyes burning hot.

The smaller of the men rummaged through her purse and

pulled out her phone. He held it to her face to unlock it and walked out of her view.

After what felt like two minutes, Maxine finally said, "Get to it. Whatever you have planned. Do it and be done."

"It's tragic what happened to your son, Samuel," the lady said.

The words landed like hammer blows. Only a handful of people knew—

"Was he radicalized before he left for Pakistan or after he arrived?"

"Who are you?" Maxine asked.

"Irrelevant," the intruder said. "Answer my question, please."

"Go to hell."

The intruder chuckled. She leaned back in her chair and crossed her arms. "After the missile hit him, was there anything left to bury, or was he just turned into humidity?"

Maxine's jaws locked so tightly that they hurt.

"You were on the Intelligence Committee at the time, weren't you?" the lady asked. "Did you see the battle damage assessment pictures?" The lady pulled her own phone out of her pocket. "I can pull them up for you if you haven't."

Yes, Maxine had seen the pictures, and no, there was nothing left. "No need. Bitch."

One of the thugs behind her smacked the side of her head. "Show some respect," he said.

The lady went on as if nothing had happened. "How does that work, exactly? When you're on the *Intelligence Committee*, how do you keep the secret that your son has turned into a terrorist?"

It was shockingly simple. He changed his name and it's not the kind of question that anyone asked. But the masked bitch had no need to know that. She remained silent. Behind her back, she heard the electronic clicking of fingers on a keyboard. Craning her neck, she saw that the smaller of the men was typing on her phone.

She jumped to her feet and reached out to grab the phone away. "Who the hell do you think you are?"

The man with the phone pivoted his shoulder to keep her away while the giant stepped between them. "I wasn't kidding about breaking your legs, Madam Senator." The timbre of his voice seemed to rattle the walls.

His glare told her that he'd broken legs before. And had probably done much worse.

Maxine sat.

"Tell us about your social media posts."

A spark of panic burned hotter in her gut. How much could these people know?

"May I call you HavvidGal, or do you prefer Maxine?"

Maxine felt ill. These intruders knew far too much, but how much could it be? "I prefer Senator Bridges," she said.

"Yeah, well, that's not gonna happen," the masked bitch said.

"And what was that other name?" Maxine bluffed. "I've never heard of that person."

"Interesting," the bitch said. "You've got all the skills to pull off a long con on America, but you suck at lying. Your face doesn't hide fear or recognition well. I'm curious, though, whether your expressed thoughts that America is Murder Incorporated and should be burned to the ground are your real thoughts, or are they a fake online persona?"

"Tell me where you're going with this."

The smaller thug behind her moved around to where she could see him as he said, "First tell me about your relationship with Solomon Pritzker."

She gasped before she could stop herself.

"The man formerly known as Omar Farook before he had his face rearranged."

CHAPTER EIGHTEEN

Omar Farook stood in the dark amid an endless sea of tents, waiting for the assault to commence. With his NVGs in place, he would be able to see everything he needed to see, and with the infrared patches on his sleeves and the infrared flasher on the shoulder of his coveralls, his team would be able to see him. They had practiced this assault eight times and they had it nailed. Nine minutes from touchdown to takeoff, maximum carnage assured. He estimated up to three hundred fifty casualties, but if he was being honest, two hundred fifty was a more likely figure.

It was all in the choreography of the assault and the execution of the details. Ten teams of two, preassigned landing zones, carefully assigned firing lanes and detonation targets. The last time they practiced this, not a single significant mistake was made by anyone.

At least not that he could see. In all the previous rehearsals, Farook had been part of the assault force, as he would be tomorrow when the assault was real. For this final rehearsal, he wanted to experience the terror from the point of view of the terrorized. Perhaps from this angle, he could identify defects in the plan, or areas where the assault could be more devastating.

The genius of this assault plan was the use of powered parachutes (PPCs) as their vehicles for infiltration and exfiltration.

Roughly resembling a small air boat of the type used in the Everglades, the base of the PPC was a four-wheeled go-cart with a caged propeller attached to the back end to provide propulsion. A parafoil—an inflatable wing that looked a lot like a parachute—extended out behind the vehicle itself. When the vehicle increases speed, the parafoil provides lift, and off you go. To descend, the pilot needed only to reduce power. Takeoffs and landings required less than two hundred feet.

Farook saw the faint twinkling of his army's IR blinkers a full thirty seconds before he heard even the faintest hints of the powered parachutes' motors. Tomorrow night, when the assault was real, they would have flown for over thirty minutes at treetop level to get to this point, but for tonight, the boys had been in the air for only fifteen minutes.

To get the true experience of what it would mean to be a victim, Farook lifted his night vision monocular off his head. The night returned to black, and without any visual reference, the noise seemed to grow louder. Surely, some people would hear the approach, but with PPCs, no one would know what they were hearing. Those who crawled out of their tents to take a look would likely be among the first to die.

Farook replaced his night vision and was startled to see that one of the ultralight aircraft was passing only ten feet off the ground and maybe thirty feet away. The pilot expertly flared the canopy to bring the PPC to a smooth rolling halt. The pilot and his passenger, both expert gunmen, exited their tandem seats from opposite sides and advanced together on their section of tents, firing three-round bursts with each step, raking the exterior of the tents at the angles where they knew the campers would most likely be lying asleep. The sound of the Simunitions cycling through the weapons was much quieter than what the real sound would be when they made the assault, and that was without the sounds of panic and pain when the lead would be tearing through viscera and bones of boys and young men.

Once among the tents they tossed their grenades to the sides, lobbing the simulated explosives over two rows of domes.

Each of his fighters carried ten thirty-round magazines and five hand grenades. The night pulsed with the sound of simulated carnage for exactly eight minutes, and then it stopped.

Each fighter would have one more mag to fight their way back to their aircraft, and from there, after a short run powered by the 100-horsepower engine, the whirling blade would push them along the ground until their parachute canopies inflated, they lifted off the ground, and they returned to the rally point.

America would never be the same.

At the mention of the name Omar Farook, Senator Bridges seemed to shrink in her seat, as if something essential had been sucked out of her. Blood drained from her face and for a few seconds, Jonathan thought she was going to faint. When she finally recovered, she looked . . . defeated.

Using her phone's history, Venice had quickly been able to trace Bridges's most recent calls, and from there, somehow broke the identities. Mother Hen's capabilities were beyond amazing.

Scouring the internet using his own phone, Jonathan took two minutes to read the history of Omar Farook.

"You've got interesting friends, Maxine," Jonathan said. "Not everyone cavorts with so many traitors to America. It seems that your friend Omar is a car bomber, too. Just like your baby boy." Jonathan swung one of the remaining chairs around and sat in it backwards, his chest leaning into the seat back. "Let's talk about that, *Senator*."

Maxine Bridges stared at the table, her lower lip trembling.

"I imagine it's helpful to have a friend on Capitol Hill when you're a terrorist," Gail pressed. "What kind of help are you able to provide?"

Bridges didn't reply. Most significantly, she didn't deny anything.

"Confession's good for the soul, Senator," Boxers said. "Hasn't anyone ever told you that?"

Jonathan shot him a glare. This was not the time to push too hard.

"Look, Maxine," Jonathan said, "you must have figured out by now that we are not police. We have neither the ability nor the desire to arrest you. But we think you've started something that needs to be stopped, and we're determined to stop it. We know that you hired an assassin or team of assassins to kill people from Irene Rivers's off-the-record contractors list. Are you going to deny that?"

"Would it matter?" Bridges asked. "You seem to have made up your mind."

"Yeah, I have," Jonathan said. "And my patience for bullshit games has dropped to zero. We have everything we need to send you away forever. We don't have the authority, but we have the evidence. I'll be honest and tell you that we didn't collect it through court-friendly processes, but we have it. There's your way out. Are you listening to me?" She was staring at a point in space in a way that made him think her mind had disengaged with this world. That can happen at times like these.

"I'm listening," she said. And she had yet to deny a thing.

"All right, here's the deal. You tell us what we need to know to get ahead of the assassins and we walk out of your life. Let the police work their own case. But first, they'll have to discover that there's a case to be worked because they won't hear it from us. If you don't cooperate, I'll be chatting with the FBI tomorrow morning, and you'll be in a jail cell by tomorrow night. Call the ball."

Bridges finally engaged Jonathan eye to eye. "You have no idea what you're dealing with," she said. "Or *who* you're dealing with."

"Are we talking about you now or about Farook?" Jonathan asked.

"Pick one," Bridges said. "I am only a pawn in a game you don't want to play." Her features had hardened into a mask of determination.

Jonathan leaned heavily into the chair back. "Are you a terrorist, Senator?"

She scoffed, "Not hardly." She stopped speaking, as if she'd said enough.

"Let me guess," Gail said. "The rest of America are terrorists."

Bridges smiled.

"And you are a patriot?" Jonathan asked. "Seriously?"

"You're clearly not a lawyer," Bridges said. "It's never smart to ask a question to which you don't already know the answer."

"Explain it to me," Jonathan said. He sensed that she wanted to make a speech.

"Look what America has become," Bridges said. "The land of the free, home of the brave has morphed into land of the censored and oppressed, home of cowards."

Jonathan sensed Boxers puff up. Probably didn't even know he was doing it.

Bridges continued, "My son did some bad things in the eyes of the United States. When they killed him, they didn't even have the courage to fight man-to-man. They sent a drone—a machine—to kill him from above. They murdered him."

"They smoked a murderer," Boxers said, earning another glare from Jonathan.

"They assassinated a freedom fighter. Samuel was a religious man, standing up for his beliefs."

"By blowing innocents up via remote control," Boxers said. "That looks heroic to you?"

"Not now, Big Guy," Jonathan admonished. They were trying to get information, not engage in a debate.

"While evading superior technology," Bridges said. "By beating the odds that were horribly stacked against them. By being brave. Only to be murdered by cowards."

"Okay," Jonathan said, "so you're pissed off. What does this have to do with the kill list?"

"Did Omar Farook reach out to you?" Gail asked. She'd been reading a running commentary from Venice while Jonathan had been grilling Bridges. "Did he see your angry posts and recruit you?"

Bridges scoffed again. "You make that sound so easy, like I was stupid. There was no *recruiting*."

"To do what?" Jonathan asked.

"To avenge my son's death. To avenge the deaths of thousands—*millions* who have died because of America's ambitions."

"How does killing a short list of contractors avenge the deaths of millions?" Jonathan asked. "You're not making sense."

The senator's eyes shifted to look straight through Jonathan. They were cold enough to trigger a chill. Then she smiled.

"I don't see the humor," Jonathan said.

"You don't see anything," Maxine said. "You have no idea."

"Is your plan bigger than the kill list?" Gail asked.

Bridges stood.

So did Jonathan and Gail.

"I need a cigarette," Bridges said.

"Not now you don't," Jonathan said.

"If you want to hear the rest of this story, I need a cigarette. As you say, call the ball."

"Where are they?" Jonathan asked.

Bridges pointed as she moved. "Right here in the drawer."

"Sit back down," Jonathan said. "I'll get them."

"Worried I'll get a gun out of the drawer?"

"Something like that," Jonathan said. "Now, sit."

Bridges exhaled heavily as she lifted her chair and slammed it onto the floor before sitting back down. "This is my house, you know." Then, as Jonathan pulled open the kitchen drawer, she said, "Get me the Lights, please. I tell myself they're better for me."

Of the two packs in the drawer, the one labeled Lights in a

bold red font was the only one that had been opened. He grabbed that and the cheap plastic lighter next to it. He noted that there was no weapon of any kind in the drawer or anywhere within reach.

He returned to the table and handed them over.

Bridges pointed to the counter. "The ashtray's over there."

Jonathan noted the absence of ashes in the ersatz scallop shell. In fact, the house didn't smell of cigarettes. "You must not smoke much indoors," he said as he presented her with the ash catcher.

"It's a disgusting habit," Bridges said as she tapped out a stick. "Probably going to kill me one day." She smiled again as she gestured with the filter end of the cigarette. "I'll tell you this. I can't live with the thought of arrest and humiliation. But neither can I live with the thought of betraying so many others."

"Who are these others?" Gail asked.

"Names I pray you will never know."

"What are we talking about, Maxine?" Jonathan asked. "Is there a terror attack in the works?"

"It was probably foolish of me to think that I could survive this," Maxine said. She'd slipped into an odd pensive state. "But big events bring big consequences. There are worse ways of dying than dying for a cause. At least I'll see my boy again, right?"

Jonathan exchanged glances with his team. This was all very strange.

Maxine brought the cigarette to her lips, but there was something wrong with the way she was handling it.

Instead of taking it with her lips like every smoker in the world, she placed it deep into her mouth and bit down on the filter with her molars.

"Oh, shit. No!" Jonathan reached out to stop her, but it was done.

Three seconds later, her facial features relaxed, her pupils expanded wide and she toppled onto the floor, dead.

"Holy shit!" Gail yelped as she jumped in her seat. "What the hell?"

Jonathan could smell the characteristic burnt almond stench from here. "Suicide pill in the filter," he said. "Cyanide."

"Now, that's some serious spy shit," Boxers said. "Be lyin' if I said I didn't admire that a little bit."

"Seriously, Big Guy," Gail said. "You should consider getting counseling."

Boxers blew her an air kiss. "What now, Boss?"

Damned interesting question. This was not at all how he'd expected this evening would end. "We toss the place and get out as fast as we can. Anything that looks like a computer, or that it might untie this knot, we take it with us. Keep the balaclavas on in case there are cameras we didn't see."

Twenty minutes later, they were done, their dump bags filled with three laptop computers, two tablets, two phones and more disks and chips and thumb drives than Jonathan cared to count.

Venice was in for another long night once they got back to Fisherman's Cove.

CHAPTER NINETEEN

Kerry Smallwood didn't know what time it was as he stepped over the ring of rocks and into the ashes to give the remains of the bonfire a stir with the end of the log in his right hand. When the white-orange embers jumped to life as flame, he dropped the log onto it and then added the one from his left hand to form a slanted X that would give the fire a surface to climb.

Feeling heat through the soles of his boots, he quick-walked back out of the fire for three more logs, then quick-walked back over the ring to add those to the fire as well. He figured he'd given himself an easy half hour, and that's about all he wanted. Just enough time to chill and watch the stars for a while.

Checking over both shoulders for witnesses, he pulled a thin box of Swisher Sweets plastic-tipped cigars out of his pants pocket, pulled a stick free, and placed the box back where it came from. As he peeled the plastic wrapper, he slipped a strike-anywhere match from another pocket and lowered his butt onto the first of three concentric rows of felled trees that served as seats.

Kerry knew that the coolest way to light the match was to use his thumbnail, but the thought of burning match shit under there gave him the willies. Instead, he ran the match under his thigh to get a light and brought the flame to the cigar. When he had a good hot cherry glowing, he tossed the match, still burning, back across the rock ring into the fire pit.

Ninety minutes ago, this place was packed with troopers. They'd had after-chow announcements and then the most talentless talent show Kerry had ever seen, until the sun went down, and then it devolved into s'mores, small-group ghost stories, and finally lights-out.

Kerry was pleased overall with the crop of kids at this year's Planetariat. Not a lot of whining, not a lot of homesickness, even from the nine-year-olds. Homesickness pissed him off.

Dear moms and dads: If your kid doesn't want to go away to camp, let him stay home. His whining embarrasses him and ruins the trip for everyone else.

Tonight, he did his walk-around to make sure all the squadrons were secure and that everybody was bedded down, and then he headed out here for his alone time.

He thrived on the quiet of the night and marveled at the sheer number of stars in the sky out here.

The night was perfect. The heat of the day had blown off. The air was still thick with humidity, but the air temperature was in the sixties. He almost needed a jacket.

With the Swisher Sweets clenched in his teeth, Kerry lowered himself onto the ground and used the felled tree as a kind of pillow to support his head as he stared into the sky.

This was where his problems solved themselves, though he didn't understand how. It wasn't as if that's what he set out to do—you can never solve a problem by thinking about it head-on—but something about the relaxation he felt out here brought contentment, and with the contentment came peace.

Then there was the sense of finality. This was the year of lasts. His last as a trooper, his last before he headed off for Annapolis, and from there to the rest of the world. Right now, today, the Marine Corps seemed like what he wanted to do after the Naval Academy. He wanted to fight bad guys for real, up close and hand to hand.

Last week, though, becoming a jet jockey seemed like the best thing. He knew it would all work itself out. Life did that. Maybe, twenty years from now, when he had kids of his own, he'd do like his dad did and double back to manage one of these Planetariats.

But probably not. That seemed like a lot of damned hard work.

As he blew a stream of cigar smoke straight up into the sky, he noted that the whole cloud of it stayed together as it rose toward the stars. He figured that must mean there was no wind at all. Or if there was—

"Can you imagine how much shit you would be giving one of your troopers if you wandered up and saw what I'm seeing?"

The voice wasn't loud, but it was familiar and the suddenness of it made Kerry's whole body jerk. "Dad!" He started to pull the cigar from his lips to hide it but realized the futility and instead just sat up. "Hi." He used his hands to press himself back up onto the seat.

"Hi? That's all you've got?" Danny Smallwood straddled the log and sat down next to his son.

Kerry smiled past the plastic tip still clamped between his molars. "Well, one of us could say, what are you doing here?" he said. "At least my answer would be obvious."

Danny chuckled and pointed at the turd in his son's mouth. "Got another one of those?"

Kerry gave him a cigar and a match.

Danny twisted off the plastic end and tossed it into the fire, then lit up. "God, these things are foul. Every young man's training cigar."

This wasn't what Kerry had been expecting. Yes, there were guys' rules on trips such as these, where accepted norms were suspended, but smoking at camp was new territory.

"Who are you and what have you done with my father?" Kerry said.

"Is there anything I could have yelled at you that you didn't already know?"

"Probably not."

"Then consider yourself yelled at and enjoy your cancer stick. If you ever tell your siblings, I'll disinherit you."

Kerry pulled on the cigar, exhaled. "Got any beer?"

"I'm going to hurt you."

They both laughed.

"Seriously," Danny said, "I came up here to make sure the fire was out. Are you here just to escape, or are you working through problems?"

"Escape. Thinking about how much I'm going to miss it."

The flickering glow of the fire made his father look older than normal. "You've got far better adventures than this to look forward to," he said. "You know I'm proud of you, right?"

Kerry didn't expect the lump to arrive in his throat. He nodded. "Yeah, I do know. And I'm proud of you, too. How did it end with Mr. Schultz?"

"You embarrassed him, and he's pretty pissed."

"He started it."

"That's kinda how World War One started," Danny said with a smile.

"Twenty troopers heard him disrespect you and me and the entire organization," Kerry said. "They're looking to me for leadership. I had to do something. It's not like I hit him."

"Sometimes there's strength in walking away."

"Not this time. You didn't see their faces. I'd already walked away from him insulting me. It would have been petty for me to push back on that. But when he insulted you, I had to speak up. Don't expect me to apologize for that."

"What do we do if he packs up his rifles and takes them all home?"

"Then we make it clear that he's the asshole I thought he was, and the rest of the Planetariat goes without a rifle program."

Danny repositioned himself so he was no longer straddling the log. "Okay, then. I guess we'll know tomorrow morning."

Kerry cleared his throat and took another hit on the cigar.

"I've got a random question for you. Have you heard from Senator Bridges recently?"

Danny recoiled from the question. "Random indeed. Maxine Bridges? Why would I have heard from her?"

Oh, shit. He didn't want to give the secret away about the wall display. "No reason."

"Come on, Kerry, that is a very specific question to ask. Where did it come from?"

"Didn't you two go to school together or something?"

"Well, yeah, but that was a long time ago."

"I thought you two were a thing."

Danny threw back his head and laughed at the sky. "Where on earth did you get that idea? Oh, Lord, no. She had no idea I existed. I wasn't allowed within fifty yards of her crowd."

This suddenly wasn't feeling right. Why would she be going to all this effort to make such a nice gift for his dad if they weren't even friends?

"Kerry? Are you all right?" Danny put his hand on his son's shoulder.

"Isn't she on the planning committee for the Planetariat? Senator Bridges, I mean?"

"Well, yeah," Danny said. "It's kind of a symbolic thing. North Carolina is her state, and when election season comes around, she's going to want to have that photograph of being surrounded by mom and apple pie." Danny leaned forward and turned his head for a closer look at Kerry. "I still don't understand why we're talking about this."

"I guess I don't either," Kerry said, taking one last pull on the cigar and throwing the remains into the fire. "Maybe I was just thinking about her because she was the one who nominated me for the Academy. I figured that was a favor to you."

"Ah," Danny said, then he clapped Kerry on the shoulder. "No, son, that's all on you. You earned that appointment all on your own."

CHAPTER TWENTY

At 04:30 the next morning, Farook assembled his army in the barn he liked to call the aerodrome. Or, sometimes he called it HQ. The men had partied hard after returning from their final rehearsal. He understood that they needed the relief, but the early meeting was notice that work came first. There was a penalty for being hungover.

The post-exercise debriefing took less than twenty minutes. He shared with each of his soldiers the belief that they had executed their tasks flawlessly, and that he had great confidence that when the balloon went up on the true assault tonight, he had every confidence that they would get in and out with no casualties at all.

The teams sat casually in folding wooden chairs arranged around wooden tables scattered throughout what Farook imagined was once a dressage arena. Signs on the heavy wooden pillars declared that smoking was forbidden because of the presence of so much wood and hay, but his soldiers smoked anyway—those who wanted to. Some were adding new whiskey or beer to last night's whiskey and beer that hadn't yet cleared their digestive systems.

These men didn't need his praise and they understood bullshit when they heard it, each of them having endured valiant military tours that for various reasons turned them bitter. And if not bitter, then burning for the opportunity to keep killing.

The ease with which these soldiers' and Marines' and airmen's patriotism could be subverted for the promise of cash surprised Farook. Why else would healthy young men risk their lives for their country if not for the love of it? And even in the case of these twenty men, that was true. He'd interviewed each of them carefully before introducing them to his compound. Each had first been identified and vetted on paper by Maxine Bridges, and in all but one case, her instincts had been spot-on. But there was no replacing a face-to-face, eye-to-eye discussion to judge a man's trustworthiness.

It was during these interviews that his war-weary recruits revealed the events that turned their patriotism to bitter anger. The details of each story were different, of course, but a common theme did run through all of them—a feeling that they were pawns in a game that American leadership had no interest in winning. These men watched their friends die yet were forbidden to strike back. Or, if they did strike back, it would be in a way that was guaranteed to hurt the fewest bad guys and bring the least criticism from the media.

The men of Farook's army were angry at their country and Farook's job was to stoke and exploit that anger to convert it into action. This thing they were about to do, he told them—this slaughter of hundreds—was not about the individual lives that would be taken, any more than a firefight in Iraq or Afghanistan was about the individual lives. The killing was about making a point, about changing minds. About focusing attitudes.

Perhaps this attack—the Event—would finally force smug, comfortable oh-so-opinionated Americans to realize that their philosophical talk about war brought with it searing-hot shards of metal, severed limbs, cries of pain and senseless deaths. For once, when Americans watched the news and saw the aftermath of slaughter, the images would be from their own backyard and feature the shredded and broken remains of children who looked like them.

"Omar, I've got a question." This came from Dax Baker, a jarhead from the west coast who seemed perpetually at half-cock, ready to pick an argument with his colleagues. "What happened to Echo?" Farook knew he was referring to Team Echo, as in the fifth letter of the military alphabet.

"I can answer that," said a voice from the back of the barn, at the exit door.

"Willy K," Farook said. "You look better than I thought you would."

"Yeah, well, I hurt like hell and feel like shit." He hobbled on his cane all the way to the front row before lowering himself into a chair and slapping his cane flat on the table. He looked across to Harley Grace, an Iowan who had custody of a bottle of Buffalo Trace bourbon. "Could I trouble you to pour me one of those?"

Harley pulled a clear plastic cup off the upside-down stack and poured in two fingers of dark liquor. As he handed it over, Willy K waved him off.

"C'mon, buddy, I've been shot. Fill that puppy up."

He didn't fill it to the rim, but it was close.

This time, when he took the cup, Willy K downed half of it with a single pull, then finished with an aggressive cough.

"You sure that's a good idea when you've been gut shot?" Farook asked.

"Missed all the important stuff. I'm good to go. What does everybody know about Team Echo?" He looked at Farook as he asked.

"Only that I sent them on a mission," Farook replied.

"Do they know what it was, or what the outcome was?"

Farook shook his head. He didn't want to distract the men from the successes of last night or the mission of tonight.

"Don't you think they have a right to know?" Willy K asked.

"What the hell's going on?" Baker insisted. "I asked about Echo, and I still haven't gotten an answer."

"They're dead," Willy K said. "Farook sent them on a mission to burgle a house and gather some contraband and apparently, they walked into some kind of a trap. Got themselves killed."

"Contraband?" Baker asked. "What does that even mean?"

Willy K looked to Farook. "Your turn again, fearless leader."

Farook had never met a man like Willy K. His smarminess, his disregard for authority were of a nature that he'd never encountered before. It annoyed the hell out of him, but the men seemed to look up to him. He was a natural leader. "There were loose ends to be accounted for," Farook said to the group. "Bits of evidence which, if it fell into the wrong hands, might have caused some problems for us and our operations."

"What kind of problems are we talking about?" Baker asked.

Farook hesitated. "I'm not sure it's important—"

"Photographs!" Willy K shouted it. "They were some goddamn photographs. Just tell 'em, Omar. Three of our men died for pictures. Plus the two in the woods that I killed, and two more after that. Not to mention yours truly getting clipped, and I don't have a clue what happened to Goldberg."

"Goldsbury," Farook corrected.

"Like I care. They must be important damn pictures. I've told you from the beginning that everybody has a right to know the full burden of what they're getting themselves into. You've wanted to sugarcoat everything, and I've wanted to—"

Willy K stopped himself and rose to his feet.

"Sit down, Willy," Farook said.

"Shove it up your ass, Omar. I get that you're the boss and we all let you lead, but don't think for a second that we actually defer to you. So, here's your chance. Do you want to tell them what's going on, or do you want me to?"

Farook ran the coming scenario through his head. If he, Farook, started telling the story himself, Willy K would interrupt enough to make him look weak. If he deferred to Willy K at the start, he thought he might look stronger.

"Go ahead," Farook said. "You've been closer to it. You've certainly been closer to the violence."

Baker shot up. "What—"

"Sit down, Dax. Jesus, not everything has to make you shout." The entire crowd watched as Willy K lifted a chair and put it on top of the table. Then, using Harley's shoulder to steady himself, he stepped onto a chair to boost himself onto the table and then sat in the tabletop chair.

"I want you to be able to see me, but I'm tired of standing. My damn leg hurts. Okay, y'all know who owns this place, right?"

"You really shouldn't do this," Farook said.

"Once people on your team start dying, the rest of the team has a right to know why," Willy K said. "Senator Maxine Bridges owns the farm. All fourteen hundred acres of it. You probably don't know it, and I know she doesn't *want* you to know it, but she's one of us. That's why we're allowed to be here and have all these support facilities. To make the deal to arrange these facilities, Omar and Senator Bridges had to meet from time to time. They were pretty good about keeping on the DL, but somehow, sometime, word must have leaked." He looked back at Farook. "How'm I doing so far?"

Farook nodded for him to continue.

Willy K continued, "Y'all remember Irene Rivers? Queen bitch of the FBI?"

A rumble of affirmative opinion rippled through the crowd.

"Yeah, I figured. So, apparently, she grew suspicious about Senator Bridges and had her followed and snooped on by private assets. There was an accountant, a computer geek, and a photographer named Farrell Sulkey. We got word that Sulkey had pix of

Bridges and Omar together—pictures that were ordered taken by Irene Rivers before she shit all over her career and everybody else."

"So, when Omar says *contraband*," Baker surmised aloud, "what he really means is damning photographs of him?"

Farook felt his blood pressure spike. "Now, wait just one minute."

Willy K held up a finger to shut him down. "Don't be a dick, Baker," he snapped. "We don't know what all they had pictures of. Which is why it was important to kill the photographer and get the photos."

"What about Rivers? Don't you need to kill her, too?"

"No," Farook said. "If she knew what she had, she'd have made an arrest. Besides, that would be far too high profile. She's persona non grata now anyway. Nobody cares what she has to say."

"So, why all the killing and the burgling?" Baker pressed.

While Farook paused to gather his thoughts, Willy K took over again. "That was on the senator. When we're done with the Event, there's going to be a huge investigation, and she figured there was a high likelihood that the breadcrumbs would lead back to Omar. If the photographer remembered what he had and came forward, those images would be a direct link between her and this American Jihad."

"You've been killing others, too," said Kelly Drake, a former Army grunt from somewhere in the Midwest.

"That's all on the senator," Willy K said. "She freaked out when she heard about that list of contractors and she went all scorched earth. It didn't matter to her whether or not the contractors were directly investigating her. If they were on the list, they were to get whacked. The hits were assigned to me and Goldberg."

"Goldsbury."

"Right. And he's in the wind as far as I know."

"Back to Echo," Baker said. "They're all dead?"

"Affirmative."

"Who killed them?"

"I don't know," Willy K said. He looked to Farook to see if maybe he knew anything, and the best Farook could muster was a shrug.

"And the photographs?" Baker said. "What about them?"

"I think we assume that the shooters got them," Willy K said. "We have to."

"So, our OpSec is shot?" Dax Baker again.

"Not at all," said Farook. "I believe that Senator Bridges was overly paranoid."

"How can you say that?" Drake shouted. "The other side—whoever they are—sent a team to the same house at the same time, presumably looking for the same *contraband*."

"So, Kelly," Willy K said. "Are you suggesting that we abort?"

"We are not aborting!" Farook said.

"I'm not asking you, Omar. Kelly Drake. Speak up. You seem upset. Put that in the form of a plan."

Farook saw what Willy K was doing. This was not a group in front of whom to declare oneself a coward.

"No, I'm not suggesting that we abort."

"Okay, then calm the hell down."

Baker raised his hand. A mocking exaggeration of a kid in class.

"Say what's on your mind, Dax."

Baker stood. "Yeah, I want to make something really friggin' clear to Mr. Farook. You, too, Willy K. You used the word *abort*. I signed on for a mission and I'm a man of my word. If a fight comes with the mission, I'll fight to my last bullet and my last drop of blood. That's the deal. That's why you're paying me two hundred fifty thousand dollars. I think I speak for all of us here."

That triggered a grumbling of general agreement around the room.

"If you order me to abort the mission, I'll do that, too, but you'd best remember that you owe the two fifty, one way or the other."

More agreement.

"I understand that," Farook said. "You will be paid, no matter what. Those funds are already poised to drop in each of your accounts." He looked frightened, Willy K thought. That was good. It meant he understood all the rules of the game he created.

"And Drake?" Baker pointed at his fellow operator. "I know you probably didn't mean nothing by what you said, but I think you and everybody else in this room needs to know that there ain't no leavin' the team at this point. Yeah? We all agree on that?"

Affirmative mumbling.

" 'Cause I don't know about y'all, but if I see one of you trying to sneak away from your duty, I'll smoke your ass. If you manage to get away without me seein' it, I will make it my life's work to kill you and everybody you love."

Willy K watched the reactions of the others in the assembled army. They clearly didn't like being lectured to, but they also hadn't heard anything they hadn't already thought on their own.

"Um, hey, Willy?" Scotty Tagget, a Signal Corps geek from DC, stood to be recognized. Generally not much of a talker, he was the tech guru for Farook's army.

"Yeah, Scotty, whaddaya got?"

"I'm pretty sure there's another team working against you. Against us. I think they might be the ones who killed Echo."

"What are you telling us?" Farook asked.

"Well, remember when you told me to hack into the security system at the Urgent Care place?"

"Of course," Farook said.

"Well, when I went in to delete the files, somebody else had already hacked in and was copying the files."

Farook felt his stomach flip. "Who? And how long have you known this?"

"I've only known it for a little while, and I didn't say anything because I think I may be able to tell you who the other party was, but I'm not there yet. The other hacker and me were only on at the same time for a few seconds, but while I was there, I got a screen shot of the metadata. If I can track him down from there, it will take a while, but the *fact* that they were there copying the files says there's another team."

"But how would they know to connect the dots from the Urgent Care to the Sulkey house?" Willy K asked.

Farook said, "There's only one way that makes sense. They linked *you* to the Urgent Care. That suggests that they knew you were wounded, and connecting the dots backwards, they somehow knew you were involved with Farrell Sulkey when you were shot."

"Is that even possible?" Baker asked.

Willy K's body sagged in his chair and he shook his head. "Shit." He stood to a crouch and sought assistance from Harley again, this time to climb back down to the ground.

"What is it?" Farook asked.

"I'm pretty sure I know what happened," Willy K said. "I screwed up. This is my mistake." After some difficulty steadying himself, he grabbed his cane and started back toward the door. "The op isn't in danger, boys. But my day's not as finished as I wanted it to be."

He pointed a finger at Scotty. "Mr. Tagget, can you hack into doorbell cameras?"

Scotty shrugged. "Sure. It depends on how secure their router and Wi-Fi are, but if it's one of the major companies, and the homeowners haven't updated the firmware—which nobody does—yeah, I could probably hack in. I'd have to be close enough to get into their system though."

"Okay, I have a job for you. I need you to drive to the Sulkeys' neighborhood and dig into as many camera feeds as you can to grab images of anyone who came and went from their house be-tween eleven o'clock this morning and one o'clock this afternoon. Record the images and get them back here."

Scotty looked to Farook for confirmation, Farook nodded. "Where are you going, Willy K?"

"I need to go talk to a babysitter."

CHAPTER TWENTY-ONE

Finding Lori Madison's house was barely a challenge. After chatting with her at the front door and learning where Farrell Sulkey and his son had gone hunting, Willy K had snapped a picture of the license plate parked in front of the house. A quick search of the dark web delivered Lori's address: a single-family home nestled into the woods on what appeared to be maybe a five-acre plot of land. It was mostly surrounded by grass, but tall hardwoods guarded the two-story structure up close. He imagined that was mostly for shade, just as he imagined that this slice of land was once part of a larger farm.

Dawn had bloomed, but the sun still hung below the trees. For an operator, this was the difficult choice—night vision or no night vision? He kept the harness with the night vision monocular fastened to his head, figuring that he'd likely need it once he got inside.

He parked fifty yards or so from the top of the drive and limped the rest of the way to the front door across the patchy lawn. The house was nice, a brick center hall Williamsburg colonial that looked like it might have been lifted from Colonial Williamsburg. No lights were on inside. As he approached closer to the front stoop, he realized that the construction might well have dated back a couple of centuries. Ripples in the old-style glass distorted his image of the inside of the house.

This was a problem. Old houses creaked and popped with every step—hell, with every occupant's heartbeat. He considered killing power to the building to give himself more advantage but opted against it. Working alone as he was, and crippled as he was, he didn't think he could pull the meter on the side of the house—which always created noise and a giant blue spark—and then get around to enter the house with enough speed to make the additional advantage pay off.

Two short brick stair risers led to a brick stoop. He left his geezer cane standing on its own and drew his .40 caliber Glock 23 as he thumbed the latch on the door handle. The unlocked door floated inward. In his experience, it wasn't unusual for people who lived in the country to neglect basic security precautions.

Leading with his bad leg, he stepped across the threshold onto the ancient wooden floor, and true to form, the house creaked like a bad horror movie. The interior was still dark as a cave.

He lowered his monocular into place, thumbed his infrared muzzle light to life and swept the foyer left to right. No sign of people, no sign of movement. Best of all, no sign of a great big dog.

Another step forward produced another groan, this one accompanied by a loud wooden *pop*. The heavy gait caused by his limp made stealth impossible. Still, he had to try.

The next loud step brought the sound of movement and voices from upstairs. There was an urgency to the tone. A male voice asked, "Are you sure?" and a female voice said, "Yes!"

Shit.

Willy K limped with more speed than he thought he could muster—and more noise than he wanted to make—to stand at the bottom of the stairs, where he waited for the inevitable.

"Is somebody down there?" the male voice called.

Willy K said nothing.

The lights came on.

*   *   *

Jonathan hadn't slept for more than a couple of hours. At 05:30, he gave up the quest for rest. He showered, dressed, and headed up to the office.

He still couldn't make any of the pieces fit. He was surprised to find the entire team slumped in the War Room, spitballing ideas as to what was important enough about those pictures to warrant a suicide pill, but nothing made sense.

"The only thing that makes sense to me," Gail said, "is that she must somehow be afraid of Omar Farook. Somehow, whatever punishment he might mete out for whatever went wrong must be worse than death by cyanide poisoning."

"Kearns is out there killing people to gather back damning information," Boxers reminded. "I think she killed herself because the information got out."

"What got out?" Gail asked. "That she had a couple of conversations with a bad guy? That's bad for a political career, but it's not against the law. It's not worth dying for."

Jonathan saw the corner of an idea peeking through the clutter in his mind. "Terrorists gotta do what terrorists gotta do," he said. "She all but confessed that Farook was planning another op somewhere. Maybe she's worried that if whatever he's planning gets traced back to him, and then the pictures are put out there, she'll be seen as an accomplice. What I want to understand—"

"Hey, Dig?" Venice said. She was scowling and leaning into her computer. "That babysitter you spoke to at Sulkey's place. Was her name Madison?"

"Yes, why?"

"Police in Harrisonburg were just dispatched to a home invasion at a house owned by a Madison family."

Jonathan felt something stir in his spine.

"That's a common name," Boxers said. "Especially in that part of the world."

Venice's computer produced the sound of a ringing phone. "It's your FBI number," she said. "Incoming call."

"Shit. I gave Lori Madison this number. Okay, put on speaker."
The line clicked open.

Jonathan said, "Neil Bonner speaking."

"Oh, my God, Mr. Bonner, he's here. He's back. The man from this morning. He's got a gun." The background vibrated with the sound of bedlam as people shouted.

The sentences that cut through all the noise were, *Please don't shoot. We're not armed. We don't even own a gun. You can take whatever you want.*

Lori's voice squeaked when she said, "Oh, my God, he's coming upstairs."

"Lori, listen to me," Jonathan said. "No questions, do exactly what I tell you. Are you ready?"

"Yessir."

"Tell him . . ."

"Everybody just calm down," Willy K said. He kept his pistol aimed at the center of the male's forehead, and he kept both eyes open so he could see the movements of everyone else. The fact that he could not see the source of the female voice he heard told him that she must have called or be in the midst of calling the police.

"You in the bedroom!" he yelled. "Come out here. Don't make me kill your husband!"

"Please don't shoot," the guy said. "We're not armed. We don't even own a gun. You can take whatever you want."

"Well, for right now, I want your wife or girlfriend or whoever the hell she is to do exactly what I'm telling her to do. Get her ass out here before I blow your brains out."

A woman in her fifties emerged from behind the man, her hands in the air. "I-I'm here," she said. "Please don't shoot us."

"You called the police, didn't you?"

The lady just stared.

"Don't lie to me."

Her head twitched with what might have been a nod.

The face of a little boy appeared from the shadows behind the woman. "What's going on?"

"Go back to bed, Rascal."

"That was a stupid thing for you to do," Willy K said, ignoring the boy for now. "Both of you get down on the floor. Face down. Hurry."

They'd just begun to move when a bedroom door opened on his left. He pivoted his aim and saw the target of his mission, Lori Madison, standing in the doorway in cream-colored pajamas holding a cell phone.

"Mr. Kearns," she said. "There's a phone call for you."

His stomach seized. She used his name. How was that possible?

"Agent Bonner said it's important that he talk to you."

"Agent Bonner." He said it aloud, as if to test the reality of what he'd just heard. He took the phone and brought it to his ear. "Yeah."

"Willy K!" a male voice said with such enthusiasm that it had to be sarcasm. "How's it hangin'? Bummer about the leg. Is my buddy Omar doing well?"

The depth and accuracy of what this guy knew left Willy K feeling a little dizzy. Then he put it together. "You're the hacker that broke into the Urgent Care video feed. You got my face. That's slick work."

"I try."

"Would have been better for you if you hadn't left an electronic footprint, though. I imagine we'll be meeting up close and personal one day soon."

"I'll put it on my calendar."

"I'll put my crosshairs on your face. You'll never know it's coming."

That comment triggered what sounded like genuine laughter from a group of people. "Good luck finding my face," Bonner said.

"I hear you're not alone. Something funny about getting shot down from a few hundred yards away?" That kind of talk *always* put an intimidating spin on a conversation like this. It *always* shifted the power. Why wasn't it doing that here?

"Yeah, but I don't expect you to get the joke yet. Give it time."

Who was this guy? He didn't believe for a second that he was FBI, but he didn't want to give the asshole the satisfaction of asking for clarification.

"Listen, Willy K, I could overhear what you were telling the family. I'm in a position to verify that the police are on their way. The only smart move for you is to get the hell out and call it a day. If you're worried about people finding out who you are, well, that's already a done deal, and the Madisons had nothing to do with it. If you're gonna try to press Lori for information on who she talked to, well, here I am. You've got zero to gain by hurting any of those people. My recommendation to you is—"

Willy K clicked off. He was tired of the banter. He had shit to think about.

"Willy K?" Jonathan bent his head up to address the speaker in the ceiling. "You there?"

"He hung up," Venice said.

"How'd I do?"

"I think you made the case that needed to be made," Gail said. "There's no reason for him to hurt that family."

"There was no reason to leave that guy in the Urgent Care a cripple, either," Boxers said. "Sick and twisted is sick and twisted."

"What's the status on the police response?" Jonathan asked.

Venice squinted and leaned into her screen. "No one's marked on the scene yet."

"What are you looking at?"

"They're on a CAD system—computer-aided dispatch. Units update their status by pressing buttons on their computer screens."

"Can we monitor their radio traffic?" Jonathan asked.

Venice typed as she said, "We can try. I'm not totally up to speed on their systems after only a few minutes, but usually dispatch channels are UHF and VHF, but when they go to tactical channels they go low band and off the internet." Something pulled her attention to her left. "Okay, the first unit just marked on the scene. There's two. And three."

"Whatever happens should happen fast now," Boxers said.

"Time to do a little defense," Jonathan said. "We've got to wipe Neil Bonner's cell phone number. Whatever Lori's status is, the cops are going to want to speak to the last person everybody talked to before they were killed."

"On it," Venice said.

"Did you give her your business card?" Gail asked.

"No, just put the number in her phone."

The speaker overhead popped and a scratchy voice said, "Forty-two to Control, status report."

"Forty-two."

"Be advised, ten-seventy times four. Suspect unknown. We're gonna need the State PD crime lab."

"That mean what I think it does?" Jonathan asked. The meaning of ten-codes varied wildly by jurisdiction, which was why many jurisdictions had abandoned them in favor of plain language communication.

While Venice was searching for confirmation, Boxers pulled it up on his phone. "Ten-seventy is a homicide. Times four. He killed four people."

"Yeah," Jonathan said.

"I'm gonna kill that sonofabitch personally," Boxers said. "I'm gonna hurt him really bad first, and then I'm gonna kill him."

"We've got to find him first," Gail said.

"Y'all leave me alone for a few minutes," Venice said. "I have an idea of how we might be able to find where he is."

"How's that?" Jonathan asked.

She gave him a look.

He backed off. "I think we should leave her alone for a few minutes."

CHAPTER TWENTY-TWO

Venice slapped the table with her palm. "Okay, I got it. I think I know where Kearns is working out of."

The team reassembled in the War Room.

"All right, here's the screen capture."

The screen filled with a bunch of numbers and symbols.

"And here we go again," Boxers said. "Screen capture of what, Venice?" He spoke the words as if he were a robot.

"This is the metadata from the other computer I met when I was hacking into the security system at the Urgent Care. Remember, he was trying to delete while I was trying to copy?"

Boxers offered two thumbs-up and a wink. "Gotcha."

"To be honest, I couldn't grab a lot of data, but I got the MAC address for the other hacker's computer, and it goes to someplace in northern North Carolina."

When she stopped, Jonathan gave her a curious look. "That's it? Somewhere in northern North Carolina? Can you drill down further?"

"Not with fact, but with reliable conjecture."

The screen filled with a picture of an expanse of land that looked like it might have been taken from a commercial satellite company. Outlined in blue, the lot appeared to be somewhere between large and huge.

"These fourteen hundred acres belong to Senator Maxine

Bridges. Well, I suppose they used to. Care to guess where they're located?"

Jonathan said, "Since she was the senator for North Carolina, I'm going to guess in context that this property is located in northern North Carolina."

"Bingo."

"Are you suggesting that Omar Farook is there as well?"

"I'm not suggesting that he is, but if that's the location of the computer that wiped the cameras at the Urgent Care, it doesn't seem like that big a stretch."

Jonathan had to agree. "But why there? Of all the places to set up, why set up there?"

"I might have something for you there, too," Venice said through a grin. "Once I had the North Carolina thread—which I confess I've had for a couple of hours now—I worked some magic with Maxine's emails and messages to filter out and capture communications going to or originating from North Carolina locations. I replicated the search across all her aliases, of which she had more than a few."

"How did you have time for that?"

Venice recoiled and made a noise that sounded like *pish*. "I didn't do it manually. I created a program to do it. Okay, I used a program I created a while ago to do it. Anyway, I ended up with hundreds of messages. So, then I ran a program for frequent words, sifting out definite and indefinite articles and linking words." She grinned and leaned into him. "If you have a super-secret and you want to hide it in plain sight, call it *And*."

Jonathan laughed. That was actually a very good idea.

She continued, "As you might imagine, there were quite a few, but one phrase that I thought resonated as fairly ominous appeared over five dozen times over the past three months. *The Event*."

"What event?"

"No explanation," Venice said. "That's what makes it ominous. Sometimes it's capitalized, mostly it's not, but the fact that *the event*"—she used finger quotes—"needs no explanation means to me that it's a code phrase."

"And who uses code phrases for good things?"

"Exactly. I think *the event* is the thing that Maxine Bridges killed herself to keep from being associated with."

Jonathan stood. He thought better on his feet than on his ass. "What do we do with this? Let's postulate that everything you just said is spot-on, so what?"

Venice grinned again. "There's more."

"Of course there is."

"Of all the times *the event* is mentioned, an associated date was mentioned only three times, but each of those times included the same date. August fifteenth."

"That's today," Gail said.

"Yes, it is."

Jonathan resumed his seat. "What was the context when the date was mentioned?"

"Nothing specific. Like, a general reference to *it won't matter after August fifteenth*. That sort of thing." She paused and tapped a few keys. "And then there's this."

The screen filled with highlighted text from an email:

After the sun sets on August 15, the world will be changed forever. There will only be before August 15 and after August 15. Some of us will be martyred heroes, some of us will live to fight again. But no matter what, we will all know the pride of being a part of something so important.

"We should alert the authorities," Venice said. "They need to know."

"About what?" Jonathan asked. "This is the crazy part of what we do. We learn stuff like this, but we don't officially *know* anything because what we learn comes from illegal sources."

"This is way beyond the mission parameters," Gail said. "We

were supposed to find and stop a killer. As in one. Or even a team. But if we're looking at a major terrorist threat, the local police need to at least be alerted."

"It's too early," Jonathan said. "Nothing we have is actionable by legal authorities. But I agree with Ven. If the computer is in North Carolina, then that's probably home base for Omar Farook and whatever he's planning."

"And what do you bet it's the hive that our asshole shooter returns to?" Boxers added.

Jonathan clapped his hands once. "Let's mount up. What's the drive time, Venice?"

She tapped. "Looks like five hours."

"That will still get us there before noon," Boxers said. "The scary email talks about *after the sun sets*. That must mean whatever they've got planned, they don't do it before dark."

Jonathan headed for the door. "Let's stop burning daylight, then."

CHAPTER TWENTY-THREE

Willy K thumped his cane on the wooden floor of the barn floor, hoping that the sound of his footsteps would cause Farook to stir before he knocked on his door. Scotty Tagget, six inches shorter and fifty pounds lighter, struggled to keep up.

"I don't know why this can't wait," Scotty said. "He hates to be waked up."

"It can't wait because it can't wait," Willy K said. "Plus, it's eleven o'clock in the morning. If he's still asleep, he shouldn't be."

"What did he say when you told him about the phone call?"

Willy K didn't answer as he continued across the expanse of the exhibition space. Scotty pulled up short. "Willy K?"

He stopped and turned. "I didn't tell him about that yet," he said.

"Why the hell not?"

"What would be the point? Without the information you have now, what would be the point of telling him about the conversation?"

"Did you tell him about shooting the family?"

Willy K spun around and started walking again. "Same story," he said.

Scotty moaned, "Oh, Jesus."

"C'mon, Scotty," Willy K said. "Not all news can be good."

For a guy who had allegedly spent time hiding in the caves of

Afghanistan, Farook had treated himself pretty well in the world of creature comforts here at the North Carolina compound. First of all, he had a door that gave him privacy, and a window air conditioner. Plus, he had a twin bed and a desk with a desk chair and then a comfortable padded chair for reading or lounging. Willy K figured that the space must have belonged to the barn manager in the building's past life.

Out of habit, Willy K stood off to the side as he rapped on the door with his knuckles.

"Who is it?"

"It's Willy K and Scotty," Willy K said. "We need to talk to you."

"Come on in."

Willy K turned the knob and opened the door. He was surprised and pleased to see Farook awake and dressed and involved with something at his desk.

Willy K moved around to take the comfortable chair, leaving the bed for Scotty.

"Did I invite you to sit down?" Farook said.

"I didn't ask. We have a problem, Omar," Willy K said. "Our cover may be partially blown."

Farook spun his chair around to face Willy K directly. "What do you mean?"

"This morning," Willy K said. "Once I heard that an outsider was aware enough to connect the incident at the Urgent Care to Sulkey, I knew that we had a leak somewhere. And the fact that the outside party was aware enough to copy the video files from the Urgent Care was particularly disturbing."

"What did you do, Willy K?"

"I took care of the problem, Omar. When I first visited the Sulkey residence, I spoke to the babysitter. She was the one who told me where Farrell Sulkey and his son had gone hunting. I connected the dots and figured that the other party—our enemy— must have had the same conversation later in the day, so I paid a visit to the babysitter at her home."

Farook put a hand over his eyes. "Oh, my God."

"I needed to know who she talked to," Willy K explained. "And don't make such a dramatic case out of it. She and her family are dead now, too."

"My God, Willy!"

"My God Willy what? We're in the death business. We control the number of witnesses. I had no choice. Why would I let her live when—"

"Fine," Farook said. "Fine. You've made your point. Thank you for letting me know."

Willy K cleared his throat, glanced at Scotty and then continued. "There's more. While I was there at the Madison place—"

Farook held up a hand. "The Madisons? Is that the family you killed?"

"Jesus, Omar, yes. The family I killed. While I was there, I was hoping to squeeze the sitter for information about the other person she talked to when she handed me her phone. It was the guy himself."

"The guy she talked to about you?"

"Right. The guy who came to the house I guess to warn Sulkey, but after I had already been there and gone. The girl had called him. He'd left his number. Said he was an FBI agent."

Farook's shoulders sagged.

"But I don't think he actually is an agent. I think he was lying to the sitter to get information."

"What was his name?"

"He said it was Neil Bonner, but I'm sure that was a lie. The troubling part is the guy called me by my name. He tried to talk me into leaving the family alone. Yada, yada. But witnesses are witnesses."

Farook looked confused. "Why are you so convinced he was not with the Bureau?"

"Because this is not the way the feds work."

"How would he know your name?"

"From the images they downloaded from the Urgent Care security files," Willy K said.

"That would require sophisticated facial recognition software, would it not?" Farook asked.

"Well, yes, but—"

"Then we will presume them to be FBI. That is the only safe course."

Willy K nodded to Scotty for his turn in the conversation.

"We've got access to facial recognition software, too, sir," Scotty said. "It's not that hard to get. It's commercially available. You get what you pay for, and we paid a lot for ours. And that's where things get really kind of creepy."

Scotty stood from the bed, shrugged out of his backpack and walked around Farook to place it on the desk. "Willy K took me along to hack into security systems and doorbell cameras in the area around the Sulkey house to see who visited during the afternoon." As he spoke, he opened his laptop, logged in and then spun the machine around so that Farook and Willy K could see the screen.

"Okay, so here's some of the raw footage from the cameras. That's Willy K right there. See how he's got his ball cap pulled down low and he's wearing shades? See the angle on his chin, looking down and off to the side? To be honest, that's borderline enough to confuse our FR software, and in fact, it did."

The images jumped to reveal two men this time, one of them the size of a tree.

"Holy shit," Farook said.

"Yeah, he's a big boy," Scotty agreed. "Now, by contrast, notice how these guys are walking. They've got caps and shades, sure, but it's a sunny day. They've made no effort to shield their features at all."

"Most people don't," Farook said.

"True. Because most people don't have to worry about it," Willy K said. "And that's because they really *don't* have anything to worry about because they live vanilla lives."

"Where is this going?" Farook asked.

"I'll show you," Scotty said. He clicked some keys and the images of the two men on the screen became indecipherable blurs. "This is what I got when I ran their images through facial recognition."

"What?" Farook said, arms extended to his sides. "There's nothing there."

"Exactly. That's my point. There's nothing there. Somehow, these guys are immune from facial recognition."

"Immune."

"It's like a standing program to keep their features from registering," Scotty explained.

"That's impossible," Farook said.

"I don't think it is," Willy K said. "I'll tell you up front that this goes way, way beyond my expertise, but I've heard that programs like this exist in the super spooky corners of crazy spooky universe. This is real James Bond, Jason Bourne shit."

"That only governments can control," Farook said.

Willy K bobbed his head. "Probably. And they were yukking it up with me that they knew we would hit this wall when we tried to identify them."

Farook stood and walked to the window, his hands thrust deeply into his back pockets. "What you're telling me, then, is that your name and activities are known by people well enough connected to the United States government to have the advantage of super invisibility. Is that about right?"

Hearing it so succinctly made it all sound dourer than Willy K had perceived it. "Yes, that's about right."

Farook stood at the window for more than a minute, staring out into the sunny day, his back to the room. He shifted his hands from his back pockets to fold them across his chest, and then he bounced a little on the balls of his feet as he clearly worked through some form of a plan in his head.

When he turned, his features looked hard. His thick eyebrows had joined to form a solid line and his lips were pulled tight. "Listen to me, gentlemen," he said. "None of the others are to know of these new developments."

"Oh, wait—" Willy K said.

"Shut your mouth, Willy," Farook snapped. "I have given you far too much leeway over these past weeks. I know that you feel loyalty to these men, but they are spending *my* money, and as of now their loyalty—and yours—must lie exclusively with me. If you cannot live with this, then I suggest you put a bullet through your own brain before I put one through it for you."

Willy K had not seen such heat in Farook's glare before. He'd not seen the raw threat.

"You are part of a cause now, Willy K. The genie, as they say, is out of the bottle and cannot be returned. The Event will happen. We will do this thing. We will change history, and the time for the volunteer soldiers in this army to change their minds has passed. To share these new dangers would only make them more nervous, and nervousness would breed mistakes. Do we understand each other?"

Willy K found himself nodding without knowing he was doing so. He found himself moved. Inspired, even. "I understand."

Farook shifted his gaze to Scotty.

"Shit yeah, I understand." Scotty looked like he might, in fact, be on the verge of shitting himself.

"Scotty thinks he may be able to find where these invisible people are," Willy K said.

Farook's eyebrows separated. "Is this true?"

Scotty hedged. "*May* be able to. Emphasis on the *may*. You see, when we were both signed into the Urgent—"

The sound of crunching gravel silenced the room.

Willy K drew his Glock and joined Farook at the window. Scotty drew a Kimber 1911 from a holster at the small of his back and joined them.

They watched as the county sheriff's Ford Expedition drove down the unpaved pathway through the uncut field to park at the edge of the fence.

"What the hell is he doing here?" Farook asked.

"He's here for the radio batteries," Willy K said. "Dax told me he finished with the modifications."

Farook pushed away from the window and walked toward the door to his room. "I'm still not comfortable with him on the team," he said. "I know Maxine trusts him, but when I see the badge, I worry about mixed loyalties."

Willy K had harbored the same thoughts. "I'll handle that," he said.

Farook stopped and turned. "Do not kill the county sheriff."

Willy K rolled his eyes. "That's not what I meant," he said. "I'm going to talk with him."

Scotty stayed behind while Willy K and Farook strolled out into the barn to greet Sheriff Morrissey at the door. The sound of the approaching vehicle had alerted others in the team, who'd materialized outside their doors, each with some form of armament in their hands.

"Stand down," Farook said.

"It's the sheriff," Willy K added. "I've been expecting him."

Morrissey entered cautiously. The latch on the door lifted and the panel opened a crack. "Whoever's aiming guns at me, please put 'em down. It's Sheriff Morrissey." He entered hands first, fingers splayed. "I mean no harm, but I got important news."

He seemed startled to see people waiting for him at such close range.

"Mornin', Ervin," Willy K said. "All things considered, an advance phone call might not be a bad idea." He meant that to be a lighthearted comment, but the sheriff's face remained dour.

"You need to gather your people," Morrissey said. "I've got news everyone needs to hear." Then he looked up and saw all the people who'd been waiting to shoot him if he'd been a bad guy. "All of you need to hear this."

Willy K watched Farook's eyes as Morrissey delivered orders directly to his army. He didn't like the free flow of information on the same day as the Event.

As the men of the army closed in on the exhibition ring, Willy K asked, "What's going on?"

"You'll hear it all in a minute, Willy," Morrissey said. "Just hold your horses."

Three minutes later, the whole crew had pulled up chairs in their regular spots, and Sheriff Morrissey commanded the center of the circle. "You might have heard that us law enforcement types are part of a tight circle," he said. "And by tight circle, that means we like to gossip like teenage girls."

The room grumbled a laugh.

"A buddy of mine from up in Northern Virginia said some big news is about to break and it especially affects everybody here."

He scanned faces to make sure everybody was engaged.

"Ready? Senator Maxine Bridges killed herself last night."

In an instant, Willy K saw the direct link to the pictures Sulkey was supposed to have of the senator and Farook, but he said nothing.

"My God!" Farook blurted. "How?"

Morrissey started to answer, then checked himself. "Take a guess, Omar. You two knew each other pretty well. How would you guess she killed herself?" His tone carried an unmistakable undertone of accusation.

Everyone in the room heard it and it triggered a rumble.

Farook's jaws locked.

"Hey, Ervin," Willy K said. "It's the morning of the day we're about to go on a hot op. We're all a little uneasy. Just say what's on your mind."

"Was it cyanide?" Farook asked.

Morrissey cocked his head and made a clicking noise with his tongue. "That was the rumor I'd heard. Since that was your guess, then I'd have to say yes. Same rumor said it was a suicide pill."

"Old-school," Farook said. "She insisted on having one. Several, in fact. She had them in the filters of cigarettes and she had one in the cap of a pen she carried."

"What the hell," Baker said. "That's sick."

"Is it?" Junior challenged. "I think it's kind of cool."

Baker looked horrified.

Junior thrust his hands out to his sides. "What? Think about it. If we're honest, don't we all have a bit of a death wish in us? We wouldn't be here taking these chances if we didn't. I'll tell you right now if things go shitty on this or any other op, I ain't surrendering to nobody. I ain't spendin' my old age rottin' away in no jail cell. I'll shoot down to the last mag, but if I'm cornered, the last bullet in that last mag is goin' through my own brain."

"And you're nobody," Harley Grace said, triggering a ripple of laughter. "I didn't mean insult by that, but you know what I mean. All of us are nobodies. We're grunts with gun skills that the world hasn't noticed one way or another for years. But Senator Bridges? Well, hell, she's Senator Bridges."

"Exactly," Farook said. "If she got linked to the upcoming event, they wouldn't just throw her in jail. It'd be a circus. She wouldn't want any of that."

"Y'all are asking the wrong question," said Ivan Slotsky, a voice rarely heard from. Burned by a Taliban IED, the skin on his face looked melted and the wounds had messed with his lip muscles, slurring his words. "The right question is why. Why last night? Why not tomorrow night and why not two weeks ago? What spooked her?"

"I don't think there's a way to know that answer," Morrissey said. "Omar?"

"The why doesn't matter," Farook said. "There's a bigger problem. With her dying the way she did, there's going to be an investigation run by about a million different agencies. And that's not even counting media outlets. By killing herself, she's all but guaranteed that people will connect the dots between her and the Event."

"Not before it's over and done," Baker said.

"Okay. And I'm fine with that if you are. Hell, we're about to flip the world on its ear, so drawing attention is pretty much baked into the cake."

"You never know when they're going to come poking around here," Morrissey said. "Senator from North Carolina commits suicide, it's not a stretch that they're gonna want to search her properties."

Willy K thought that was the best point to be raised so far.

"We've got to bug out," Baker said.

"You're absolutely right," Farook said. "We start now. Take everything down. I'm confident we have a few hours, right, Ervin?"

Morrissey smirked. "They'll probably contact me to assign some deputies to keep people out of the property until feds can get here from Raleigh. Yeah, you've got a few hours. I wouldn't dawdle, but you don't have to kill yourselves, either."

"Where are we going to go?" Harley asked.

"You can use my farm," Morrissey said. "It'll even move you a little closer to the target since tonight's the night and I don't have to keep you under wraps."

Farook clapped his hands once. "There it is, gents. We're almost to the finish line. Let's leave this place looking like we were never here."

As the room stood, Willy K put a hand on Morrissey's shoulder. "The batteries are finished. Come with me." He beckoned for the sheriff to follow as he led the way to one of the supply vans. He opened the back door, leaned in, and slid out two three-by-four-foot gray Pelican cases with handles.

"This one's the batteries," Willy K said, tapping the case on the left. "And this one's the cell signal jammers. They are timed to activate at twenty hundred hours. All you have to do is distribute them around the campground. Do you have a plan for that?"

"I do."

"What is it?"

"I'm going to do a security walk around this afternoon and drop them off as I do."

Willy K liked it. Sometimes, simplest was best. "Perfect," he said. "Let's go." He kept the cases and headed toward Morrissey's vehicle, doing his best to ignore the pain in his leg.

"Whoa, Willy. Where are you going?"

"With you."

"Why?"

"Is there a problem?"

"No. I just—"

"You can show me the sheriff's department headquarters."

Willy K kept limping.

CHAPTER TWENTY-FOUR

They'd driven hard to get to Maxine Bridges's country house in North Carolina, knowing that the window of opportunity would shut fast and hard once someone found the senator's body. Working with gloved hands, Jonathan inserted the Y-shaped tension bar into the north-south poles of the keyway and was preparing to insert the half-diamond pick when Gail placed a hand on his shoulder.

"I'll say it again," she whispered over the air because it was the easiest way to communicate quietly. "By doing this, we are setting ourselves up as key suspects in Senator Bridges's demise."

"She committed suicide," Boxers said.

"Nobody's going to believe that," Gail pressed. "The conspiracy theorists are going to force a different kind of all-out investigation, and this burglary plays right into their hands."

"I appreciate the thought," Jonathan said as he inserted the pick. "Just as I appreciated it the last two times." He kept upward pressure on the tension bar with the inside of his left forefinger as he probed the pin tumblers of the old lock with the pick. When the bottom row of tumblers pressed out of the way, he turned the pick upside down and worked the top row.

"I just happen to believe that the potential reward of finding the smoking-gun clue is worth the risk. I've been wrong before, but I hope I'm right this time."

The last of the pin tumblers fell out of the way and the keyway turned.

"We're in," Jonathan said, keeping the knob turned so the lock wouldn't reset. He scanned the circumference of the door one more time for evidence of an alarm system. "Last chance to point out any alarm contacts," he said.

"Looks clean to me," Big Guy said.

"Me, too," Gail agreed.

"Mother Hen?"

"I've run her emails and finances, and I don't see any payments to an alarm or security company," Venice said. "That's as close to an answer as I can give you."

"I heard that as your personal guarantee of safety," Jonathan said. "Here we go." The instant when the door panel unseated from the jamb was always the most unnerving. That's when whatever's going to happen is going to happen, and often with great noise.

In this case . . . silence.

"Okay, we're in," Jonathan said. "Same as before. Electronics, low-hanging fruit. A signed manifesto would be nice."

"Now you're talkin'," Boxers said with a chuckle.

"Photograph everything," Jonathan said. "Minimal impact."

The problem with a mission such as this was the total lack of focus. Without knowing what they were looking for, it was impossible to know the significance of anything. The trick lay in identifying patterns or outliers. They weren't looking for hardware, necessarily, but rather for indicators pointing to frame of mind. Or hints about what the target might be.

Jonathan's search brought him to a room at the end of the center hall, off to the right of the foyer and across from a very elaborate powder room. Given its towering bookcases and ornate desk, this had to be the senator's office away from the office. Measuring twenty feet across, the space felt like a turret, nominally round—octagonal, really—with two sides consumed by windows that rose all the way to the top of the fifteen-foot ceiling.

A leather wingback chair and footstool occupied the space across from the desk. The small adjacent round table and articulating lamp identified this as her reading nook. In addition to volumes of popular fiction and nonfiction, her bookcases featured an assortment of family knickknacks—most featuring photos of the same toddler, then little boy, then adolescent, then teenager, then young man. Jonathan figured him to be Maxine's son, Samuel.

Stitching together a narrative from the more than two dozen photos and accompanying paraphernalia, the kid was a talented soccer player and a devoted outdoorsman. He loved large-scale camping trips, as indicated by photographs of him smiling, communing with others in outdoor settings and playing among a multicolored backdrop of A-frame and igloo style tents. In a few, he and his friends wore odd uniforms that invoked a science fiction, space travel theme. There were some photos of solo trips, as well, but they were few.

A plaque on one bookshelf thanked Samuel Bridges for his "invaluable service as the student coordinator for the North Carolina Regional Planetariat," as recognized by the International Brotherhood of Starlighters. Whatever the hell that was, he must have shown leadership qualities before he surrendered to whatever poisonous bug crawled into his head and turned him into a jihadi.

Jonathan couldn't begin to imagine the torture that Maxine Bridges must have gone through during that period. He didn't sympathize with the cause, but he'd have to be a monster not to sympathize with the humanity. The fact that this office was such a monument to her son spoke volumes.

For all the tributes, though, there were no family photographs, no academic triumphs. Jonathan didn't know what that meant,

but it had to mean something, right? And there was nothing—
nothing—to indicate Samuel's descent into terrorism or his mother's
support thereof.

Jonathan opened the drawers of the desk and riffled through
the contents but ultimately found nothing of interest. Some bro-
chures for yet another regional Planetariat, and some takeout menus,
but nothing that jumped out as plotting for the next Ground
Zero.

"Is anyone finding anything?" Jonathan asked over the air.

"Just really good housekeeping," Gail replied.

"Uh-oh," Boxers said. "Take a peek out the windows, folks.
We've got a cop approaching."

"Everybody out," Jonathan said.

A vehicle was, indeed, approaching, but it was coming from
a direction other than the road, from deeper within the property, and from the slow speed and the way the chassis was bob-
bing up and down and swaying, smart money said they were
four-wheeling.

"Where is he going?" Gail asked. "He's not headed this way."

"Let's take that as a win," Jonathan said.

"A better question is where is he coming from?" Boxers said.

Jonathan said, "Mother Hen, Scorpion. Have you been monitoring our radio traffic?"

"Every word. What direction is that vehicle coming from?"

"Call it south, southwest of the house, and heading due north
toward the road. What's back there?"

Twenty seconds later: "A lot of nothing," Venice said. "I mean,
all I have is the same commercial satellite data as everybody else,
but as of whenever those photos were taken, there's nothing but
farmland all the way down to the river."

"What's on the other side of the river?"

"More farmland."

Jonathan laughed at the absurdity of the conversation. "Where's
the nearest bridge?"

That took another few seconds of silence. "Looks like three miles and change to the east, downriver."

Jonathan let those details stew. *So, what the hell is going on?*

"Whatever he's been doing, he's been doing it deeper into the senator's property," Gail said.

"Maybe he busted a still," Boxers said.

"He wouldn't do that alone," Gail said.

"Maybe he bought product from a still," Boxers said.

They watched in silence as the squad car finally rolled from the grass onto the driveway, and from there, back out onto the roadway.

"Scorpion, Mother Hen," Venice said. "More news. The media is reporting that Senator Bridges has been found dead."

"Copy that," Jonathan said. He turned to the team as he switched his radio to PTT. "I want to know what's going on down there by the river."

"Before long," Gail said, "police will be swarming all over this house. We can't go driving down there."

"No, we can't," Jonathan said. "We need to pack up and relocate to somewhere off property. We can launch Roxie from there and look around."

Roxie was the name given by Boxers to every drone in the air corps of flying whirligigs he had acquired over the years. In the early days of Security Solutions, surveillance was dependent upon the team's ability to physically sneak up close enough to their adversaries to get a good look, or to repurpose a commercial satellite system owned by a friend of Jonathan's to give them a distant peek.

Now, with the growth of drone technology, combined with camera technology, they could survey large swaths of land to find the small details they wanted to examine, and then zoom in closely enough to read the labels on bottles. In the dark.

The most recent Roxie variant was munitions capable, with the ability to drop explosive devices (or tear gas, or smoke, or any number of other options) with precision that increased with proximity—the closer to the target, the more accurate the drop. In the case of an explosive payload, a truly accurate drop would prove suicidal for Roxie.

Boxers perked up when he heard his quadcopter drone mentioned. "Isn't there like a thousand acres?"

"Fourteen hundred," Jonathan said. He pressed his mic button. "Mother Hen, Scorpion. We need a place to hole up out of sight as close to the senator's property as possible where we can launch Roxie."

As he waited for his answer, they loaded up the Batmobile and turned around in the driveway, lights off.

"How much security do you need?" Venice asked. "How invisible do you need to be?"

"I think the answer to that is always *as much as possible.*" To Boxers, he pointed right out of the windshield. "Just drive. We don't want to just sit in the driveway."

"Big Guy, Mother Hen. How much range does Roxie have?"

Boxers and Jonathan exchanged looks. Venice rarely communicated with him directly. No reason, she just didn't. "It depends on factors," he said, "but two miles is a good number. If conditions are right she can go to three."

"What happens if she flies out of range?" Venice asked. "Does she crash?"

"Roxie never crashes," Boxers said. Jonathan didn't know if that tone was pride or disdain. "If she starts to lose signal, she comes home. Same if her power gets low. She's a survivor."

Honest to God, when Big Guy spoke of his drones, he spoke of them the way that other men spoke of their children. Jonathan found it simultaneously creepy and entertaining.

"Is there a point to all this?" Jonathan asked over the air.

"You sprang this on me out of nowhere," Venice said. "I'm working my way through the problem and trying to learn the parameters. I know that Big Guy is very close to his toys, and I didn't want to make him cry if it got lost."

Jonathan was going to let that one go if everyone else would. It was too early and everyone was too tired to poke fun at Boxers. Sometimes he didn't like being poked fun at and when you crossed that line, it was always unpleasant.

After five minutes of silence, Jonathan keyed the mic again. "Mother Hen, do we still have signal?"

"We have signal and we have a problem," Venice said. "The senator's property is massive, and I presume you can't be squatting on any part of that. Am I correct?"

"Affirmative."

"Okay, the adjacent properties are also quite large. Even if I parked you on one of those, there is no one spot from those properties where Roxie would have the range to explore every corner of the senator's property. Plus, you'd be in the open, trespassing on a stranger's farm. There's a lot that can go wrong in that scenario."

"I copy," Jonathan said. "Let us know when you get something."

"I'm working on an idea now," Venice said. "Give me a few."

"Let's talk for a bit about William Kearns," Gail said from the back seat. "I've been thinking about him in the context of the Event, whatever that means. What are the chances that he *is* the event, and that we're seeing it play out in real time?"

"It doesn't feel big enough," Boxers said. "Wasn't there some reference to everybody would be dividing time into two parts— *before* the Event and *after* the Event? Offing a few contractors one at a time doesn't even raise eyebrows."

"I agree with Big Guy," Jonathan said. "I think Kearns is part of the Event. He might even be the main perpetrator of it. But whatever it is, I think it's pretty clear that it hasn't happened yet."

"But you think it's headquartered here?" Gail asked.

"I have no idea. I kinda hope so because the fuse is so short on whatever the hell it is, and this is where we are, but we're just shooting in the dark."

"Speaking of dark," Boxers said, "how dark do you want to go in conspiracy theorizing?"

"We can't go a lot darker than holes we've already traveled," Jonathan said.

"Let's go with the working assumptions on the table," Boxers said. "We know that the late Maxine Bridges was up to her implants in whatever this terror plot is, and that car bomber Omar Farook is a part of it, too. If that's the case, what better place to hide out than on a thousand-acre outpost in the middle of friggin' nowhere?"

"There's no sign that anyone has been in that house," Gail said.

"A fact that plays even deeper into my twisted plot," Boxers said. "When you've got over a thousand acres, you're gonna have a bunch of buildings, right? Some of them might be suitable for housing and hiding a pet terrorist after he's had his features fixed."

"Makes sense to me," Jonathan said.

"Of course it does."

"How is that particularly dark?"

"It's particularly dark because we just saw a sheriff's department vehicle driving home from the morning terrorist planning meeting."

"Oh, now that's a stretch," Gail said, but her tone belied her words.

"You've said it yourself a million times, Boss. Ain't no such things as coincidences."

The best Jonathan could muster was, "Huh." Boxers had a point. When two unusual occurrences happened within a short sleeve of time, they were somehow always related, even if the relationship was not obvious.

If, in fact, they were near the epicenter of a terror attack, and the sheriff's department were somehow involved, the consequences would be unimaginable. If deputies didn't respond, what would be the next line of defense?

"That doesn't sound plausible to me," Gail said. "I'll stipulate that one or two or a few local law enforcement officers could be drawn that far to the dark side, but an entire department?"

"The days of the KKK aren't that far in the rearview mirror," Boxers said. "I hope I'm wrong, but Digger's wisdom about coincidences is pretty powerful magic."

"Scorpion, Mother Hen. Okay, I've got something for you. It's a bit of a drive, but ultimately it will get you in close."

CHAPTER TWENTY-FIVE

"W̶hy are you doing this?" Willy K asked. "This is a lot of ugly bloodshed. What's in it for you?"

Ervin Morrissey looked to his right across the center console. "You first. Answer your own question."

Willy K scoffed. "For me, it's the money. Hard stop. When I calculate all the time I put in over the years, I killed men, women and children for Uncle Sam for, like, fifteen bucks an hour. I got over the killing part a long time ago. This thing's putting two-fifty large in my account tax-free, and I'll still have my pension from Uncle. Cha-ching, dude." He let the words rest for a beat. "Your turn."

"Same, but different," Morrissey said. "It's about the money."

"There are far easier ways to make it," Willy K said.

"No there's not." Morrissey shot him an annoyed glance. "Look, you don't know me, and this is none of your business, but I've got a kid with serious medical needs. He'll never live a real life, and I'll never be able to afford to pay for the kind of live-in care that he deserves. Medicaid barely pays for his ass to get wiped. Maxine was very generous. The annuity she put together for him will give him first-class care for the rest of his life."

"After this, you won't be able to be a part of it."

"He doesn't know who I am anyway."

"What about the blue brotherhood?" Willy K pressed. "Or

whatever the hell it is you call that special relationship cops have?"

"What game are you playing, Kearns? How is any of this any of your business?"

"No game. I'm dead serious and just making sure you are, too. Today is showtime, and we can't afford last-minute changes of heart."

The sheriff looked back to the road. "You don't have to worry about that from me."

"Then answer my question. Gotta be honest. You're about to betray a whole bunch of fellow cops who trust you with their lives. I'd be crazy not to not to wonder about your trustworthiness."

Morrissey took his time answering. Willy K watched as he thought through how to deliver his words. "It's best just to spit it out," he prompted.

"They're the means to the end, okay?" Morrissey said, finally. "Collateral damage. I wish it could be some other way, but it can't." He looked back across the center console and his eyes were wet. "It helps that I won't actually be the one doing it. I'm just facilitating it. I know, I'm parsing here, but . . . well, it helps."

They drove in silence for a while. Ahead, the rural road was giving way to the encroaching town. This was just outskirts, a Baptist church across the street from a concrete-block tavern that called itself Tommy D's. A single green pickup truck sat nose-in at the handicapped space just to the right of the door.

"That's Cope Singleton's ride," Morrissey said. "Must've passed out in the booth again and Tommy locked him inside." He laughed. "I don't know if I'm gonna miss this place or not."

"How old is he?" Willy K asked.

"Cope? Shit, I got no idea."

"Your boy. Your son."

"Damn, son, you got a real problem stayin' in your lane, don't you?"

Willy K waited.

"He's fourteen, okay? His mama was a meth head and a whore and I made a mistake, and Trevor is God's way of punishing me. There it all is, laid out bare for you. Like what you see?"

"I'm not here to judge you, Sheriff."

"The hell you ain't."

"I swear to God I'm not. I'm just trying to figure things out. Who to trust, who to not. And I appreciate you being honest with me."

Morrissey scoffed. "Well, if I've earned your appreciation, then I guess I can die a happy man."

"How many years does he have left?"

"As many as God gives him. There's no end in sight. It's not like that. He's not unhealthy. He just can't walk or think or wipe his butt." His voice broke on that last part.

"I'm sorry," Willy K said. "That's tough. Horrible."

"I don't need your sympathy."

"Did you ever think about killing him?"

Sheriff Morrissey yanked the steering wheel hard to the right and stood on the brakes, screeching his cruiser to a halt in the gravel along the shoulder.

"Out," he commanded.

Willy K made a gentle waving motion with both hands. "Wait a second, Sheriff."

"Get out of this vehicle. Now."

"No, Sheriff, I don't believe I will."

Morrissey's jaw slackened. Clearly, those were not the words he'd been expecting.

"Instead, I believe I will sit right where I am and wait for you to answer my goddamn question. Because here's the thing, *Ervin*. You might have figured out that I'm not the most compassionate guy in the world, but even I'm having a hard time untying the knot that is you. You're the parent of an adolescent kid who's essentially a human potato spud, about whom you don't seem to give a fraction of a single shit, yet you're willing to commit an epic act of terrorism so that he can spend the next fifty years staring at the fluorescent tubes over his bed. Do you see my problem here?"

Morrissey stared, eyes wet and red, his breathing chuffing like a steam engine.

"From where I sit, it would seem a hell of a lot easier just to off your kid and walk away. I mean, murder is murder, right? Why kill hundreds when you accomplish the same goal by killing one?"

Morrissey's eyes burned with murderous intent.

"Go ahead and speak your mind, Sheriff. Say it out loud. Tell yourself the truth." Willy K pointed ahead. "In any case, keep driving."

The cruiser rolled back onto the roadway.

"I'll do it for you, then, Sheriff. When you cut through all the bullshit, you're just like all the rest of us. You're in it for the money in your own pocket. You're rolling the dice that you can get away with it, that hell's not a real place, and that you can live large for a long, long time. There's no shame in it. But don't try to sell me on some lofty notion of a more noble goal."

Willy K thought it was important for people to understand the full ramifications of what they were about to embark on in times like these. Excuses were easy when H-hour was still days away, but as the clock ticked down to zero, and all that remained was the reality of what they were about to do—the wonder of it, the *horror* of it—the window of opportunity for conscience-driven second-guessing was shut.

"You're not a monster for this, Sheriff," Willy K said. "People are going to say that—the media is certainly going to portray it that way—but you're just a guy doing a dirty job in a professional way. I can even take a religious spin on this if you're interested in hearing it."

"That should be interesting."

"I think it is." Willy K turned sideways in his seat, hooking his left ankle under his right knee to get a better look at the sheriff. "I grew up as a Baptist. We were all about God's plan. Predestination, right? I never believed any of that, but, just for grins and giggles, let's say I do. Let's say that half the people in that crowd tonight are going to believe in it."

He stopped, waiting for Morrissey to see it for himself.

"And?" the sheriff said.

"And if they're right—if their Bible-pounding faith isn't all bullshit—then whoever lives and dies during the Event is just fulfilling God's plan."

Morrissey's throat issued a low chuckle as he rolled his eyes and shook his head. "Man, and you say *I'm* rolling the dice that there's no hell."

A few minutes later, they arrived at the headquarters building for the sheriff's office, and Willy K handed over the Pelican case with the batteries in it.

"These are standard battery cells for the radios," he explained, "just shorter lives. When the balloon goes up, it'll make comms more difficult, and then there'll be that special surprise. Just change them out with the regular batteries."

Morrissey took the case. "What's your plan? You staying out here?"

"Yeah, I think that's probably best. I'll keep a low profile. I'll make some phone calls and then we can head out for Ground Zero."

Venice sent Jonathan and the team eight miles east to cross the river and then back nearly eight miles west and then through serpentine back roads and narrowing lanes till they finally ended up in the Anders and Villa Mobile Home and Camp Ground. A throwback to times long gone, this thirty-acre facility was built for the kinds of vacations that Jonathan didn't think people took anymore.

The most prominent feature, just inside the front gate, where a carved wooden black bear stood sentry next to a carved wooden buck, was a double-wide trailer marked with three signs, each stacked on top of the other:

REGISTRATION
PARK MANAGER
☺ PHYLLIS MCCLENDON ☺

"The smiley faces are a tell that Phyllis is a total bitch," Boxers said as he swung the Batmobile to place Jonathan's door at the foot of the stairs to the trailer.

"And that's why you get to stay in the vehicle," Jonathan replied. "I'll just be a minute." He opened his door, slid to the ground, and entered the front door to the office after making sure his jacket covered his firearm.

A linoleum-tiled foyer allowed just enough room for the swing of the door, and beyond that lay someone's home, divided off only by a hinged counter supported on four-by-four posts. A single glance brought him a view of a living room and dining room decorated in old-school cannons and guns Early American fashion. The rest was closed off by doors.

He tapped the little domed bell that always made him feel like an asshole and waited.

"In a sec!" came a large female voice from behind the door on the left. Ten seconds later, it opened to reveal a woman in her forties who might have been a wrestler at some point in her past. Closing in on six feet, with gut and shoulders of equal girth, she wore an enormous, nickel-plated revolver in a cross-draw shoulder rig.

"Are you Boner?" she asked.

"Bonner," he corrected, but the smirk told him there hadn't been an error. "Do you need ID?"

She scoffed out a laugh. "As if it would be real. No, the transfer cleared, and that's all I need. Did your handler give you the safety talk?"

"My what?" He regretted leaving Big Guy behind. He would have loved this gal.

"Seriously? You're gonna play the bluff to the end? Okay, fine.

You be you. The safety talk goes like this. Your . . . *secretary*"—finger quotes—"insisted on a place as close to the river as possible and with real walls and a roof. So, you got the safe house."

"Is that a problem?"

"Not for me, it's not. I don't give a shit what you do. You paid a stupid amount of money, and that gives you the right to friggin' torture puppy dogs for all I care. But it does mean you're gonna be doin' shit you're either ashamed of, afraid of, or otherwise need to hide. Again, I don't care."

Jonathan stood a little taller and put his hands in his pockets, an effort designed to reveal the presence of the Colt on his belt while not making a threat. "So, what are we talking about—Phyllis, is it?"

"I'll be Phyllis if you want. What we're talking about—what we're *going* to talk about—is your neighbors. Your *secretary* assured me that you and your friends are not cops, and while I don't give a shit about that, either, it's hard to overstate how important it is that that be true. This is the last place in the world you want to be if you have a badge. Are you following me?"

"No, I don't think I am. Not that I'm a cop, but I don't understand the rest."

"Just mind your own business, Mr. Boner. Maybe that's the point. Whatever you see, hear, smell, unless it's touching you, your key to survival is to leave it alone. I don't know how to put it any plainer than that."

"What about me and being left alone?" Jonathan asked.

"Rules are rules," Phyllis said. "If they apply to you, they apply to everybody else." She fished a key out of the pocket of her jeans and used it to open a box safe on the wall perpendicular to the foyer. She withdrew a larger key with a fob fashioned out of a .50 caliber BMG round. "This'll open the gate and the front door. The Safe House is the farthest structure back."

Jonathan took the key and nodded at Phyllis's holstered revolver. "That's quite the cannon you've got there."

"One of three on my person and about a dozen within reach," she said with a crooked smile. "It's the clientele."

"Yeah, about that," Jonathan said. He'd changed the timbre of his voice to add a touch of gravelly menace and he leaned in to put the weight of one elbow on the folding shelf. "I like your style. I like everything you just had to say, and I hope you meant every word because you and everyone else here in Anders and Villa Mobile Home Park and Camp Ground need to understand that killing you and everyone else here wouldn't bother me a bit. Look in my eyes and tell me if you believe me."

Phyllis cocked her head and scowled, as if unsure what to do.

Jonathan danced his eyebrows as he waited.

Finally, she locked in on real eye contact, and he saw something change in her demeanor.

"Yeah?" he asked.

Phyllis had lost some of her edge. "Yeah."

"Good," Jonathan said. He offered his hand in friendship and she took it, albeit with hesitation. "I want us to be friends," he said. "If only because it would be so terrible to be enemies." He held her gaze as he held his grasp. "Don't you agree?"

He let go and Phyllis retrieved her hand as if it had been stung. "I absolutely agree," she said. "The Safe House is paid out for the whole three-day minimum. Just put the key out there in the box when you're done."

The interior spaces of Anders and Villa revealed themselves to be a mishmash of trailer and RV hookups and flat spots for tents, each lot marked by a predetermined place for a campfire, as indicated by a ring of concrete blocks with an expanded metal grate stretched across the top. Only two of those spots were occupied, each by a Spam-can travel trailer that looked like it hadn't been moved in years.

Boxers piloted the Batmobile along the perimeter road, keeping the open camping lots to the left. On the right, nestled into scrubby woods, people had built cabins and vacation homes on what appeared to be quarter-acre rectangular lots. While the styles ran the gamut from log cabin to A-frame to ersatz Tudor, they all sat far back on their lots and appeared to be around two thousand square feet. Several stood on stilts, which struck Jonathan as a good idea, being this close to the river.

Most of the homes and cabins appeared to be empty, but a few had cars in the driveways and yards, and one in particular must have been having a party because the yard was choked with at least ten vehicles parked at random angles.

They drove with the windows open, and as advertised, the breeze brought occasional whiffs of weed and one particularly strong blast of methamphetamine in production.

"Do we assume the police know about this and just look the other way?" Gail asked, having been read into Jonathan's chat with Phyllis.

"I go back to my previous theory," Boxers said. "When civil servants don't make a lot of money to begin with, they're very affordable to buy. Everybody makes money, nobody gets hurt. Sweet deal when you think about it."

"Sweet deals like that always fall apart," Gail said.

"I wish I agreed with you," Jonathan said. "There's our gate right up there." He pointed to an overgrown chain-link fence along the road up ahead. The sign on the gate, predictably enough, read, SAFE HOUSE.

"Where do you think the name came from?" Boxers asked as he pulled to a stop.

Jonathan opened the door to get the gate. "I think it's where they stashed Elvis and JFK while they were convincing the world that they were dead."

With the gate opened, he waved the Batmobile through and walked the rest of the way. They joined up at the front door and he opened that, too. Inside, the cabin defined an open-concept plan. The foyer sat slightly elevated from the rest of the interior, and from there, they had a spectacular view of the river through the back wall, which was nothing but floor to ceiling glass. Beyond the glass lay a deck and beyond the deck, the world dropped off sharply to the riverbed.

"Phyllis said I spent a lot for this place," Jonathan thought aloud. "At least I know why."

"No idea what the number is?" Boxers asked.

"Nope. Doesn't really matter, does it?" He checked his watch. It was already 08:30. "All right, let's get to work. I don't want any of the duffels left in the Batmobile. Let's bring it all in, establish comms, establish a perimeter and get Roxie in the air."

CHAPTER TWENTY-SIX

Kerry Smallwood was still munching on the final arc of his bagel with cream cheese as he entered the admin tent and walked to the front to join Fleet Admiral Smallwood at the whiteboard that served as the focus of everyone's attention.

These afternoon meetings were a daily affair, designed to identify problems and fix them before they spun out of control.

Kerry had lost sleep worrying that he was going to have to address the loss of the rifle program and explain how it was his fault—even though he believed to his bones that it was not—but Mr. Schultz had backed down from his promise to quit, albeit with the condition that Kerry relinquish his position as assistant instructor. He thought that was unfair, but it was a noble sacrifice if it kept the entire Planetariat from being robbed of a popular program.

"Tonight's a big night," Danny said. "Fiddler Joe and Clem will be performing here, and that's always a good time."

A pained groan rolled through the assembled commanders. The words *lame* and *corny* jumped out clearly.

"That's enough of that," Danny said. "They are coming, and they are guests of this community. As such, they will be treated with great respect. Are we clear on this?"

More grumbling.

"I'm sorry, are we clear on this?"

In unison: "Yes, sir."

"Now, I understand that their music is not for everyone, but there's never an excuse for rudeness. Troopers who do not wish to attend the concert are free to refuse, but they will be confined to their campsites. We will not have troopers wandering around during the night. Is that understood?"

"Yes, sir."

"Commodore Smallwood, stand up, please."

Kerry stood.

"The commodore will be in charge this evening for the concert. Make sure that your troopers are aware of that, and that he speaks with my authority."

Squadron Commander Athan Farmer raised his hand to be recognized. "The troopers are going to want to know why, sir."

"The County Commission meets this evening, and they have asked me to come and give a short presentation on the Starlighters and what we're doing here. It's the kind of invitation to which it's hard to say no." He turned to Kerry. *It's your meeting now.*

"Does anyone have any other business?" Kerry asked.

No one raised a hand.

"All right, then. Y'all are dismissed. Go out and tame the chaos and make sure your troopers are staying hydrated."

Kerry waited till the others were filing out before he moved to join them, but Danny stopped him.

"Hey, Kerry. I need a minute." He looked very serious. And he called him by his name, not by his rank.

Danny led him to a corner and pointed to a chair while he sat down himself. "Have a seat, son."

"You look like something's wrong," Kerry said. The hairs on the back of his neck stood at full attention.

"Last night," Danny said softly, "you asked me about Maxine Bridges. Why did you do that?"

Kerry's cheeks flashed red-hot in an instant and his dad saw it.

"What is it?"

"It's nothing," Kerry said. "It's stupid. I don't want to talk about it."

"I think you need to, son."

Kerry shot a look back toward the rest of the room to see who was listening. They were still alone. "No."

"I'm serious, Kerry. What's going on?"

"Why is this so important, Dad? I don't have to share everything with you. I never have."

"I worry this time is different," Danny said. This time, he was the one to cast the nervous look around the room. "She's dead."

Kerry physically jumped at the sound of the words. "What? Who?"

"Senator Bridges. Maxine Bridges. She committed suicide. But apparently, the police aren't sure that's true."

Kerry stood.

Danny reached out for his arm, but Kerry pulled it away.

"Kerry, what's wrong?"

What the hell? What the actual hell? How crazy was that bitch?

Suicide?

"How did she do it?"

Danny stood, too. "I heard it was with a cyanide pill."

There was only one way to play this. He didn't know if he could pull it off, but it was the only way. Kerry straightened his shoulders, stood tall and said, "Thanks for letting me know."

"Are you okay?"

"I'm fine," he said. "It's a little startling. I mean, she was a nice lady."

The door to the tent opened, mercifully shifting attention away from Kerry and his emotions. Sheriff Morrissey entered with another guy dressed in civilian clothes.

"Good afternoon, folks," the sheriff said. He cocked his head. "Looks like I'm interrupting something."

"Not at all," Danny said quickly. "How can we help?"

Kerry locked eyes with the civilian. They knew each other, but he didn't know how.

"Nothing, really," Morrissey said. "I just want to wander the area and do a security check. None of us wants to hear from another complaining mother."

"Help yourself," Danny said.

Then Kerry got it. This was the guy who visited Maxine Bridges when Kerry was mowing her lawn.

CHAPTER TWENTY-SEVEN

After two hours of watching an aerial view of nothing happening, Gail was the first to speak Jonathan's thoughts aloud.

"Maybe we're in the wrong place. And if that's the case, the clock is ticking down on the right place."

"Too soon to make that call," Boxers said. "This is a lot of ground to cover and we don't know what we're looking for. That cop car was coming from someplace."

Jonathan saw no need to cast a vote. They were here, so it made sense to exploit the location for every asset it might turn up. If they moved away now, they'd never know what they left behind.

Boxers had been very methodical in conducting his survey of the property, piloting Roxie in precise grids and documenting her route on the computer screen. She was flying at three hundred feet with her camera lens zoomed to two hundred feet and the unrelenting sameness of the imagery was impossible for Jonathan to watch without his mind drifting.

"Tell you what," Jonathan said. "Let's pull way up for a wider establishing shot of a part of the property we haven't seen yet. This watching grass grow is killing me."

"There's only one right way to conduct a grid search," Boxers protested.

"We're not looking for a body, Big Guy. We're looking for

some sliver of an idea of what a terror plot might look like. We're not going to find that in the grass roots."

The ground dropped away quickly as Boxers launched Roxie higher into the sky while zooming out the camera lens.

"It's tough not knowing where the lot boundaries are," Gail mused aloud.

"With this much acreage, I figure if you can see it, it belonged to Senator Bridges," Jonathan said. "Hey, what was that?" He shot his finger to the upper-right-hand corner of the screen. "I thought I saw something move."

The image raced left and down to reveal what at first appeared to be a patch of garden, separated by fifty or sixty yards from some outbuildings.

"Have we seen that before?" Jonathan asked.

"I don't think so," Boxers said. "At least, it never jumped out before."

"There are people!" Gail said, pointing. Her excitement was clear, and Jonathan shared it. This was why you never gave up early.

"Zoom in but stay high," Jonathan said. "Don't give us away."

"Aye, aye, Captain Obvious," Boxers said.

As the image grew larger on the screen, it became clear that what might have been a garden was man-made, and that the people moving about were in the process of either putting something together or taking something apart.

"I'm open to anybody's opinions," Jonathan said.

"Let's start with the permanent structures," Big Guy said, pulling the image away. "That looks like some kind of a show barn to me. I think that's what you call them. You know, like you'd have at a county fair?"

Jonathan saw it, too, a series of pens for the animals surrounding a larger covered structure. "That's pretty big," he said.

"Why would Senator Bridges have something like that all the way out here? Are we even still on her property?"

Boxers leaned in closer to his screen. "The long-lat readings are right there in the corner," he said. "Roxie's getting her data from satellites, so she's right. I'm assuming that the boundaries that Mother Hen sent for the property are also right. I'm sure as hell not going to question her."

"Wise man," Jonathan said.

"So, the question remains," Gail said. "Why build a show barn out here?"

"Go back to the activity," Jonathan said.

The image shifted again.

"I see two trucks," Gail said. "Upper-left-hand corner, concealed by the shadow of the barn."

"Got 'em," Boxers said.

"Spitball what you see," Jonathan said. "Trucks and people. Only males. Twelve of them. No, fourteen. No, seventeen." They kept moving in and out of frame, and in and around shadows. "All fit, and all of fighting age."

"Sounds like we might have found our terrorist army," Boxers said.

"Or a bunch of fit ranchers or farm workers," Gail countered. "Nothing about their physical characteristics screams terrorist."

"You mean they don't look Middle Eastern," Jonathan said.

"You're such a racist," Boxers said.

"On the contrary," Jonathan said, "they share all the physical characteristics of the fellows we encountered at the Sulkey residence."

"Let's not forget William Kearns himself," Boxers added.

"Points all well-taken," Gail said. "I'm just trying to get ahead of any plan that might be bubbling in Big Guy's brain to drop bombs on these guys just in case."

"Jeez, mom, you never let me have any fun," Boxers said.

The image rotated as Roxie circled overhead.

"I'm not getting any faces," Big Guy said. "It's as if they've been trained not to look up in case of satellites."

"Who looks up while they're working?" Jonathan asked.

"I see sidearms," Gail said. "Not on everyone, but on some."

"Life in the country," Boxers said.

"Okay, pull out more," Jonathan said. "What are they working on? Are those tents?"

"Yes," Boxers said. "That's exactly what those are. And a bunch of them."

Now that it was clear what they were looking at, it was hard to see how they could have been confused. These were decent tents, though not military grade. The kind that people would take on a camping trip. Looking down from Roxie, they appeared to be made of synthetic material—nylon, probably, and while all had been taken down, not all had been stuffed back into their carry sacks. Where they hadn't been, the poles and stakes were plainly identifiable.

"There must be a hundred of them," Boxers said. "Maybe more." And they were strewn over a wide area, every bit of fifteen or twenty yards.

"We all agree that they're packing them up, not deploying them, right?" Jonathan said. "That means they've already been deployed."

"That's what I see," Gail said. "Yeah, that guy there is loading an armload onto the back of the truck."

"So, where are all the other people?" Jonathan asked. "That many tents, there should be a lot more people. Pull out again, Big Guy. This little area isn't where they were set up. They must have broken this shit down from somewhere else and dragged it here or driven it here."

The ground fell away again.

"And where's all their stuff?" Gail asked. "We've got tents, but what about cots or sleeping bags or camp stoves or the thousand other trinkets that go with setting up a camp?"

Jonathan thought that was a very good question.

Gail pointed at the screen. "I see tire marks in the grass." Funny how obvious things became when you knew what you were looking for.

The tire tracks led them away from the barn and seemingly out into a field. Where they stopped, the grass appeared to be matted in a wide swath that covered several acres of area.

"What the hell are we looking at?" Boxers wondered aloud.

"Kind of looks like those alien UFO crop markings you hear about," Gail said.

Not quite, Jonathan thought, but he got the reference—the hint of concentric circles. "I think this was their campsite," he said. "The one the tents came from."

"A circular camp?" Boxers said. "That's a new one for me."

For Jonathan, it rang a bell, but he didn't know why. "They sure as hell were neat," he said. "There's not a lick of trash left behind."

"Where's the chow hall?" Boxers asked. "Where's the latrine? I mean, they're just now taking this stuff down, right? They had to eat and take a dump. And that many tents means a lot of people, which means significant food and waste facilities. Those things would leave footprints. Where are they?"

A lot about this was wrong, and the harder Jonathan looked at it the more things didn't add up. When a camp of this size is set up even for a couple of hours, travel lanes develop along the most efficient lines to get from one place to another. They start as matted grass, and after a day, the grass gives way to a dirt path. None of that existed here.

"It's almost like it was a prototype or something," Gail said. "A proof of concept, maybe."

Jonathan thought that was as good as any other wild-ass guess.

"Have Roxie take us back to the people at work," Jonathan said.

Thirty seconds of flight time later, they once again were watching the process of loading equipment onto the trucks.

"Hey, look who's back," Gail said, pointing to the screen.

The sheriff's department vehicle had reappeared, and Roxie had arrived in time to catch someone in a sheriff's uniform disappearing into the barn.

"Again, no face," Boxers said. "This is frustrating as shit."

"We picked up an eighteenth man, too," Jonathan said. "Notice the green jacket."

"Our own William Kearns?" Gail wondered aloud.

"I believe it is," Jonathan said.

"Good," Boxers said. "So, we can kill him now."

"No, we can't," Jonathan said. "He's now our link to the Event, whatever the hell that is. If we kill him, we lose the link."

"The involvement of the sheriff's department makes legal intervention tricky," Gail said.

"I'd say that makes them a part of the plot," Boxers said. "We could try to snatch him."

"I don't like those odds," Jonathan said. "Especially not during the day. Eighteen against three."

"We've faced worse," Boxers said.

"Not on purpose," Jonathan said. "And it's likely worse than that. I figure the sheriff or the deputy, whichever it is, must be talking to somebody inside the barn."

"I see stacked rifles," Gail said. As the sun continued to shift, so did the shadows, revealing items that had been previously concealed.

Jonathan leaned into the screen. "And I see . . . Is that a dune buggy?"

Boxers worked the controls and the image shifted violently to the left and the lens zoomed down to a level of maybe ten feet. A vehicle of some sort sat along the fence. Two tandem seats sat on four wheels surrounded by a tubular metallic frame.

"Weirdest dune buggy I've ever seen," Gail said. "There's no steering wheel."

"No motor, either," Jonathan said.

Boxers tapped the screen with his finger. "I think I know what this is. I think this is the base for a powered parachute. Digger, it's a thing you would hate, but they're getting more and more popular with the base-jumping crowd."

"People who parachute off of buildings?" Gail clarified.

"And bridges and cliffs. They clip a parachute to the frame, hook a big fan to the back and you make your own wind to go hang gliding."

"So, we've discovered a hang-gliding camp," Gail said.

"Smart money says no to that," Jonathan said.

"Yeah," Boxers said, "our guesses have to account for the assassin piece, plus all the weaponry."

The radio broke squelch. "Scorpion, Mother Hen."

He keyed his mic. "Go ahead, Mother Hen."

"I think I might have something on your crop circles."

"Oh yeah? Have you been monitoring Roxie the whole time?"

"Monitoring and recording. It is my job, after all."

Venice had been so quiet—so *uncharacteristically* quiet—that Jonathan had forgotten she was even on the net. "So, what have you got?" he asked over the air.

"I just forwarded something to you all," Venice said. "Take a look at it and see if you think it looks as much like that matted grass footprint as I think it does."

Jonathan pulled it up on his phone—they all pulled it up on their phones. It was a diagram of squares and rectangles arranged in four concentric circles, pretty much exactly what they had just seen.

"What are we looking at?" Jonathan asked.

"This is a diagram requested from a Kerry Smallwood by Maxine Bridges," Venice explained. "It was contained in an email he sent to her about two weeks ago. It replaces an earlier version that he apparently hand delivered, if I read the shorthand of the email correctly."

"I don't understand," Jonathan said. "The shorthand?"

"There's no formality to it," Venice said. "They're clearly familiar with each other. The accompanying letter says, *Here's the final drawing you asked for with the landmarks marked. Dad's really gonna be thrilled with the poster.*

"Then, it gets a little weird. He writes, *About the other stuff, I'm really not embarrassed. I really thought it was great. I can't thank you enough for everything.*"

Lots of raised eyebrows among Jonathan's team members.

"Is Kerry a boy or a girl?" Gail asked.

"I'm assuming boy," Venice said. "I hadn't questioned. The spelling is K-E-R-R-Y, which prints as masculine to me, but now that I think about it, I guess it doesn't have to be."

"Do you know anything about him or her?" Jonathan asked.

"Only that they're high school age. There are several references along those lines in previous emails. Kerry was trolling for an appointment to the Naval Academy."

"Whoa," Boxers said with a chuckle. "I don't think I've ever wanted anything enough to sleep with the likes of that."

"Big Guy!" Gail scolded.

"What? Like there's any other reasonable interpretation of not really apologizing for something he thought was really great? Nothing wrong with that, really. The wannabe squid got somebody to play with his ink sack."

Gail looked horrified. Jonathan's guffaw made it worse.

Jonathan held up his hands in surrender. "Look," he said through his laughter, "I'm sure there's a non-prurient explanation for what young Master Kerry wrote, but at the moment, I can't think of one."

He thought of *ink sack* and started laughing again.

"In your own time," Venice said over the radio. "'Slinger, let me know when the boys are ready to be men again."

After a few seconds, Jonathan cleared his throat. "Enough of this joviality. On with the business of death and slaughter."

"Now you're talkin'," Boxers said.

Jonathan asked, "Is there any further mention or clarification in other emails on the business of the poster, or Kerry's dad, or why his dad is going to be happy?"

"No. But I did find one reference to a contact phone number for Kerry. From what I can tell, the senator never called it."

Jonathan sat taller. "Have *you* called the number?"

"I thought you'd want to have a plan first."

"Good idea," Jonathan said. "Let's talk it through. What do we want to know other than what the drawing is?"

"Why did he share it with the senator?" Gail said.

"What does any of this have to do with his father?" Boxers added.

"How about who is he and who is his father?" Venice said.

"Tell you what," Jonathan said. "Mother Hen, how about you make the call and conference us all in via the satellite? I'll take the lead."

CHAPTER TWENTY-EIGHT

Kerry was going to swallow his pride and suck up to Mr. Schultz and bargain to get his job back as an assistant instructor. Without that job, he really didn't have much to do during the day and being second-in-command under his dad, while his dad was present, was merely being named a senior adjutant, and he wanted none of that.

Mr. Schultz knew that he was good at what he did, and knew that he understood how to operate a safe firing line. Frankly, they both knew that he'd have a hard time finding someone with equal talent.

As he walked, he tried to wrap his head around what the senator had done. Why would she do that?

What would drive a woman as successful as Maxine Bridges to take her own life—and in such a terrible way? He didn't know if it was painful, but he'd read that it was quick. It was the way that spies killed themselves. And because of that, the method she used was going to be the main thing that people talked about.

Kerry knew it was stupid to think this way, but he somehow felt responsible. So much about her didn't make sense—not including the sex stuff. Why would she lie about his dad?

"Hey, Commodore!" Up ahead, Alvaro Santana, a twelve-year-old trooper, was waving to get his attention. He jogged closer. "Is it true there's no free swim if our tent don't pass inspection?"

"Who told you that?"

"Billy Prescott."

"Isn't he your wing commander?"

"Yeah."

"What did he tell you?"

"He said that my tent was a shithole and that I had to clean it up before I could have any free swim. Can he do that?"

"Is your tent really a shithole?"

"No."

Kerry put his hands on his hips and waited.

"Well, it's not completely neat, but it's not a shithole."

"Yes, he has that authority," Kerry says.

Alvaro kicked at the dirt. "That sucks."

"As so much of life often does. Have a good day, Ensign Santana." Kerry walked on. He knew better than to be drawn into this kind of an argument. "Where are you supposed to be right now?"

"My flight's all down at horses."

Kerry stopped and turned. "Are you AWOL, trooper?"

"I don't like horses."

"Perfectly nonresponsive," Kerry said. He put a hand on the boy's shoulder. "C'mon, I'll walk you back."

"Am I gonna be in trouble?" They turned and started walking toward the tree line, and the horse paddock beyond.

"Do you think you should be? Don't you think Billy Prescott is worried about you?"

"I don't even think he knows I'm missing. He doesn't like me very much."

"Why would you say that?"

Alvaro shrugged and looked away. "It doesn't matter."

"Okay," Kerry said.

After a few seconds, Alvaro looked back up at him. "Aren't you curious?"

"I'm curious about a lot of things."

"I mean about why I think Billy doesn't like me."

"You said it doesn't matter," Kerry said. He could play this game all day. Just another three minutes would take him the rest of the way to the horse paddock and then he could make the handoff official.

"I think I'm too much of a challenge for him."

Working with kids in this kind of environment made you a psychologist without a degree. That statement was specifically designed to get Kerry to ask another question, and Kerry wasn't going to give the kid the satisfaction.

Alvaro wasn't done. "I think—"

Kerry's pocket vibrated. *Thank God. Perfect timing.* "Sorry, Alvaro," he said as he pulled out his smartphone. "I've got to take this."

"You didn't even look at the screen yet."

"You know the rest of the way," Kerry said. He turned away and connected the call. "Hello?"

A male voice he'd never heard before said, "Hi, is this Kerry Smallwood?" He sounded like he was on speakerphone in a big room.

"Who's calling?"

"Is this Mr. Smallwood?"

"Kerry Smallwood, yes. Who is this?"

"This is Neil Bonner, special agent with the Federal Bureau of Investigation. Have you got a few minutes?"

Oh, shit! "Um, not really."

"Well, do yourself a favor and make a few minutes. I want to talk to you about your relationship with Senator Maxine Bridges."

Kerry couldn't move. Couldn't breathe. How could they know?

"Kerry? Are you there?"

He thought maybe he was nodding, but he wasn't sure.

"You did know the senator, did you not?"

Kerry tried to form words, but they got stuck. He cleared his throat and tried again. "Um, do I need a lawyer?"

"No, Kerry. You're not in any trouble. I should have told you that up front. We're just trying to gather some information."

"I-I didn't kill her." *Jesus! Why did you say that?*

"Oh. Okay, good to know. But that's not why we're calling."

"Do you know who did?"

A pause. "Do you have a suspicion?"

"Not really. I mean, no. I heard it was suicide. But that doesn't make sense, does it?" He lowered his voice, and walked into the tree line, hoping to disappear into the foliage.

"So, you did have a relationship with her."

"Why do you say that?"

"Listen to your own words, Kerry. One, you're clearly upset that Senator Bridges is dead, and two, you know her well enough to say that she didn't seem suicidal."

Kerry fell silent. He'd said too much. "I should hang up."

"Please don't do that," Agent Bonner said. "I really need you to answer some questions. I hope you can give us some important information that we need to know. I can't share the details, but I promise you it will doubtless save lives."

"*Save* lives? Whose lives?"

"That's complicated. A couple of weeks ago, you sent an email to the senator—"

"Wait. You're reading my emails? Who gave you the right to read my emails? Don't you need a warrant to read my emails?"

"Calm down, Kerry. Come on, think about it. No matter what you hear in the news, we're the good guys. We're not reading *your* emails, we're reading Senator Bridges's emails, and yours numbered among them."

"And how did you get my phone number?"

"Seriously?"

Kerry hated the arrogance in the guy's tone. "Oh, because you're the FB-Friggin'-I you get to—"

"Your phone number is in the signature block of your emails, Kerry. I mean, don't get me wrong. There's all kinds of stealthy code-breaking shit we can do, but dialing the number you provide doesn't even make the table of contents for Detective 101."

Kerry felt himself blushing. He was grateful that no one could see. "Oh."

Bonner said, "Yeah, oh. Now, tell me about that relationship."

Oh, God. "*Relationship* makes it sound like so much more than it was. I went to her house in Arlington to interview for an appointment to Annapolis. During the PT portion—"

"Wait," Bonner interrupted. There was muffled noise in the background. "The what?"

"The PT portion of the interview. I'm sorry, the physical training portion, where you do the push-ups and sit-ups—"

"Stop talking." A new voice interrupted him. A female. "This is Agent Culp. Agent Cantata is in the room as well. That road you were about to go down is not part of our investigation. You should not speak about that without an attorney."

"No, it was okay," Kerry said. "It was legal. I'd turned eighteen."

A long period of silence followed. Every bit of thirty seconds, if not longer. "Hello?"

The line came alive again, with the first voice back in charge. He cleared his throat. "I want to talk to you about an email you sent a week or so ago. It was one of the last emails to the senator's personal account. You attached a drawing of some sort. What can you tell me about that?"

Kerry had only emailed one thing to her, so he knew exactly what they were talking about. "Why is the FBI concerned with a bunch of tents?"

"So, it *is* a drawing of a campsite?" Agent Bonner seemed happy about that. "I thought that's what it looked like. It's pretty big."

"The biggest yet," Kerry said. "Three hundred twenty-eight troopers."

A beat. "Troopers?"

"Right. From as far north as Maine, as far south as Florida and as far west as Mississippi."

"I'm sorry, Kerry, I'm confused," Agent Bonner said. "What are we talking about?"

Kerry got an uneasy feeling again. It felt like this was something the FBI should already know if they were asking these questions. "It's the five-year Eastern Regional Planetariat."

The silence that followed seemed to last way too long.

Jonathan muted his phone. Over the radio, he said, "Mother Hen, can you make sense out of the phrase, Eastern Regional Planetariat?"

"Here it is," Venice said. "Large gatherings of members of an organization that calls itself the Starlighters. I'm reading this cold, but it looks like if you think Boy Scouts you won't be too far off."

"Hello?" Kerry sounded annoyed.

Jonathan took his phone off mute. "Sorry, there, Kerry, but you caught me off guard. I knew about the Starlighters, of course—"

Boxers mouthed *Liar!*

"But Eastern Regional Planetariat threw me off. I had to look that one up. Is it fair to think of it as sort of a scouting jamboree?"

"Right."

"And troopers are scouts?"

"Exactly."

In an instant, Jonathan saw the ripeness of such an event for a terror attack, but it was no riper than any other large gathering of innocents. "Why did Senator Bridges want you to send the plans for the campground to her?"

"She wanted to make a wall hanging for my dad. He's the guy in charge of the whole Planetariat. It's a huge job and there's no pay. It was a way to say thank you."

"Why didn't she go straight to him?" Jonathan asked.

"She wanted it to be a surprise. You know, her being the senator from North Carolina and them going to school together, she wanted to do something nice."

This struck Jonathan as odd, but he couldn't put his finger on why. Gail's face turned into a giant O as she turned her phone around and showed it to Jonathan. It was set to the Planetariat website. Jonathan felt a chill.

"Uh, Kerry, is the Planetariat going on right now? As we speak?"

"Yes, sir. Is that a problem?"

Jonathan didn't know what to say. Yeah, it could be a huge problem. Or, no, it could be no problem at all. Either way, this was way out of his zone of responsibility.

"Tell you what, Kerry," he said. "This is all I need for now. Keep your phone close, okay? I may be getting back in touch with you later today."

"For what?"

"I don't know yet. More information, certainly. Maybe something else."

"You said something about saving lives," Kerry said.

"Yes, I did," Jonathan said. "And we're going to work very hard to do just that."

"Should I be concerned?"

"No," Jonathan said. "And I didn't mean to make you nervous. I promise to let you know if the time comes when you need to be concerned."

After they dumped Kerry from the call, Mother Hen stayed on.

"Why the hell would you tell him not to worry?" Boxers asked. "He should be worried as shit."

Jonathan shook his head. "We don't know that yet."

"We're looking at a training facility here, Boss. The place for a dress rehearsal."

"And all indications are that this is the night it goes down," Gail added.

"I know what it looks like," Jonathan said. "And I don't disagree with your assessment. But take it to the next step. What are we supposed to do? And let me remind you that the county's chief law enforcement officer appears to be part of the conspiracy."

"We can't stand by and do nothing," Venice said over the satellite link.

"I agree," Jonathan said. "But getting a teenager spun up about a terrorist attack that he can do nothing to stop is going to do what? The extremes I can think of are he'll be ignored or he'll spark a panic, neither of which outcome advances our cause."

"So, what do we do?" Gail asked. "The clock is ticking."

"I'm aware," Jonathan said. "Mother Hen, I need you to dig up everything you can find about this Planetariat thing. And about Starlighters, too. At a minimum, what do we know about where it's being held?"

"I've already got that," Venice said. "It's a place called Davis Farm. A pretty big spread about fifteen miles south of you."

"Great," Jonathan said. "Now, everybody riddle me this: Why are those guys on the ground bugging out now? I mean, *right now*?" He thought he knew the answer, but he wanted to hear it from someone else, too.

"Because this is the night of the Event," Gail said. "Assuming this is their training ground, they don't need it anymore."

"If you're going for the specific timing," Boxers said, "I'd say it has to do with the senator's untimely demise."

"Exactly," Jonathan said. "Bridges's whole purpose for killing Sulkey and the others was to get rid of the connection between her and Omar Farook. There was no connective tissue between the Event, as they call it, and this place. But now that she's dead, they have to know that cops are on their way."

"But the police are in on it," Venice said.

"The locals, yes. Or, we assume as much. But when a senator dies—especially under circumstances such as these, the feds are going to take charge."

"Okay," Big Guy said, "all of that makes sense. We'll assume it to be true. So what?"

Jonathan wanted to nail down one more detail before he got too far out over his skis. "What's the range on those powered parachutes?"

"Depends on a lot of factors, not least of which is weight load and fuel, but more than you'd probably think."

"Thirty, forty miles?"

"Cakewalk."

"Okay, here's what I think," Jonathan said. "I think this was not just a training location. I think this was their staging area. They were going to launch their attack from here and return to here. With no tie to the senator, there'd be no need to pull up stakes like this. Located all the way back in the middle of the estate, flying in and out—especially at night—there'd be no trail to follow. It's kinda perfect when you think about it."

Gail's face brightened. "Senator Bridges's suicide threw everything off. Maybe they've scrubbed the whole thing."

"Not likely," Jonathan said. "Too much money promised to too many mercenaries, and this is a unique opportunity."

"They need to find another staging area," Boxers said. "One way or another, an op like this can't just evolve. It'll need an organized launch."

"Exactly," Jonathan said. "If we find out where that is, we can hit them there while they're still disorganized."

"That's a big *if*," Venice said. "How are you going to find the new staging area?"

Jonathan looked to Big Guy. "How much juice does Roxie have left in her?"

Boxers squinted as he leaned into his screen. "About forty-five minutes. But there's a bigger issue, and that's the distance between her and the control unit. I presume you're going to suggest that she follow the bad guys as they bug out, and that's fine. But to keep a signal, we need to stay in range with her, and we've got a river between us."

"Shit." Jonathan and Gail said it together.

"Now, I can lock her onto a target and have her follow it autonomously," Boxers said. "She has a built-in locator signal tied to GPS so if she stays airborne, we'll be able to catch up. If she runs out of power, she'll try to find home base, and if she can't she'll land someplace safely."

"Will you be able to see the path she flew, so at least we'll have a good compass direction?" Jonathan asked.

"The alternative," Venice said, "would be to bring Roxie back now, give her a fresh battery and send her back out."

"But that risks missing the moment when they leave, and then we'll have nothing," Gail said.

"I think we've covered all the bases," Jonathan said. "All the options."

"I say we lock her on and let her stay," Boxers said.

"Mother Hen, which side of the river is this Davis Farm on? Our side or their side?"

A few seconds passed. "It couldn't be simple, right?" Venice said when she came back. "The river splits the senator's property."

Jonathan laughed. "Of course it does. Have we already gone over the nearest bridge?"

"That's a negative, Scorpion. That nearest bridge is another . . . call it ten miles from where you are."

"And when we get to that bridge, how close will we be to the Davis spread?"

"Three, maybe four miles."

Jonathan thought through the options. Staying put here, on the side of the river opposite from where the bad guys were, seemed

silly. Equally silly, he thought, would be to backtrack to the senator's land where they knew the bad guys were leaving, and where
law enforcement would no doubt soon be arriving. This was a
choice of bridges.

"It only makes sense to pack up and drive to the next bridge,"
he said. "Staying true to our underlying assumptions, if they're re-
locating to a staging area, they're moving closer to the Davis
Farm, not farther away. Mother Hen, I want you to find us another staging area, too—a place where we can stay out of sight in
case we need it."

"Ooh, I dunno," Venice said. "Just looking at the map, it gets
super-rural super quickly out there. Are you willing to trespass, or
do you insist on keeping it legal?"

"Surprise me," Jonathan said.

"Whoa!" Boxers exclaimed, pointing at his screen. "Look!
We got him. This is it."

Jonathan darted around to Big Guy's side of the table to see
what he was looking at. Sure enough, there was Omar Farook,
walking out of one of the wooden structures with William Kearns
on one side and a guy in a sheriff's uniform on the other.

"Mother Hen," Jonathan said, "are you watching the feed?"

"Affirmative," she said. "I'm running facial recognition on the
cop. Wow, that didn't take two seconds. You're looking at Sheriff
Ervin Morrissey."

"The elected sheriff?" Gail said. "Not a deputy?" Having
been a sheriff herself, she seemed exceptionally appalled.

"I think that's why the results came back so fast," Venice said.
"He was just elected to his second term back in November."

If Jonathan's suspicions were correct, this impending *Event*
just took on a whole new, much larger dimension. A national-level
politician working with a local politician to bring havoc to a
campground filled with innocents was beyond unthinkable.

"We just moved beyond our paygrade," Jonathan said. "This
is way more than what we signed up for."

"Ya think?" Boxers scoffed. "You're just now coming to this conclusion?"

"We can't just walk away," Gail said.

"I have no intention of walking away," Jonathan said. "We just need to call for reinforcements. Mother Hen, can you spoof me a phone number, please?"

CHAPTER TWENTY-NINE

Kerry found his dad in the administration tent, just as he expected, on the phone, looking stressed as he listened far more than he spoke. He caught only snippets, but he guessed that the party on the other end of the conversation was a parent, and that the subject had something to do with sunscreen or sunburn or maybe both. As far as Kerry knew, they hadn't had a serious case of sunburn yet—despite perpetually clear skies.

When Danny finally clicked off, he turned to one of the adjutants. "Ensign Brannen, find out who the squadron commander is for Stacy Allen and have him check every day to make sure Ensign Allen is wearing sunscreen."

"Aye." Brannen said.

"That's creepy," Kerry said.

"Yes, it is. Welcome to my world."

"We need to talk."

"Now? You look serious."

"I think I am," Kerry said. "But I think we need privacy. Let's step outside." Kerry didn't know if he was being stupid or responsible, but if it was the former, he wanted the fewest possible witnesses. He led the way to the announcements board and stopped.

"You're actually scaring me a little bit, son."

"I got a weird phone call about an hour ago and I don't know what to do about it," Kerry said. "It was the FBI."

"What?"

"Yeah."

"Why?"

"Senator Bridges wanted to make a present for you as a thank-you for running the Planetariat. So, when I went to her house for my Annapolis interview—"

"Wait. What? You went to her *house*?"

This wasn't at all where Kerry wanted the conversation to bog down. "Well, yeah. For the interview. And because you guys were such good friends growing up—"

"I told you that was not the case."

"But I *thought* it was. She *told* me it was. You guys were buddies. Is this really important now?"

Danny shrugged. "I don't know. It just seems odd—"

"She told me that it was routine, okay?" Kerry said. "That doesn't matter to what I'm trying to tell you. She said she wanted to give you a big picture for your wall as a tribute to the Plane-tariat. It was going to be the layout of the camp, so she asked me to get her a copy of the final plat."

Danny scowled, as if he'd tasted something awful. "Why did she need that from you? It's been posted online for weeks."

"Not the final one. She wanted the most accurate layout possi-ble. The only other person to get that from would be you, and if she did that, there'd be no surprise."

Danny shook his head, clearly confused. "Why did she say you had to come to her house for the interview?"

"Jesus, Dad, I didn't ask. I just went."

"What kind of questions—"

"Don't you want to hear about the call with the FBI?"

Danny's head bobbed rapidly. "Yes, of course. Sorry, I got drawn a little off track there."

"They called me because they found my name in her phone—

or on her computer, or whatever—along with the attachment, and then they asked a lot of questions about the Planetariat and about Starlighters."

None of this was easing his dad's confusion. "Are you in some kind of trouble for something? Because I don't see where you did anything—"

"No. In fact, they were very specific about that. They told me that I was *not* in trouble."

"Yet you look very, very concerned about something."

Kerry broke eye contact and cleared his throat. If he was going to make a fool of himself, this was where it was going to happen. "They told me that they were working to save many lives. I think that was the exact quote. *Save many lives.* Combined with the questions about the Planetariat and the plat showing the tents, I didn't know if, you know, maybe ..." He was hoping his dad would say the last words so he wouldn't have to.

"If maybe what?"

Kerry sighed and threw his hands to his sides. "I don't know. You know, if maybe somebody was planning a terrorist attack on us."

Danny took a step back, as if pushed. "Did they say anything about a terrorist attack?"

"No. Just about saving lives, and that I shouldn't worry."

"Well, there you go, then."

"But they also told me to keep my phone close in case they needed to get back in touch with me."

"About a terrorist attack?"

"About saving many lives."

Danny's scowl deepened. "Huh."

"I know they told me not to worry, but this still felt like something I shouldn't keep to myself."

"And you're right. I get that. I think the sheriff has left, but let's give him a call and see if there's anything to worry about."

"Yeah, about that," Kerry said. "The guy that was with him when he visited a little while ago?"

"Yeah."

"I've seen him before. At Senator Bridges's house." God, he hated this.

"While you were doing your interview?"

Kerry sighed and closed his eyes. "No, while I was mowing her lawn."

"Her lawn!" Danny looked startled by his own tone and he dialed it back. "She made you mow her *lawn*?"

"She didn't *make* me, exactly. I sort of volunteered."

"Kerry, this is getting very strange. Why would she—"

"Can we not? You know, just . . . not?" His face and ears felt hot enough to ignite. "You were going to call the sheriff."

"They're movin', Boss," Boxers said. "The last of their shit is packed up and they're on their way to wherever they're going."

"Hold off on making that call, Mother Hen," Jonathan said. "Which way are they headed?"

"It's too early to tell, but it has to be roughly the direction you're talking about. Assuming we're right about their strategy, they're not going to move farther away."

"I'll gather the perimeter monitors," Gail said, and she headed for the door.

"I've got the duffels," Jonathan said.

Eight minutes later, they were on the road again, headed to God knew where.

Willy K rode in the shotgun seat of Sheriff Morrissey's Ford Interceptor, eyes closed, hoping to get some sleep and to will away the pain in his leg. "Why do you keep eyeballing me?" he said.

Morrissey scoffed. "What?"

"I can feel it. You keep turning your head like you're going to say something but then you don't."

"You know this with your eyes closed?"

Willy K opened his eyes and rolled his head to look over at the driver. "In my line of work, knowing what's happening even when your eyes are closed is a survival skill. You gonna deny it?"

"No, but that's creepy as shit." They were driving through nowhere on the way toward a spot only Morrissey knew. The rest of Farook's army followed behind. "I was wondering if you had your escape thoroughly planned. Like, down to the last detail."

Willy K closed his eyes again. "I do, but I also understand that no plan ever survives reality. They all go to shit. The more important the plan, the faster and more thoroughly they go to shit." His wasn't even that complicated. By sunrise tomorrow, he'd be somewhere in Florida, on his way to Miami, where he would take a flight to Nassau, where he would begin his life as a permanent expat.

"Care to share what it is?" Morrissey asked. "Your plan, I mean?"

"Absolutely not." He chuckled but then checked himself. He got it. Morrissey had never done anything like this before. "Are you open to advice?"

"Of course."

"You've got the hardest job of all of us," Willy K said. "Your best chance at not getting caught is to stick around and do everything you'd normally do. Go through with the investigation, cooperate with the feds, talk to the media. Be sure to attend as many of the funerals as you can."

"That's going to be really hard."

"That's why Farook is paying you really well. More than anyone else on the team."

Morrissey stared at the road, lost in thought.

Willy K continued, "Your worst mistake would be to spend the money you're getting in a way that anybody can see it. Your neighbors are going to be mourning the shit out of what we're about to do. They're going to be paranoid, and they're going to be pissed that you didn't do anything to stop it."

"What would they have expected me to do?"

"Specifics won't matter when people are hurting. They're going to be super-alert to anything you do that's out of the ordinary. That's all I'm telling you. After a year or so, you can resign your job and move away to obscurity."

"You sound like you've done this before," Morrissey said.

"Not this, exactly, but close." His kill missions for Uncle Sam often required him to make himself a part of a community and then to disappear again. But the sheriff didn't need to know the details.

A phone rang and the display on the dashboard read *Smallwood*.

"Oh, shit," Morrissey said. "This is the third time."

"Who is he and what does he want?"

"He's the guy in charge of the Planetariat."

"Why is he calling?"

"I don't know. I don't want to talk to him. For *obvious* reasons, if you know what I mean."

"Normality, Sheriff. Remember that. You need to keep doing whatever you would normally do."

Morrissey sighed and shook his head. Then he pressed the connect button on the steering wheel. "Sheriff Morrissey speaking."

"Yeah, Sheriff, this is Danny Smallwood down at the Davis Farm site for the Planetariat. We might have a situation here that you need to know about."

"If it's an emergency, you need to call nine-one-one," Morrissey said. "I'm out of position here."

"No, it's not an emergency. Not exactly, anyway. It's just that my son, Kerry, got a phone call from the FBI, and it was really strange."

Willy K felt a chill.

"What do you mean by *strange*?" Morrissey asked.

"Well, he talked about saving a lot of lives, and he asked a bunch of questions about our campsite here. I'm just wondering if there's any cause for concern. You know, if there's some kind of chatter about terrorist activity or anything?"

For five long seconds, Morrissey and Willy K just stared at

each other—long enough that the sheriff had to pull his vehicle away from the gravel shoulder where it had wandered.

"Sheriff?"

"I'm here," Morrissey said. "Just trying to make some sense out of it. To answer your question, no, I haven't heard any rumblings about a terrorist incident. And to be honest with you, if the FBI or any other agency had such a concern, I would be the first to know."

"So, I can settle my imagination down?"

"Absolutely. I'll make some calls, just to be sure, but don't worry about anything. If I think you're in danger, I'll let you know."

"Thanks, Sheriff. I really appre—"

Morrissey cut him off.

"Is that true?" Willy K asked. "If the feebs got a whiff of a rumor about what we're about to do, would you really be the first to know?"

"It'd be me or the state police. Those are the only choices around here. By definition, I'd be number one or number two. Do you want me to call the FBI field office and check?"

"No. Absolutely not. That would invite too many questions, and after the fact bring attention back to you. No, the feds aren't involved."

"Who made the call, then?"

"It has to be the same people who've been dogging us all along." Willy K tried to piece it together in his head. "Smallwood said the call came to his son, right?"

"Right. Kenny, I think."

"Kerry," Willy K corrected. "Kerry Smallwood."

"You say that like you know him."

Willy K dropped his chin to his chest and shook his head. This was why you never let yourself become a part of an operation run by religious zealots. They took stupid chances.

"I don't know him," Willy K said. "But I know who he is. Against my fervid objections, Farook insisted on the most accurate possible intel on the layout of the campsite for the Planetariat. Maxine Bridges had a weird relationship with Kerry Smallwood, and she leveraged it to get drawings. That's the only possible connection I can think of to the director's kid, and it's too strong to be an unrelated coincidence."

"I'm not following."

"There's a paper trail somewhere," Willy K said. "Or an electronic trail. These assholes who've been making my life miserable somehow connected the dots."

"So, they know everything," Morrissey said. His voice carried a tinge of panic.

"No, clearly, they don't," Willy K said. "Or else you'd have heard."

"Or, if they know, maybe they don't care," Morrissey said.

"Oh, I think they care. Remember our guys at the Sulkey house." Willy K bolted upright in his seat as the next thought occurred to him. "Stop the vehicle. Now."

Morrissey responded without questioning, pulling onto the shoulder. The three trucks behind them did likewise.

"What are you doing?" Morrissey asked.

"Think about it," Willy K said as he got out of the car and moved around to open the back door. "If they know about Maxine's involvement, then it's an easy connect to her property." He reached for the rifle bag, unzipped it, and withdrew his Browning X-Bolt, chambered in .308. It was the wrong gun for what he had in mind, but it was the best of the options available.

Morrissey slid out of the car, and behind them, so did Omar Farook.

"What the hell are you doing?" Farook called.

Willy K didn't owe anyone an answer. He wasn't even sure that he had an answer to give, but that shadow he saw before seemed more important now. He shouldn't have ignored his instincts then. He sure as hell wasn't going to ignore them now.

Leaving the rifle on the seat for now, he started with his phone, pulling up the camera app and pressing the filter to reverse the exposure, making the world look like a photographic negative, where lights were dark and darks were light. It was a trick he'd learned from an acquaintance he'd met at a hotel bar who made his living as a network cameraman, mostly covering professional golf. The trick to tracking a golf ball in flight, he said, was to reverse the exposure in the viewfinder. Our eyes are better suited to tracking a black dot on a white screen than the other way around.

If it worked for tracking golf balls, then it made sense that it would work to find a drone in the sky.

It took all of seven seconds to find the little four-rotor drone hovering over their caravan.

"I'll be damned," Willy K mumbled. "We're being followed."

"What?" Farook and Morrissey said it together.

It wouldn't be there for long. Now that he knew in which corner of the sky to look, the rest should be easy.

"You really think you're going to shoot a drone out of the sky with a rifle?" Morrissey teased.

Willy K grabbed his rifle and his gear bag and carried them across the street to an outcropping of rocks. He used his telescopic, digital range finder to mark the distance to the target. Four hundred fifty yards. A challenge, but doable.

He moved to the most vertical face of the outcropping—one that rose six or seven feet above the ground—and he leaned his belly against it. With his rifle now tucked into his shoulder, he was essentially mimicking a prone position, but with his muzzle nearly vertical.

He dialed in an extra degree of magnification, bringing it to 5X, settled the crosshairs just one MOA above the body of the drone and pressed the trigger. The suppressed report registered as a loud clap and the recoil lifted him away from the rock face for just an instant. When he tried to reacquire the sight picture, the sky was empty.

"Holy shit!" Morrissey exclaimed over the noise of the war whoops and applause from the others who were watching. "That was a shot!"

"I didn't see the hit," Willy K said. "Where did it land?"

"Everywhere," Farook said through a grin. "It blew completely apart on impact. At least half a dozen pieces."

Willy K wanted to collect the pieces, if only because it seemed like the professional thing to do. But his leg was hurting, and the news from Danny Smallwood left him feeling overexposed.

Morrissey approached Farook. "Omar," he said, "there are some things we need to talk about."

"Not now," Willy K interrupted. "Not out here. Let's get to the new staging area. We can set up and talk about things there."

"What's wrong?" Farook asked, his curiosity clearly piqued.

"A wrinkle in the plan," Willy K said. "But just a wrinkle, I think. Not a tear. This isn't the place to discuss it."

"I'll ride with you, then," Farook said.

"That's not a place to discuss it either," Willy K insisted. He was pissed that Morrissey had said anything. You couldn't just dump things like this on Farook. He had a panic reflex with a hair trigger. He could feel the nervousness in the man and knew that his instinct would be to do the wrong thing, selected from a long list of potential wrong things. Problems had to be presented with finesse.

"If this mission is endangered in any way, you have an obligation to tell me," Farook said.

"The mission is a go," Willy K assured. "You couldn't get the genie back in the bottle now even if you had to."

CHAPTER THIRTY

Jonathan kept his phone on speaker as Venice placed the call for him. The technology involved made her involvement necessary. The person on the other end answered on the second ring. Jonathan anticipated the speed, but not the enthusiasm in the voice.

"Special Agent Paul Boersky speaking."

"Howya doin', Paul? This is Scorpion, your favorite venomous insect speaking."

"What the hell?"

"Yeah, I know. Not what you were expecting." Venice had spoofed the number for the office of the attorney general of the United States.

"Good God," Boersky said. "This is inappropriate on about a thousand levels."

"I assure you it's important."

"You are not to contact me directly." Boersky's voice had modulated to a shouted whisper. If he was trying to be inconspicuous in his surroundings, it would be difficult to draw more attention to himself than by speaking that way.

"Chill out, Paul. We've got a situation brewing and you need to know about it. I figured if I called under my own identification you wouldn't have picked up."

"You're damn right I wouldn't. Because this is—"

"Inappropriate. Yeah, I got that. What I've got to relay is pretty hot stuff. Are you in a place where you can talk?"

"Give me a minute. Let me find an empty conference room. Call me back in—"

"Nope. I'll stay on the line," Jonathan said. He wanted to hear everything that Boersky did and said. Paranoia does that to you.

While they listened to the sounds of movement, they watched the North Carolina landscape buzz past their windows. Trees had largely given way to broad expanses of farmland, and the number and steepness of the hills surprised Jonathan, whose association with the state dealt mostly with the eastern counties and the Outer Banks.

"Okay, I'm ready," Boersky said.

"Are you alone?" Jonathan asked.

"Why does that matter?"

"Because I want to know what I'm dealing with," Jonathan said. "Given what we're about to discuss, I don't think you want an audience."

"Take heart then," Boersky said. "I am alone. And you?"

"I am with my entire team," Jonathan said. "No one you're not aware of. I'll cut to the chase, Paul. I think the clock is ticking down on a big, very ugly terror attack in North Carolina tonight. I think Omar Farook is the leader, and I think it's going to involve a campground full of kids."

"You *think*?"

"It's what all my instincts tell me. All the evidence points to Senator Maxine Bridges being part of the plot."

"*What?* Why?"

"Why do we think it or why is she involved?"

"Both."

"Did you know that Uncle Sam killed her only child in a drone attack a few years ago?"

Silence for a beat. "I'd heard rumors to that effect," Boersky hedged.

"Don't play me, Paul. You're the FBI. If you didn't know, then you should have. Everybody kept it quiet because she was an ally of the president and part of his party. That gave her all the cover she needed to keep the story out of the press. Right? Give me a simple answer."

"Right."

"That didn't hurt too badly, did it?" Though it certainly sounded as if it did.

"You think she plotted a terror attack to avenge her son's death?"

"That's exactly what I think. But let's talk about what I *know*. I know she hired at least one hitman to take out Irene Rivers's OTR contractors. Ask me what her motive was."

"Seriously?" Boersky's annoyance vibrated through the phone line. "Okay, why did she have the contractors killed?"

"In at least one case because he'd taken pictures of Senator Bridges hanging out with Omar Farook."

More silence. It was a lot to digest. "Who knew about the photos?" Boersky asked.

"Beyond the photographer and the senator? I have no idea. Though, I'd bet my Corvette that Wolverine knew, too."

"Well, that would make sense because she hired the photographer. But she never took any action, and now she *can't* take any action since she's been PNG'd. Why contract murders to control a situation that's already stabilized?"

"I can't give you a firm answer for that," Jonathan said. "But my guess is that she saw the pictures as a loose thread that would link her to the terror event that doesn't seem to concern you all that much."

"Don't put words in my mouth, Scorpion. It's hard to be overly concerned about something that makes no damn sense. How are the murders of the OTR contractors linked to a terror event?"

"Most of those answers need to be extrapolated from the senator's emails and messages."

"Wait," Boersky commanded. "How did you get access to Maxine Bridges's emails and messages?"

Boxers shot Jonathan a glare and shook his head. Certain details could never be shared.

"You're gonna have to trust me. Sooner or later, your techs will find the same information we did. Only we have it now, *before* hundreds of children are dead."

"Hundreds of *children?*"

"That's what I said. That's what we think. Ages nine to eighteen. That's what the evidence points to."

"Yet you can't tell me what that evidence is?"

"Oh, I can tell you what it is," Jonathan said. "I just can't share it with you or tell you how we obtained it."

"You're not making this easy," Boersky said. "Tell me what you can."

Over the course of the next five minutes, Jonathan shared what they'd learned about the senator's property being used as a rehearsal space and likely staging zone for an attack that would involve powered parachutes.

"We suspect the attack will come tonight because Bridges said as much in her emails. She said that this date will change America forever."

Boersky listened quietly through the entire recitation. When it was his turn to speak, he said, "There's a piece missing here, and I think it's buried in the parts you don't want to talk about. There's a level of conjecture here that concerns me. Your projected terror plot is built entirely on facts that are not in evidence. You're projecting motives that might not exist, and however honestly you came to your conclusions, you may still be wrong."

"I'd be thrilled to be wrong," Jonathan said. "The whole world should be thrilled if I'm wrong. But if I'm right, the carnage is unthinkable. You've got to do something."

"Based on what?" Boersky's frustration shimmered. "Your word? No, I can't even quote your word. I cannot marshal the resources of the federal law enforcement community to address a threat I can't define."

"This is Gunslinger," Gail said. Seemed she couldn't contain herself any longer. "Is it your suggestion that we do nothing? Just let this slaughter play out?"

"Come on, folks. Don't pretend that you don't understand my dilemma. I could alert the local police to keep an eye out for unusual activity, but you tell me they're part of the conspiracy. I don't know what—"

"Wait," Jonathan said. "I've got it. I don't know why I didn't think of it before. Thanks for the chat, Agent Boersky." He clicked off. "Mother Hen, I need you to spoof me another phone number."

"Before I do that," Venice said, "you need to know that Roxie is dead. No signal at all. I haven't been watching the video feed, but I'm going to guess that they shot it down."

Boxers' shoulders sagged and his chin dropped to his chest. "Damn them."

Jonathan looked back at Gail, who rolled her eyes. Big Guy seemed genuinely saddened.

"Sorry for your loss, Big Guy," Jonathan said.

"This isn't a good time to mock me," Boxers growled.

"There goes our chance to find the staging area," Gail said.

"I think you might be wrong," Venice said. "While I was researching a place for you to hole up, I found a property not far from you that looks pretty much perfect. Care to guess who owns it?"

"I really don't," Jonathan said. "Just tell me, please."

"The tax records say it belongs to Ervin Morrissey."

"The sheriff?"

"One and the same. It's free and clear of mortgages or liens. Probably been in the family for generations."

"How far is it from the Davis Farm?" Boxers asked.

"About twenty-four miles, as the crow flies."

"That's easily within their roundtrip flight range," Boxers said. "How big is the property?"

"Well, that's the bad news," Venice said. "Almost six hundred acres."

Jonathan gave a low whistle. "As night falls, without Roxie."

Esther Jeffries had just begun the second hour of her shift in the Wellington County Emergency Operations Center when every light on the switchboard lit up with incoming calls within a five second period. They were all bullshit, and as soon as an operator hung up on one, another came in to take its place.

"All right, people," she said to her team. "We've been hacked again. We'll do our best to ride it out."

CHAPTER THIRTY-ONE

Kerry Smallwood sat on a front row log for the concert, next to Marcus Elliott, a trooper from Henderson, Nevada. They were the same age, but Marcus had made the decision never to advance through the leadership positions to attain higher rank. Kerry thought he was a nice enough guy but he had a hard time mustering respect for someone with so little ambition.

Much to Kerry's surprise, Fiddler Joe and Clem were a hoot. Equal parts standup comedy and country music performance, their act had the audience howling with laughter and bouncing with the rhythms of the music. Dressed like hillbillies in denim coveralls and T-shirts, Fiddler Joe shredded his bows on the strings while Clem picked and strummed a mean banjo and guitar.

It was a shame, Kerry thought, that so few of the troopers decided to attend. It was a boomer act, you see—something designed for their parents and grandparents. To attend the Fiddler Joe and Clem performance would risk being hit with social media scolding.

Kerry hated that shit. He wondered how many of those self-proclaimed cool kids were straining to hear the music while regretting their decision to stay behind.

Presently, they were killing a long version of "Foggy Mountain

Breakdown," with Clem working the bow on Fiddler Joe's fiddle, while Fiddler Joe worked the strings on Clem's guitar, all while seeming to get their limbs tangled. Honestly, it was one of the funniest—

Kerry's phone rang in his pocket, earning him harsh looks from all directions.

"Sorry, sorry, sorry," he whispered as he fished for the smartphone. Who the hell would be calling him? Who calls anyone anymore anyway? It's all about texting these days. He moved to dump the call by reflex when he saw the number from the FBI guy—Bonner, right?

He pressed the connect button and said, "Hold on till I get to a place where I can hear."

Now, the front row felt embarrassing as he sorry'd and excuse-me'd down to the end so he could break free. And walk around to the back of the stage where the noise level would be lowest. When he was about fifty yards away, nearly to the War Room tent, he brought the phone to his ear again. "Hello?"

"Where the hell are you?"

"At the Planetariat, where I'm supposed to be. There's a concert going on."

"This is Agent Bonner, Kerry. Do you remember me?"

"It hasn't been a day yet, so yeah. And before you yell at me, yeah, I told my dad. I thought I had to."

"I don't care about that. Remember when I talked to you about saving lives?"

Kerry felt a chill. "Yeah."

"Good. Because all the lives we're going to save are right there at your campground."

The chill became a shiver. "Who is it?"

"All of you unless you get everyone to a safe place."

"Where is that? What are you talking about?"

"Trust me, Kerry. I hear my own words. I know it's a lot and it doesn't make sense, but there's a terrorist attack coming your way and it's coming by air in machines called powered parachutes. Because it's nighttime, you probably won't see them until it's too late."

Kerry's head swam. It was too much to think about, too much to understand. "There's hundreds of boys here. They're all over the place. If I say terrorist, they'll panic."

"That's good, Kerry," Bonner said. "You're thinking the right way. To keep people from panicking, you need to give them direction. Tell them where to go."

"But I don't know where to go."

"Where is a place that is not on the map you gave to Senator Bridges? Maybe an outlier spot that everyone would know?"

"Is the plat I gave her part of this?" Kerry asked. "Am I part of a terrorist plot?"

"You've done nothing wrong. Answer my question. Think. Where is a safe—"

"The horse paddock," Kerry said.

"How far is that from the area with the tents?"

"I don't know. Two hundred, three hundred yards? Maybe more? Maybe less? But it's for sure not on the map."

"Okay, tell them to go there."

"Why me? Why not the police?"

The long pause before answering terrified Kerry. "Let's just say that I know I can trust you. Time is really of the essence here, kid. My team and I are racing to get there to fight back at the bad guys, but we can't stop them from getting there first. Y'all are going to be on your own for the first few minutes."

Kerry stood still, the phone pressed against his ear as he stared at the sea of tents that lay spread out before him. He didn't know that he could move, wasn't sure that he could speak.

"Kerry?" Bonner asked. "You still there?"

"Y-Yeah."

"You know what you need to do, right? And not to put too much pressure on you, but this is not a joke and it's not a drill. The shooting starts in fifteen minutes or—"

The call dropped. *Shit.*

Fifteen minutes or less, right? That's what it had to mean. That's how much time he had before some unknown terrorists were going to fly in and start shooting people for no reason, based on a map that he gave to the lady who stole his virginity. All this on the word of a stranger.

Kerry needed to talk to his dad, find out what he thought about this. But Dad was away and the phones were down.

Screw it. One of the fundamental principles of good leadership was to trust your gut. Kerry believed this guy. If he turned out to be a liar and all of this was a prank, then Kerry would take his lumps for acting the fool. But if his gut was right—and Bonner was right—he had to move his ass.

Fiddler Joe was in the middle of a beautiful solo that Kerry associated in his head with a movie about concentration camps when Kerry climbed the center stage steps and pulled the microphone stand away from the performer.

"Excuse me," Kerry said.

Fiddler Joe looked confused, but Clem looked *pissed.* "Who the hell do you think you are?"

"I'm sorry," Kerry said quickly, backing away from what he thought was going to be a punch to his face. "An emergency has come up." He pulled the mic stand closer, cleared his throat, and said, "I'm sorry to interrupt the concert, but there's an emergency situation that needs to be dealt with. Wing commanders and squadron commanders, I need you to gather your troops and lead them down to the horse paddock right away." The calmness of his voice surprised him, because inside, he was just half a click short of sheer panic.

"What's going on, kid?" Fiddler Joe asked.

Kerry shook his head.

"We've got to move quickly, people. Don't go back to your tents, don't worry about your stuff, just get yourselves to the paddock area and stay there. No matter what happens, stay down there. Wing and squadron commanders, make sure you've got good headcounts for your troops."

"What is this, Kerry?" someone asked from the crowd. It was impossible to see past the stage lights.

He didn't know what to say. Situations like this weren't in the training manuals. Most important of all, he couldn't lie. If he did that, he'd lose all credibility forever. But if he told them that an attack was on the way, there'd be no way to contain the panic.

"Let's just leave it as an emergency, okay?" Kerry said. "The clock is ticking, and we need to—"

"There's no cell phone signal," another voice said. "What's happening?"

"Is somebody jamming our cell signal?"

"Commanders, you have your orders!" Kerry announced. "Go do your duty, please."

Shielding his eyes from the stage lights, he watched as the senior staff rose from their log seats, ostentatiously annoyed that they needed to go back to work when they would rather be here relaxing at an evening concert.

"Troopers! Join up by squadron and fall in behind your leaders."

Clem grabbed a fistful of Kerry's uniform shirt and pulled him back, away from the microphone. "What's goin' on, kid? What about the concert? Our contract calls for another half hour."

"It's canceled," Kerry said. "Pack up your stuff and get to safety."

"Who the hell are you to even say that?" Fiddler Joe asked. "We don't work for you."

"Hey!" It was a roadie with a beard that started under his eyes and extended to his navel. "What in God's name is happening here?"

"This kid just canceled our concert," Fiddler Joe said.

Clem added, "Sent the audience to go horseback riding."

The confrontation had paused the evacuation, with all the troopers and their leaders choosing to stick around to listen to the conflict.

The roadie's glare turned white hot.

"That's not what happened," Kerry said. "Look, I don't know who you are, but I just got word from the FBI that an airborne terrorist attack was on its way in less than fifteen minutes. Well, probably ten minutes now."

"Terrorist attack?" Clem and Fiddler Joe said it together, more than loudly enough for the microphone to pick it up. The rumbling through the crown of young troopers was immediate.

"What's going on here?" The two deputies assigned to provide security for the Planetariat had wandered up to join the party. They stood at the base of the steps that led to the front of the stage. They stood with identical postures, sort of a parade rest, but with their hands in front, resting on their heavy black belts—in front of their pistol on one side and in front of their radio on the other.

"That's what we're all trying to find out," the roadie said.

"We don't have time for this, people," Kerry said. "I know you don't want to believe it, but have you looked at your phone? Try to make a call. Go ahead."

All of the men around him drew their phones. "I've got no signal," a deputy said. Lines of concern creased his forehead. "That's really odd."

"Because the attackers are jamming the signal. This is stupid to stand here and argue about—"

The radios on the deputies' belts made a loud squealing sound, not unlike feedback.

Two seconds later, the radios exploded, ripping the deputies in half.

Willy K hadn't counted on the campsite being lit up like a city in the middle of a pitch-dark landscape. He sat in the rear seat of Farook's powered parachute, cruising at thirty miles per hour, about two hundred feet off the ground. The details were clear and obvious, even from a mile and a half away. Everything looked exactly as it did on the map.

His earpiece broke squelch. "Charlie, Alpha."

That would be Dax Baker. "Go ahead, Alpha," Willy K said.

"Something's wrong up there. Look at how they're moving. It looks like they've been alerted."

Willy K saw it, too. "I told you no plan works once you look away from the paper," he said to Farook off the air. He pressed the mic button in the center of his ballistic vest. "The plan remains the same. Target concentration is reduced, however. Feel free to chase down and take out targets of opportunity."

"Whoa! Did you see that?" Farook howled, pointing ahead. "Two people just exploded. Those must be our deputies."

As soon as Farook stopped talking, Willy K heard the distant booms. He was happy and not a little surprised that the sheriff came through with his part of the mission.

"About three minutes to touchdown," Farook said over the air. "Everybody start your descent."

Kerry saw the burst and felt the pressure wave simultaneously. It staggered him, pushing him back two steps. The roadie and Clem fell all the way to the stage floor, but Kerry kept his balance. He watched a leg pinwheel through the air till it disappeared into the dark beyond the wash of the stage lights.

Kerry pushed the microphone stand out of the way and strode quickly to the stage right apron, where the troopers had gathered to eavesdrop and were now scurrying about like bees in a hive, but without purpose.

"Wing commanders and squadron commanders!" he yelled. When he got no response, he stepped back to the microphone, pulled it from its stand, and returned to the edge of the stage.

"Everybody shut up and pay attention!" he yelled.

That got most of them, but not all.

"Hey! Shut up! If anybody near you is still making noise, shut them the hell up!" After five seconds, he had their attention. "Wing and squadron commanders, you have your orders. Everybody—

and I mean Ev. Ry. Body. Get your asses to the horse paddock and stay there."

"Why are people attacking us?" someone asked.

"Let's worry about that after they're gone and we're still alive. Now, git."

Kwamee Smith leaned into the edge of the stage and pounded it with his palm. "Hey, Kerry."

Kerry saw him beckoning with his fingers for him to come closer. Kerry walked over and stooped to listen.

"Half the troopers aren't here. They didn't come to the concert."

"Yeah, I know. I'm gonna go get them, clear them out."

"No, you take care of your wing. That's plenty to do."

Kerry stood to break off the conversation. The clock was ticking, and he had things to do. He headed for the steps.

"Where are you going?" Kwamee asked.

"Gotta check the tents to make sure they're empty," Kerry said without looking back.

He descended the stairs and tried not to look at the horror of what remained of the two deputies. There are some images he just didn't need to have living in his head.

They've got guns.

Kerry spun on his heel and returned to the shredded remains of one of the deputies. His body lay on the ground in the shape of a V, hinged where the explosion of his radio had eviscerated him. On the side opposite the explosion, his pistol remained in its holster on his hip. The smell of shit and blood made him gag as he kneeled in the blood pool and unsnapped the leather safety loop and slid the dead deputy's Glock 17 free from the leather sheath.

He was familiar with the platform—he'd shot his dad's Glock 19 many times, a largely identical weapon but for its size. He ran his finger along the chamber indicator on the slide and was pleased to find that a round was in the chamber. The weapon was ready to shoot.

* * *

The Batmobile smashed through the gate as if it wasn't there, sending slivers of shattered wood and aluminum flying like a starburst.

"Jesus, this place is lit up like a movie set," Boxers said.

"'Slinger, where's their power coming from?" Jonathan asked. "Is it on the plat?"

"There's a building called *Utilities*. I guess that could be it. I don't see anything that says *Generator*."

"Utilities it is, then," Boxers said. They needed to kill the lights to bring darkness to the campground.

"Where is it?"

"Tent Number Ten," Gail said. "Make a hard right—"

The sound of two detonations in rapid succession cut her off.

"A hard right where?" Boxers yelled.

"Behind the stage. It will be the first tent past the stage. It looks like a big one."

Even with the windows closed, the sounds of mayhem filtered into the Batmobile.

"The attack has started," Jonathan said. "We're late."

Even with the headlights doused, the ambient light from the stage and the surrounding campground made driving simple. "God, I hope this is the place," Boxers said. "Otherwise, I'm gonna break shit and hurt people that shouldn't get broken or hurt."

Big Guy slammed on the brakes and slid to a halt just feet from the front flap opening of tent 10. He grabbed two GPCs from the bag on the center console and got out of the vehicle. Jonathan followed to provide cover, but he knew that was mostly muscle memory. Who was he going to protect him from?

The instant he was free from the sound protection of the door, he knew they'd come to the right place. The generator turned out to be a beast. Jonathan figured it to be at least twenty years old, as evidenced by the rust streaks along the side of the massive metal machine, and it sounded like it was screaming to keep up with the load.

Boxers wasted no time and no effort to slap the charges in place. "Don't linger, Boss," he said. "I'm setting these fuses for twenty seconds."

"Do you see the sign on the wall above you, Big Guy?" Jonathan asked. "It says DANGER: GENERATOR POWERED BY PROPANE."

"Don't worry about that," Boxers said. "Propane just makes it more exciting." He pulled the pin to ignite the first fuse, and then he did it for the second. "I'd love to stand here and chat," he said, "but . . ."

Jonathan flipped him off, then together, they ran back to the Batmobile. They hadn't yet closed their doors when Big Guy stood on the gas pedal and launched them toward anywhere but there. "You're likely to hear a little bang in a few seconds," Boxers said.

"To hell with the little bang!" Gail said, pointing through the windshield. "Look at the sky. We've got incoming."

"My God, they're wearing infrared flashers," Boxers said.

"Shit," Jonathan said. "That means they've got night vision, too." The flashers were a way for the attackers to pick each other out and to not collide in the sky.

Kerry sprinted toward the tent village, yelling as loudly as he could. "Everybody wake up! Everybody out! This is an emergency! Get to the horse paddock now!" As he shouted the words, it occurred to him that maybe he shouldn't be revealing the plan to the attackers who might somehow be listening. He changed to, "Wake up! Get up! Out of your tents! Form up on me!"

When he arrived at the village, he turned right and hopped over the snake fence to land on the edge of row Juliet, the rearmost of the ten parallel rows of tents that defined the tent village.

"Wake up! Get up! This is not a drill!"

To his right, the flap of an A-frame pup tent opened, and a weary boy of about ten crawled out in his underwear. Kerry recognized him as an ensign—a new kid—but could not remember his name.

"Get to the horse paddock now," Kerry ordered.

"Lemme get dressed first."

"We don't have time for that."

The kid didn't care. He disappeared back into his tent. Up ahead, more kids—older ones—started spilling out of their tents and onto the path. "Get to the paddock," Kerry said. "Stay together. Grab a wingman and make sure you stay together."

"Let us help wake the others," one of them said. He wore the uniform of a captain, but he wasn't part of Kerry's wing so he didn't recognize him.

"What's your name, Captain?"

"Tommy Williams, sir."

"Give me a hand getting the troopers down to the horse paddock. I don't have time to explain, but we are under attack."

Williams gaped.

"Now, Captain."

"Where do you want me to start?"

Kerry cast a glance over his shoulder and was happy to see Fleet Captain Farnsworth wrangling troopers from rows India and Kilo to get them headed in the right direction.

"Start at row Golf and work forward toward Alpha. Make as much noise as you can and gather as much help as you can. We need everybody at the paddock *yesterday*, understand?"

"Sir."

When the ensign from the pup tent reappeared, he was in his summer dress uniform, but with flip-flops. "What's your name, Ensign?"

"I'm Hunter O'Bri—"

The world flashed bright white as the utilities tent disintegrated. Less than a heartbeat later, the concussion of the explosion punched Kerry in the chest. As he reflexively dropped to the ground, he pulled Hunter with him.

After the flash came near absolute darkness, illuminated only by shimmering light cast from a vertical jet of flame launching from the remains of the utilities tent.

CHAPTER THIRTY-TWO

Boxers hit the brakes hard and all three of them piled out into the night. Jonathan's NVGs combined with his four-power scope gave him a perfect view of the incoming aircraft hanging from their wing-shaped parachutes as they slowed to land in parallel lines, flanking the cluster of tents. Jonathan didn't know what their strategy or intent was, but he knew it was deadly, and that with all these crumb crunchers running around, the OpFor's target opportunities were endless. By his count, there were ten aircraft, and each appeared to be occupied by two gunmen.

"I've always dreamed of human skeet shooting," Big Guy said. "I figure a hundred fifty yards."

"Fire at will," Jonathan said. "Note their night vision." He switched his M27 to full-auto and fired a three-round burst at the leading aircraft of the group coming in on the right. He held a little high on the theory that if he missed his intended target, he might hit the one behind it.

Yes, it was irresponsible to launch bullets into the air that would impact someplace a mile downrange, but the benefit of injuring or unnerving the incoming enemy outweighed the tiny likelihood of a random bullet hitting a random stranger.

Boxers blasted away with single aimed shots at the group floating in on the left. On his third, he let out a war whoop, followed by, "Got you, you son of a bitch!"

And he kept shooting and whooping.

Gail's voice said over the radio, "Scorpion, Scorpion, check behind you. Friendly visitor."

Annoyed, Jonathan broke his aim to see a bloodied teenager in what looked like a uniform from a science fiction movie. He held a Glock pistol in his hand, but he wasn't threatening with it.

"Agent Bonner?" he said. "I'm Kerry Smallwood. What's going on?"

Willy K and Farook were only eighty feet from the ground when the explosion ripped the night and the lights went out. They had already dropped their throttle nearly to zero and were drifting exclusively on the parachute. The blast must have startled Farook because the aircraft jerked hard to the left and then overcorrected to the right.

"Easy there, Omar."

"What was that?"

"Beats the hell out of me," Willy K said. "Keep your head in the game for the next thirty seconds, and then we'll be on the ground."

The campground had transformed into a mass of swirling shadows in the dancing light of the towering fire. Willy K guessed it was people running around, but he couldn't be sure.

"Twenty seconds," Farook said over the radio.

The radio broke squelch again with, "Holy hell, they're shooting at us! Charlie team is taking fire. Shit!"

"Do you see any muzzle flashes?" Willy K asked.

Farook howled in pain as a hole appeared in the back of his seat. He spun to his left and tumbled free of the aircraft.

Willy K hugged his arms and his rifle to his chest, brought his knees and ankles together and prepared for impact.

The parachute continued to control the descent, but now the airframe was twisted sideways, relative to the direction of travel. When it hit, it was going to be a mess.

The right-hand side caught the ground first, flipping the airframe and rolling it over Willy K's fetal form. If he'd sustained more wounds, he was unaware of them, but the previous wounds had awakened to their full brilliance.

"Bravo team is on the ground," he heard over the radio. "I believe Alpha One is dead. Alpha Two is down."

Alpha Two meant Willy K, but he wasn't willing to recommit to this goat rope yet. It had the feel of an operation that was coming unzipped, and if that was the case, maybe no one needed to know his status.

"Delta team on the ground. Shit! Delta Two is hit! Incoming fire! Incoming fire!" From the far side of the tent village, Willy K heard a long rip of automatic weapons fire. "Ah, shit. Delta Two is dead. Head shot. Ah! Uh! I'm hit! Delta One is . . ."

"Who the hell is shooting at us?" a voice yelled at the night.

"Golf One, Golf Two, both hit!" There was no sound of gunfire after the transmission. Willy K took that to mean death or incapacitation.

That's when the panic set in and Farook's entire army opened fire on the night, shooting randomly at targets they couldn't see.

Jonathan hadn't expected the wall of random gunfire from the invading army. He dropped to his knee and brought the teenager down with him. "Nice to finally meet you," he said. "This shit's about to get ugly. You need to get everybody's heads down right by God now because there's about to be about a shit-ton of bullets exchanged."

He admired the speed of the kid's response. Kerry spun on his knee, then stood. "Campers! Troopers! Stay down! Wherever you are, stay there! Get down on the ground!"

"What about the paddock?" someone asked.

"I said get down!"

"Hey!" Big Guy yelled. "Am I workin' alone here?"

"Do we agree that all aircraft have landed?" Jonathan asked.

"I don't see anyone else in the air," Gail said.

"We got to stop this spray and pray shit," Jonathan said. "Let's go full-auto ourselves and keep their heads down. While we advance. Then we pick them off and end this thing."

Through his NVGs, Team Jonathan could see everything in high relief. The OpFor appeared to have old-school monocular NVGs that were better than no night vision, but only barely. Jonathan and his team had the advantage of the fire behind them to flare out the monoculars, but the fact that they had any night vision also meant that Jonathan and his team couldn't use their IR flashlights or laser sights. If they did, the bad guys would simply have to trace the line back to the shooter to kill the target.

Bent at the waist, with his M27 pulled tight into his shoulder, Jonathan let himself fall into the zone. He was aware of the kids and the tents and the noise, but he didn't care. He knew that Boxers would be advancing to the aircraft on his right and that Gail would be hanging back to provide overwatch, but he didn't care about that, either. His whole soul was focused exclusively on stopping whoever these people were from doing whatever they were planning to do.

His thumb found the fire selector switch and pulled the trigger all the way back to the trigger guard to fire thirty 5.56 millimeter bullets downrange in less than two seconds.

Without breaking his slow, methodical stride, he fingered the mag release with his right forefinger as his left hand fished a fresh mag out of the carrier on his vest and guided it into the mag well and thumbed the bolt closed.

To his right, Big Guy was hammering the atmosphere with his HK417, no doubt shredding people and machines with its 7.62 millimeter NATO rounds.

The whole point at this phase was to scare the shit out of the bad guys, and in the process to give Team Good Guys an advantage. If he hit somebody, that was fine, but it would also have been pure dumb luck.

With their weapons suppressed, the reports of each round fired sounded more like a hand clap than a gunshot—though there was no suppressing the boom of the supersonic projectile—but the real advantage came with the absence of muzzle flash. At night, the bad guys never knew where their incoming fire was coming from.

The lead airframe, closest to Jonathan, had crashed on landing and its occupants were missing. Jonathan didn't know what that meant, but that was for later. The night teemed with many more bad guys awaiting their opportunity to be killed.

Willy K knew within thirty seconds that it was over. That they were screwed. They'd never planned for effective return fire. That was the whole rationale behind taking out the deputies first. They should have scrubbed the Event as soon as they found out about the security breach. In retrospect, there was no such thing as a little lapse in OpSec. Either your operation was secret or it wasn't. Not that it mattered much anymore.

As he listened to the teams call out their wounded and their equipment damage over the air, he knew that the Event had transformed into a suicide mission. With the damage being inflicted to the powered parachutes, there no longer existed a reliable means for exfiltration.

The American Jihad was literally an abortion—killed before it took its first breath. As far as Willy K was concerned, each operator was on his own to determine how best to eat this giant shit sandwich. With clean escape no longer even a possibility, would they fight to die—and in the process take as many innocents to the grave with them as they could, in the style of the OG jihadi—or would they fight to save themselves and find a way to safety?

For Willy K, the choice was simple. He didn't kill for free, and this paycheck would never clear. He'd kill in a heartbeat to stay out of a jail cell, but he drew the line at killing kids for free. And he imagined most of the rest of Farook's army felt the same way. Fact was, when you replaced those seventy-two virgins with eternal damnation, homicidal suicide got a lot less attractive. He figured that was maybe why the world saw so few Anglo-Saxons with vests of dynamite strapped to their chests.

For now, for him, life was all about getting the hell out of there, the sooner the better. He figured his best shot at moving without getting noticed was while everybody else was shooting at each other.

If his memory was correct, some of these troopers were old enough to drive, and the keys to their cars were stored in a cabinet in the command tent, which had to be the great big tent that hadn't just exploded.

The hard landing had torn open the wounds on his belly and his leg. He didn't think it was anything serious, but the pain spike had doubled and he could feel the hot blood on his skin. For sure, he would be leaving a blood trail, and for double-sure, walking away from this was not an option.

So, he needed a car. Once he had that taken care of, he'd have to reevaluate the rest of his plan, of which carefree retirement was no longer a part.

Jonathan had emptied his second mag and was ready to start picking targets when he saw a muzzle flash from the Number 3 airframe and heard a bullet whiz past his ear. He threw himself flat on the ground, then log-rolled to his right three full turns while the bad guy stitched the patch of dirt where Jonathan wasn't anymore. He was still trying to untangle himself from his gear when he heard two shots from behind him.

"Shooter's down," 'Slinger said over the air. "Scorpion, are you still whole?"

"Whole with no holes," he said. "I'm advancing."

Two minutes into the war, now, the OpFor were beginning to organize their diminishing manpower. They must have had comms because no one was shouting orders. The operators from the line of airframes on Jonathan's side were piling out to form a skirmish line, holding their fire until they could concentrate it. Jonathan understood the theory, but the strategy was terrible. This was not the time for them to be careful.

The enemy fired at the night on full auto as they attempted to form a line and advance. They didn't seem to understand that every muzzle flash provided a new target.

Jonathan thumbed the fire selector to single-fire, changed out his partially spent magazine for a fresh one and started picking targets as they scurried from their vehicles, blasting away like Rambo with too much caffeine. Every muzzle flash brought another kill.

One of the attackers produced a hand grenade from a pouch in his vest. Jonathan waited till he'd pulled the pin to shoot him through the jaw. When the grenade exploded, it took out the guy standing next to him. Nothing about this was a fair fight.

In less than three minutes it was over.

"Scorpion, Big Guy."

"Go ahead."

"I've got a runner, what do you want me to do?"

"Does he have his weapon?" These were the calls Jonathan hated to make. He knew all of the hazards associated with allowing an enemy to live, but sometimes—He looked back at the spared pilot and saw that he was gone. *Shit.*

"Affirmative on the weapon. Man, he's running *fast*!"

"Smoke him if you want," Jonathan said. "Or you could—"

The pulse of two suppressed rifle shots interrupted his words.

"I'm sorry, Boss, what was the other option?"

When the shooting started, Kerry yelled for the troopers to all get on the ground. "On your faces! Now! Make yourselves small! Don't look up!"

He didn't know what to do with the Glock in his own hand. Should he go up and join the fight? As the acting commanding officer, wasn't that his responsibility?

But if he walked up there and joined them, how would they

know that he was friendly, and not one of the enemy? If they saw a stranger with a gun they might just as well kill him as welcome him, right?

"Get down! Get down!" he yelled.

As the troopers fell, he wondered if it was because of his orders, or because they had been hit by a stray bullet. How could he know the difference? If they'd been shot, they needed immediate attention. That fell on him.

"Is anybody hurt?"

Without any warning, somebody grabbed him in a bear hug from behind and threw him onto the grass between two tents, damn near impaling him on a metal spike. It was Jay Pendergrass from his own squadron.

"Listen to your own orders, Kerry!" he shouted. "Who the hell do you think you are, standing tall shouting orders? You're gonna get yourself killed!"

Is that what he'd been doing? Kerry had lost track of time and his movements. He had things he needed to do. Protecting the troopers was his only responsibility.

"But you can't do that if you're dead, can you?" Pendergrass said.

Kerry didn't realize he'd spoken his thoughts aloud.

Three inches taller and fifty pounds heavier than Kerry, Jay Pendergrass threw his body on top of Kerry's so he couldn't get up again.

Kerry lay there, with that weight on his back, listening to the shooting and then an explosion, and then . . . quiet. After ten seconds of quiet, he started bucking under Jay Pendergrass.

"Move. Move. Let me up."

"I'm not gonna let you kill yourself." Somehow, Jay made himself heavier.

"They've stopped shooting!" Kerry yelled. "I can't get killed if they're not shooting!"

Jay took his time, but he rolled off, allowing Kerry to breathe again. "Thanks for caring," Kerry said. As he rose to his hands and knees, he gasped at the carpet of motionless troopers sprawled along the ground. "Oh, shit. Oh, my God."

He scrabbled to his feet and ran to Hunter O'Brien, whose white summer dress uniform was now smeared dark in the flickering light of the burning utility tent. "Hunter!" he yelled as he grabbed a fistful of uniform fabric and rolled him from his stomach to his back. "Where are you hit?"

Hunter jerked to a sitting position ready to throw a punch. "Let go of me."

"Are you okay?"

"I'm fine. What's happening?"

Kerry looked to the other troopers who were scattered across the grounds. "Listen up, everybody. Sit up, or wave, or give me some kind of sign if you're okay."

Every trooper he could see indicated that he was okay. That wasn't everybody at the Planetariat, but it was a lot. How was he going to find out about the others? Did they get to the paddock? With the power out, were some of them wounded and dying in places that would be invisible until the sun came up? He couldn't let that happen.

He couldn't let any of this happen, yet it was happening anyway. And he didn't even know what *it* was.

"Hey, look!" Jay Pendergrass pointed toward the main gate. "That's one of the terrorists."

Kerry's gaze followed Jay's finger. A man he didn't recognize, armed with a rifle, fought a bad limp as he half hobbled, half ran toward the administration tent.

"Come on," Kerry said. "We need to stop him."

"Are you crazy? He's got a friggin' rifle!"

Kerry held up his acquired Glock as if it were a prize. "And I have a pistol. That asshole is trying to kill everybody."

"Exactly," Jay said. *Duh.*

Kerry didn't have time to argue. If the urgency of stopping the terrorist wasn't obvious to Jay, there was nothing Kerry could do to explain it to him.

"Stay here," Kerry ordered. "Better yet, take some of these troopers with you down to the paddock and take roll. We need to see who we have and who we don't."

Without waiting for an answer, Kerry spun on his heel and jogged off to confront the enemy. With each step, he wondered if he was doing the right thing. Had he just delegated the most important task—keeping the troopers safe—to someone else? He sure as hell couldn't ask someone else to confront the killer, but was he being foolish by confronting the killer himself? Should he just let the guy keep killing? Let him run away?

He didn't remember any answers to questions like these in the leadership handbook.

The silence almost hurt Jonathan's ears.

"Did we get them all?" Gail asked.

"Ah, c'mon," Boxers said. "There've got to be a couple more."

Jonathan let his rifle drop against its sling while he kept his hand on the pistol grip, just in case. "Big Guy, you and 'Slinger get pictures and prints for Mother Hen. I want to check in with the campers."

Willy K had never been a fan of monocular night vision, even back in the day when it was cutting edge and he was fortunate to have access to it. His brain just wasn't great at adapting to the split input. But it was better than no night vision at all, and for this application right now, it was . . . adequate.

Here, inside the camp's administrative office, he didn't need to aim at anybody or shoot at anybody. All he needed to do was find a set of car keys for a vehicle he could use to drive himself to safety.

Whoever was running opposition against him—whoever was in charge of Team Asshole—was damned good at what he did, and sooner or later, Willy K was going to find the sonofabitch and boil him in oil.

Before then, though, he needed to get the hell out of Buttscratch, North Carolina, and on to someplace where he could deeply disappear for at least a couple of years. This abortion of an operation was going to make huge headlines, and in all the ways Farook had hoped it would not: "Yet Another Terror Effort Foiled"; "Sleeper Cell Elements Exist in USA"; "International Fugitive Omar Farook Attempts to Kill Children."

When acts of horrific violence are successful, they have impact because the public is frightened. When they fail, however, they become the focus of derision and laughter.

Either way, though, successful or otherwise, the memory of the law is very long, and Team Asshole knew his true identity. Did they share it with law enforcement authorities? How could he afford to believe otherwise?

Car keys.

Where the hell were the car keys?

Reading with night vision was a bitch. The light enhancement capabilities allowed him to make out shapes, and even faces, but without benefit of an infrared flashlight, writing appeared mostly as a smear. Thus, to find the cabinet with the car keys, he would have to open every single—

What was that?

In the quiet after that wild cacophony of gunfire, he thought for sure he heard voices.

CHAPTER THIRTY-THREE

With the electricity out, Kerry opted to approach the administration tent via the paved path instead of across the grass. It would take a little longer, but there was less chance of tripping over something or twisting an ankle.

When he heard footsteps approaching through the grass behind him on his right, he pivoted, dropped to a knee and brought the Glock up, ready to fire.

"Jesus, it's me!" Jay Pendergrass whisper-shouted as he slid to a stop. "Put that thing down."

Kerry's heart pounded so hard that it hurt. "What are you doing here?" His finger had been on the trigger, for God's sake.

"I can't let you do this alone," Jay said. "Which is my way of guilting you into not doing it at all."

"I gave you an order," Kerry said.

"Call it a mutiny," Jay said. "I'll get to it. Are you really doing this?"

"I have to."

"I don't suppose you have an extra pistol?"

Immediately, Kerry's thoughts went back to the second mutilated deputy and his bloody pistol on the sidewalk.

"No, I don't," he said.

"Can't blame a guy for asking."

"If you're coming with me, walk behind me on the path. It's quieter."

"Gotcha."

They were still twenty, maybe thirty feet away from the tent door when Jay put his hand on Kerry's shoulder. "Wait a sec," he whispered, barely audible.

Kerry turned, waited.

"What's the plan, exactly? Are you just going to go in and shoot the guy? What's the W here? The L is a hole blown through us, but what's the W?"

Kerry couldn't explain because he didn't know. There'd been so much violence. He knew people had died, but he didn't know how many or whether he personally knew who any of them were. He'd call the police if telephones worked, but that wasn't an option because something had been done to block the cell phone service.

Maybe he should go back and get Agent Bonner to take care of this, but damn, he looked so busy.

In the end, Kerry didn't say anything. He had no idea what he would do. But it was time to do it.

With the pistol clutched in his right hand, he reached with his left hand for the knob in the darkness—rather he reached through the darkness for the spot where he knew the knob should be—and he tapped his fingers gently along the door panel until he found it.

As always, it stuck a little, and when the latch finally cleared its seat, he inched the door open. He didn't know why. He didn't know anything. He was hoping that maybe the lights from the computer screens would help him see, but then he remembered that there was no damn electricity to power the computers.

Jay stayed right with him as he opened the door the rest of the way, his hand on his shoulder.

They stopped in the doorway as Kerry scanned the blackness.

There was nothing there. Just blackness staring back at him.

Then from his left side, close enough that he could feel the heat and moistness of his breath on his cheek, a man said, "You're going to drop that pistol and help me find some car keys or I'm going to blow your head clean off your shoulders."

Jonathan considered lifting the night vision array off his face to look less intimidating as he approached the milling assembly of children and teenagers but opted to keep them in place for the additional acuity in vision. At first glance, he didn't see any injuries.

"I'm with the FBI," Jonathan lied as he approached the campers. He wanted to get ahead of any panic that might be triggered by the silhouette of an amphibian-looking man festooned with weaponry. "What's everybody's status here?"

If any of the kids heard him or understood him, none of them made any indication.

Jonathan tried again. Louder, this time. "Is anybody hurt? Anybody shot? Bleeding?"

"I don't think so," said a kid dressed in a muddy white uniform. "I think we're trying to figure that out. A lot of the troopers—maybe most of them—went down that way to the horse paddock to be out of the way when the shooting started. Is it all over?"

"I think so," Jonathan said.

"You're not sure?"

"My people are still—" Jonathan checked himself when he realized he was making excuses to an eleven-year-old. "Where's Kerry Smallwood? He's the man in charge, right?"

"Yeah," the kid said. "He was here just a minute ago." He turned to other campers. "Anybody know where Kerry went?"

"Him and Jay Pendergrass were just arguing a little while ago," someone said.

"About what?" Jonathan asked.

"I don't know. A lot of people were shouting orders all at the same time. Plus, all the shooting. Hard to pay attention. Last time I saw them they were headed that way." The kid pointed.

"What's down there?" Jonathan asked.

"That's the administrative tent. You know, the front office."

Jonathan didn't say anything, but he wondered why in the hell a kid who seemed so responsible would leave all the people he's responsible for to go chase down something in the front office. What the hell, it could only take so long.

"Tell me about this evacuation down to the horse paddock," Jonathan said. "Is anybody down there counting heads, seeing if there are injuries?"

"Where are the rest of you?" a kid asked. "Where are all the other cops and ambulances and stuff?"

"They're on the way," Jonathan said, reminding himself that they needed to be finding their way out of here. He keyed his mic. "Mother Hen, Scorpion, what is the status of emergency services notifications about all of this?"

"So far, nothing," she said. "Do you want me to make an anonymous call?"

"Negative. Put this on Boersky. Tell him what went down while he was pretending everything was normal and let him make the tough calls."

Another gunshot punched the night, followed by another. Followed by more.

"Ah, shit," Jonathan said over the air. "Big Guy, 'Slinger, on me down at the main gate at the front office tent."

Kerry reacted instantly to the sound of the voice. He knew the terrorist was hurt and he knew the guy had no reason to let them live, so the only option was to hurt him more and try to kill him first. Kerry whirled on the sound and rushed it, shoving his hands where he thought the guy's face would be, in hopes of gouging an eye or breaking a nose.

Instead, in the dark, his left hand wrapped around what felt like an old camera lens and he knew right away that it had to be his night vision—he'd seen it on television. As Kerry drove the man back toward what he knew to be the standing coat rack, he twisted the lens and ripped it from the man's face.

They hit the rack hard and then they were on the ground.

Kerry remembered that he had the pistol and he fired a shot toward where the guy should be, and then the guy fired a shot that creased the fleshy part of Kerry's ear as the muzzle flash burned his cheek and the muzzle blast deafened him.

Kerry grabbed the barrel of the rifle and pushed it toward the ceiling as the attacker fired again. And again. Somehow, somewhere in the fight, Kerry had dropped his Glock. Shit, he was unarmed!

But he had the advantage for now, if only because his attacker was on the ground. He remembered the spot of blood on the attacker's shirt. With both hands wrapped around the rifle barrel as it fired two more rounds into the ceiling, Kerry dropped his knee into what he hoped was the terrorist's belly. It felt soft, and he got the pained reaction he'd hoped for. He did it again, then ground his knee into what he hoped were the man's guts.

Where the hell was Jay? Even as the thought formed in his mind, he realized that he didn't want Jay to be involved. He would be another target, another person to be responsible for.

The rifle shifted violently in Kerry's hands, and the barrel jerked free from his grasp. Something hit him hard in the side of his face, and then the attacker heaved to the side and launched Kerry onto the floor.

Kerry spun as he fell and became disoriented. He no longer knew where he was in the room. The darkness in the tent remained absolute, and as Kerry heard his attacker moving around in the dark, no doubt searching for his night vision, Kerry realized that his only advantage might be to remain quiet.

That's when Jay Pendergrass whispered, "Kerry, are you okay?"

Even in the darkness, he could hear the attacker pounce. Then there was the scream that followed.

* * *

Jonathan sprinted toward the tent that sounded like war. The shooting he heard was all rifle shots—all bad news because to his knowledge, young Kerry was armed only with a pistol. "'Slinger and Big Guy, find the back door or make one. I'm going in the front."

Jonathan was only six feet away from the door when he heard an agonized scream that motivated him to do something stupid. He kicked the door and entered an unknown space all by himself, letting his inner cowboy ignore the tactical advantage that his backup would be able to provide if he'd waited another ten seconds. Thousands of body bags had been loaded with the remains of operators who had done the very same thing.

But sometimes you get lucky.

At a glance, Jonathan could tell that the others were blind in the dark. As he burst in, he first saw Kerry Smallwood on the floor, shrinking from the noise, but then quickly regrouping and preparing for a fight. To his left, he saw a mess of broken furniture and a Glock pistol on the ground.

Keeping his feet planted in place, Jonathan pivoted to his right on the balls of his feet as he simultaneously dropped to his knees to make himself an unreliable target, and what he saw at first confused him. A tall, stocky kid about Kerry's age stood very tall, and in the darkness he appeared to have four legs.

Then Jonathan got it. An attacker had grabbed the kid from behind and was using him as a shield.

"I just want to get out of here," the attacker said. Jonathan recognized the voice. "I came here for car keys. That's it. I don't want to hurt anybody else, but I will." He had a striker-fired pistol pressed under the kid's jaw hard enough that the front sight had drawn blood. When he'd opted to take the kid as a hostage and use him as cover, he'd inadvertently pinned his hostage against his slung rifle, essentially taking it out of service.

The back door opened. Jonathan watched as Boxers and Gail silently spread out. No one said anything for fear of giving Willy K a target to shoot at.

From this angle, even though he was at bad breath range, Jonathan didn't have a good shot. All he could see was the tall camper and a tiny ridge of Willy K's head.

Jonathan pointed across the tent to Boxers and indicated a thumbs-up. *Do you have a shot?*

Boxers replied with a thumbs-down and made a vertical swiping motion with splayed fingers. *Hostage is blocking the shot.*

Jonathan fired a thumbs-up at Gail and got an immediate thumbs-down along with a gesture that might have been a salute with her forefinger, starting at the center of her forehead. *My bullet will go through to hit the hostage.*

"If you don't want to see this boy's brains, somebody better say something," Willy K shouted.

It was a bluff. And if it wasn't it should have been. The hostage was the only reason Willy K was still breathing.

"Say something, goddammit!"

Jonathan recognized the signs of a man reaching the end of his tether. This had to end now.

He looked again at the two sets of legs. The ones in shorts belonged to the hostage camper. Jonathan extended the muzzle of his M27 until it was maybe twelve inches away from Willy K's left knee.

But he couldn't risk the shot while the pistol was pressed against the camper's head.

In a voice barely above a whisper, Jonathan said, "I'm right here, Willy K, and you're an asshole."

The gunman reacted instantly, whipping the pistol away from the camper's head to shoot at the source of the voice. The muzzle hadn't cleared the boy's orbit by an inch before Jonathan pressed his trigger and all but amputated Willy K's leg at his knee.

As part of the same motion, Jonathan heaved himself up,

grabbed the camper by his belt buckle and yanked him down to the floor.

In the two seconds that Willy K's body remained vertical before it collapsed in a heap, Boxers and Gail shot him six times.

Jonathan keyed his mic. "Time to go."

"Just like this?" Gunslinger said. "We should evaluate their status, at least."

"Not our job," Big Guy said. "Hell, *this* wasn't our job."

Jonathan set the example by exiting through the door. "We've fixed what we could. Nothing we do from here can be of meaningful help to them, and everything else we do here will be meaningfully harmful to us. This is not up for discussion."

As he strode back across the campground toward the burning propane that marked the spot where they'd left the Batmobile, he heard running steps approaching from behind him. He turned as he walked and was not at all surprised to see Kerry Smallwood.

"Excuse me, Agent Bonner, but where are you going? You can't just leave things like this."

Jonathan didn't break stride and he didn't say anything. Words would only make things worse. No explanation would make sense. One way or another—either through a call by Boersky or one by Venice—civil authorities would soon be here to help Kerry and his troopers sort things out, but if Jonathan told the kid that, then he would have to explain how he knew.

Kerry grabbed Jonathan's shirt sleeve and pulled. "Wait!"

Jonathan whirled on him, a reflexive response. The kid recoiled and Digger checked himself. "Look, kid," he said. "Kerry. Stop asking me questions and don't ever touch me again. You did a good job here today. There are a lot of dead bad guys out there right now who would have created a lot of dead good guys out of you and your friends if you hadn't shown good leadership. Don't forget that part when you tell the authorities what happened."

"But I don't even know what happened!" His frustration had brought him nearly to tears as Gail and Boxers caught up and they formed a group.

Jonathan gave Kerry's cheek a paternal—maybe patronizing—tap with his gloved fingertips. "Good. And that's exactly why we need to stop talking."

Kerry slapped his hand away.

Jonathan smiled. "Good for you," he said.

With Roxie dead in a field somewhere, there wasn't much to pack as they loaded back into the Batmobile. Quickness mattered because they were being watched, but not by as many people as Jonathan would have expected under the circumstances. They put their rifles on the seats and kept their NVGs in place as they drove back through the main gate with their headlights off.

"I didn't hear any screaming from among the kids," Gail observed. "A lot of chatter and a lot of excitement, but not the kind of noise I'd expect if any of the troopers had been hit."

"Team Angel, this is Mother Hen," Venice said over the radio. "Be advised that a sheriff's deputy and state trooper have been dispatched to the Davis Farm to do a wellness check. A parent hasn't been able to get through to her son on his cell phone."

"I copy that, Mother Hen," Jonathan said. "And did that concerned mother look anything like you in the mirror?"

A pause. "If she did, the call taker certainly wouldn't know it."

CHAPTER THIRTY-FOUR

Fisherman's Cove Police Chief Doug Kramer was sitting on the bench in the tiny War Memorial that stood on the street corner outside the front of the firehouse when Jonathan finished his morning jog along the river. It was hot as hell and the humidity was nearly thick enough to be visible, but it was cooler now at 8:00 a.m. than it would be at any other time of day.

Doug stood as Jonathan drew near. With the physique of a fireplug, he was in much better shape than he looked, and he could throw a hell of a punch. Back when they were growing up together Doug could beat the hell out of Jonathan. That wasn't the case anymore, not that there was any inclination to fight. In fact, Jonathan considered Doug to be among his best friends.

He wasn't too happy with the look on the chief's face, though. His eyebrows had knitted together, and his lips were pressed into a tight line.

"Good morning, Doug," Jonathan said in his most cheerful tone. "You're out and about early."

"I wanted to catch you before you went into your office."

"You look like I'm in trouble," Jonathan said with a smile.

"Let's walk," Doug said.

"Can I shower first? I'm kind of disgusting."

"No, now is good," Doug said. He started walking up the hill on Church Street.

Jonathan joined him, shoulder to shoulder on the chief's left side. "I feel a speech coming on."

"Dig, you know I've never looked too hard into the work you do, partly because it's none of my business, but mostly because I don't think I want to know. I know that you disappear for periods of time, and when you reappear, you're bruised and sometimes you're limping. I remember that *fall* Gail took a while back." He used finger quotes. "Took her a long time to recover."

"I appreciate your concern, Doug, but the key phrase there is *none of your business.*"

Doug continued as if he hadn't heard. "I cut you a break on minor violations because we're friends and because I know that in your heart, you're always doing the right thing."

"Where is this going?"

"I've been reading in the news about that big shootout in North Carolina at the space camp thing."

Jonathan's stomach flipped.

"One of the things I found interesting about the American Jihadists was all of the bad guys' ties to military service. I mean, most of them even dressed like military with all their tactical gear."

"Huh," Jonathan said.

"And then there's the whole mystery around who the rescuers were. I mean, that's quite a feat—getting in quickly, saving the day, and then getting out. That takes special expertise, wouldn't you think?" Doug pivoted his head to glare at his friend.

As they passed the church for which Church Street was named, Jonathan said, "St. Kate's is looking great, don't you think? The new sod really made a difference."

"The change of subject is damn near an admission to my ear

that you and your team might have been the mysterious rescuers."

"I guess we very well might," Jonathan said with a shrug. "So might you. So might Irma at Jimmy's Tavern. In the absence of proof, everybody *might* be involved."

"Fair enough," Doug said. "To be honest, I wish I stopped thinking about things there. But my cop's mind works on its own sometimes. Did you read or hear anything about the body found in Chesapeake County the other week?"

"That's Maryland, right?"

"Right. Very rural, not much population. Used to have a chicken processor out there, but it caught fire years ago and was never rebuilt. Now, there's just a lot of nothing out there. A report came across my desk with details of an incident where a young man in quasi-tactical gear was found dead in a cornfield. I haven't seen the autopsy report, but the guess is that he died of some combination of blood loss, dehydration and exposure."

Jonathan kept his poker face. "Okay."

"Any of that mean anything to you?"

"I don't pay much attention to local news," Jonathan said.

Doug kept eyeballing him for a solid ten seconds before he returned to eyes-front. "The decedent's name was Richard Goldsbury, recently of the United States Marine Corps. Kind of a parallel to the North Carolina incident."

"There are a lot of people in the Marines, Doug."

"I'll grant you it was not a strong parallel, but it got me to thinking. The body had a hood over its head, and his hands were tied. Well, one of them was tied and the other one was useless. Apparently, he'd been shot in the elbow. He was barefoot."

Doug stopped walking and turned to face Jonathan. "Now, there's one interesting detail about that wound. Whoever tortured him and left him to die in a field—that's my assessment of what happened—did a very competent job splinting the wounded arm, using a wire splint." He paused, waiting for a reaction.

"What do you want me to say? Whoever put the splint on must have known what he was doing."

"See, here's the thing," Doug said, looping his thumbs into his Sam Browne belt. "Most people—you know, the everyman on the street—wouldn't have access to a wire splint. Most people would use a piece of wood. Even most rescue squads would use padded board splints. To use a wire splint, you need to be someone A) with training, and B) with that kind of equipment on hand."

Doug's glare burned hotter.

"Look, Doug, if you've got something to say, say it. If you have an accusation to make, make it."

The chief started walking again up the hill. Resurrection House was now on their right—the sprawling mansion that had once belonged to Jonathan. He'd sold it to St. Kate's for one dollar on the condition that it always be a school for the children of incarcerated parents.

"There's one more mystery swimming in my head," Doug said. "That spot of woods that you like—the one that Mama Alexander christened Jonny's Point. You been out there recently?"

Warning bells clanged in Jonathan's brain. "Yes. A week or two ago, with Gail. We shared a bottle of wine."

"Was that before or after somebody shot the shit out of the place?" He waited a beat. "Or perhaps *during*? Shattered wine bottle and glass are all over the place up there."

"Yeah? Oh, that's a shame. I need to go take a look—"

"Did somebody shoot at you two when you were on the point?" Doug's eyes were red with anger.

Jonathan had to be careful here. "Seriously? Doug, you've known me your whole life, almost. You know I carry a weapon every day. You know I'm very good with it. If somebody shot at me, don't you think I'd shoot back?"

"I think that's exactly what you did," Doug said. "In fact, I think you shot him in the elbow. I think you somehow got him to a place where you could ask questions about why he shot at you, and to get him to talk, I think you gave him combat medic quality first aid care. How am I doing?"

Jonathan said nothing and he forced his face to remain neutral as his heart hammered in his chest.

"I think you then drove him to a remote place and left him to die."

Jonathan shrugged. It made no sense to utter a word at this point.

Doug leaned in close and lowered his voice to a whisper. "Dig, I love you like a brother, man. I'm closing this door in my mind and not digging any further because I think the world is a better, safer place with you in it, doing whatever you do. But torture is a step too far. I'll stipulate that Mr. Richard Goldsbury was a bad hombre and deserved to die for whatever he did, but nobody deserves to die that way. This is your bye. I won't look away from the next one."

Jonathan felt equal measures of relief and fear—emotions he wasn't accustomed to.

Doug pulled back and in a normal tone said, "Now, so I can live with myself, I need you to tell me that you have no idea what I was talking about just now."

Jonathan hesitated.

"Digger, listen to me. I don't give a shit if it's true or false, but please say the words so I can hear them."

"I have no idea what you were just talking about," Jonathan said. His voice sounded hoarse.

After a beat, Doug tapped him twice on the chest with an open hand. "Great. I figured that would be the case." He turned and started walking back down the hill. "Have a great day, Dig. Give my best to your team."

Jonathan didn't move. He wasn't sure he could. He felt emotion pressing behind his eyes as a sense of shame draped over him like a blanket. Doug Kramer was absolutely right. No one should be left to die that way.

He stood there for a minute or so, working the problem through his head, trying to figure out what to do. Then he realized that the answer lay just down the hill. He turned and headed for the St. Kate's rectory. Yeah, it was early, but Father Dom would be up by now making coffee.

Six weeks had passed since the events in North Carolina.

Jonathan sat at his desk, scrolling through his laptop for the single news story that interested him. The media had been consuming itself for the past month and a half, trying to figure out who the good guys were who killed so many bad guys on the "attempted massacre at Davis Farm." That seemed to be the phrase the media preferred for the event. They'd tried 8/15 for a while, but that seemed disrespectful.

Survivors of the event spoke of warnings by the FBI, but the FBI denied any involvement, thus sparking conspiracy theories that the feds had secret emergency response teams that operated outside the boundaries of the law.

Like so many other fictions that the news presented as truth these days, they'd find a comfortable narrative, and then high-end investigative reporters would write the *definitive account* of that which they would never understand.

And the people who truly did understand would remain silent.

As the details settled out, though, Jonathan thought it important for Paul Boersky to know that Jonathan was not the only party with secrets to be kept. Boersky himself had some exposure, and to protect that exposure, Jonathan presented only one demand. It was the confirmation of the demand that he was searching for now.

And there it was: a picture of fourteen-year-old Jason Sulkey, his arm still bound by an elaborate array of splints and slings, but with a broad smile on his face as he accepted a medal of valor from the United States Department of Justice, and his mother accepted the posthumous award on behalf of his father.

According to the details of the story, the boy would fully recover from his wounds. He spoke of a rescuer with blue eyes, but that's all he could remember.

Turn the page for an exciting excerpt from *Burned Bridges*, the first Irene Rivers thriller by John Gilstrap, available now from Kensington Publishing Corp.

CHAPTER ONE

Thirty-five years ago

When Martin and Finn first slid Mark's body out of the bed of the pickup truck, he felt like nothing, even factoring in the dead weight. Skinny in life, Mark was even skinnier in death, so he weighed, like, nothing. Finn chose to carry the legs because he could use the cuffs of the guy's jeans as handles, leaving the heavier torso for Martin, but then Martin figured out a way to lace his arms around the corpse's arms and carry the load like it was nothing at all. God, that pissed Finn off.

Now, twenty minutes into this guy's trek through the woods in the dark while getting torn up by sticker bushes and hoping not to step on a coyote or break a leg in a sinkhole, his bag of bones was getting very damn heavy.

"Are you sure this is what your daddy told you to do?" Martin griped as he huffed from the effort. Finn was surprised he'd been able to keep his trap shut this long. "He told you to walk to the end of the world and get rid of this guy? We couldn't have just taken him out on the river and rolled him overboard tied to a rock?"

Finn's forearms had been cramping up for the last five minutes. He didn't want to argue, because he didn't want to encourage Martin to go on one of his whining sprees.

"What I'm sure of is my daddy told me two things. One was to get rid of the body where no one would ever find it. Never means forever, and in a river, you never know when a dredger or a propeller or a diver is going to turn up anything you've buried."

"Like you've done this so many times before, Mr. Teenage Gangster-man." Martin laughed.

Finn ignored him. Fact was, they'd both done more gangster shit in their seventeen years than most full-time gangsters did in their whole lives. "The second thing was to make sure that if he is found, no one will be able to tell who he is."

"He's not even from around here," Martin said. "Who's going to know who he is?"

"The FBI can do that shit, man. You ever heard of fingerprints?"

"Of course. I'm not an idiot."

He *was* an idiot, Finn thought, but he was a useful one and Finn enjoyed his company. "It's not much farther up here," he said.

This section of woods belonged to an older couple who let him hunt here, and over the years, Finn had explored pretty much every inch of the place. He was looking for a patch of ground he'd seen, maybe a quarter of an acre in size, that was lined with caves that were covered with tangles of impenetrable vines and thorn bushes. A body dumped in one of those caves was as good as buried in the center of the earth.

"I can't do this a lot longer, Finn."

"And you won't have to because we're here."

"Seriously?"

"Yep."

Martin released his grip and flung his arms wide. The corpse hit the ground with a heavy thud and the momentum pulled Finn off balance, causing him to fall back and land on the body. A shiver shook Finn's core as a bubble of bile came halfway up his throat.

Finn launched on his friend, punching him hard in the face and sending him to the ground.

Then the darkness came. Finn wasn't in charge anymore. His rage ran things now, the way it did sometimes—like last week, when it got him suspended from Shotsburg High School forever—and before he knew what he was doing, the hatchet he'd brought along to do that other thing was in his hand and held high in the air over Martin, who was trying to scrabble away.

In the light of the moon, Finn could see that Martin was trying to say something, but he only heard sounds. The rage was swallowing the words. The rage wanted him to kill.

Finn didn't see how he did it, but somehow, Martin had gotten to his feet and was face-to-face with him. Blood streaked from his nose across his lips, and as he continued to try to speak, bits of bloody spittle hit Finn in the face.

Martin had both hands on Finn's hatchet, trying to control it, and in the struggle, he must have done something wrong because the blade had left a vertical cut in his cheek, deep enough to expose the white fat cells below the skin.

"Finn, you're okay," Martin said.

There, he finally heard the words. The rage finally let them come through.

"You're okay. You feel it? You feel it, right? You're okay. That was a joke making you fall. A bad joke. I'm sorry."

Finn nodded. Yeah. Yeah, he was okay. He was back.

"You sure?" Martin pressed. "You need to sit down or anything?"

"No, I'm good." Martin was a good friend for putting up with the rage when it came. Not many people would. "Thanks."

Martin watched him in the dark for a little longer. Finn hated being stared at like that, but he knew that Martin meant only the best.

"We need to get back to work," Finn said. "You make a big enough path that we can get him stuffed into a hole and get out of here."

"What are you going to do?"

"I've got to make it so the body can't be identified."

That was the whole purpose of bringing the hatchet. First, he needed a log—not a hard thing to find in a forest. Something light would do because its only purpose was to serve as a backstop to protect the blade of his hatchet. Hopefully, this wouldn't take much time.

He placed the log on the ground next to the body, and then draped the body's arm over the log at the wrist. He wanted a good clear view of the joint. With the proper care and aim, he was confident he could sever Mark's hand from his arm with a single blow.

Visit our website at
KensingtonBooks.com
to sign up for our newsletters, read
more from your favorite authors, see
books by series, view reading group
guides, and more!

Become a Part of Our
Between the Chapters Book Club
Community and Join the Conversation

Submit your book review for a chance to win exclusive
Between the Chapters swag you can't get anywhere else!
https://www.kensingtonbooks.com/pages/review/